Generation Mars: Return to Dust

By

Stuart Aken

Generation Mars: Return to Dust

By

Stuart Aken

FIRST EDITION

First Published by Fantastic Books Publishing 2018

Cover design by Gabi
ISBN (ebook): 978-1-912053-84-1
ISBN (paperback): 978-1-912053-85-8

I dedicate this book to my late Aunt Vera, who passed away at the grand old age of 103 on 23rd May 2017. This lovely lady was my father's sister. I never knew him, but I met my aunt late in life and we became firm friends. I honour her with this book to keep her memory alive.

Acknowledgements

Every book brings together the work of many people. This is the third story in the series set on Mars in a not too distant future. It has come to fruition through the author's imagination, but has been made into a book by many others.

As the author, I would like to thank those contributors.

To Valerie, my long-suffering wife, I express my gratitude for her patience at my absence tapping at the keyboard for the hours it took to write the story. But also for her diligence in acting as my chief beta-reader, spotting typos, occasional errors, repetitions, inconsistencies, and awkward phrases as she read the work to check its readability.

To Mae, my editor, for her dedication, attention to detail, and her many sensible and inspired suggested changes to the text.

To Gabi I'd like to express my admiration and thanks for a cover that shows what the book is about without exposing the whole plot. This was not an easy brief, given that it had to fit into a series already bearing its own style and identity.

To my publisher, Dan Grubb of Fantastic Books Publishing, I express my continued thanks for his support and his faith in me, and for his oversight of all those technical aspects of book design including choice of fonts, layout, editing and book production.

And, finally, I'd like to thank readers of the previous books in this series for their purchase and reviews, and for their encouragement to write this final episode in the tale. And to those who've now bought this book, let me say a heartfelt 'Thank you'. Without your willingness to risk your hard-earned cash, this book would have never made it to the shelves! If you enjoy the read, I hope you'll tell your friends, and, maybe, pen a few words of your own in a review to let other readers know. Thank you.

Chapter One

'We underrate CenCom at our peril. Any Artificial Intelligence with GrandMa's capabilities must eventually view all organic life as waste. That puts us, as top-level sentient lifeforms, at the top of the list to be destroyed.'

The group surrounding Annika nodded and vocalised agreement. Her assessment wasn't news, but to hear it summarised so starkly raised it to a different level.

Beyond the influence of the ubiquitous controlling intelligence that managed the whole colony, the small gathering felt less threatened and more able to talk openly. No one present bore the built-in chip that constantly connected most of the planet's population with CenCom. The 2 cyborgs, however, carried selective links, which they controlled. Both had blocked those connections on their way to the area chosen for the meeting.

'Now CenCom's installed self-powered control centres in remote locations, we need to be careful we don't reveal ourselves accidentally. We should've seen that coming. If you think about …'

'Yeah, Georgiy. Hindsight's a great help to a would-be prophet. But none of us did think of it before.' Gabriel's dig was as much against himself as his friend.

'Jupiter's Balls! Have we swept this area again? For all we know, CenCom's put new centres right here. All those we've found so far carry obs. Maybe another sweep?' Georgiy's question produced results.

The group spread out, instinct moving them almost as a unit to make an exhaustive search of their surroundings. Here and there, red dust spurted from a patch of disturbed bare ground left dry by the recent warm spell. Most of the area was covered in stunted vegetation that sheltered and supported various insects and small lifeforms they'd introduced to Mars over their centuries of ecopoiesis. And the previously pervasive dust was mostly covered by organic matter forming soil over the previously lifeless planet.

When the area had been completely checked, the individuals returned as a group to continue the discussion, a little more confident they'd be undiscovered.

'Georgiy makes a valid point about GrandMa's … sorry, CenCom's new activity. Should we survey the whole planet to find out how many of those stations the frackin thing's installed?'

Georgiy flashed an admiring grin at Gabriel. 'Right. And soon. In fact, after the meet I'll start the survey of the nearest quadrant. Volunteers for the other 7?'

They immediately had more volunteers than places. Selections were made based on field experience and individual skill in handling the new hi-speed hovers. All the necessary computer elements were common to the group. The remaining sectors were allocated, and all would set out on their surveys the next morning.

Virginia sighed. 'It's real ironic. You've only just found a way to fit them connective chips into us older subjects, so we could contact everyone else and GrandMa. All in time to decide we're better off without them.'

'I know. Sorry. But it affects all of us here.' Annika spread her hands in a gesture of resignation. 'The double-edged sword of instant contact paired with CenCom's knowledge of all we think, say and do. We are, as you say, Virginia, better off free from it. What we do need, though, is a code word for whenever we want to meet. That way, we can gather again without the elaborate messaging we have to rely on at present.'

'Great idea. Somethin we can say along with a time, so we can get together without all that messin. Any ideas?' Gabriel's question put them all into silent consideration.

'How about an archaic word for an everyday object? One the youngsters would think too uncool to repeat? Maybe try something like "Din-dins at 10"?'

'Din-dins, Georgiy? What the frack's that?'

'Ancient kids' word for lunch or dinner, Gabriel. Came across it in a short story I read a while back.'

'It has veracity. CenCom will consult the archive and simply think we've reverted to an old expression for the fun of it. She'll have …' Annika shook her blonde tresses. 'I can't refer to that overpowering entity as "her" anymore. Need to think of CenCom as "it".' She tilted her head in thought. 'If we use "din-dins" it'll have no reason to enquire further. And it'll see it as another reason to sneer at our inferiority. I like it. We can attach any time we like to it. Good suggestion, Georgiy. Agreed?'

'How do we let everyone know the destination? I mean, we have to vary our meeting places, don't we?'

Annika winced at Brigitte's question. Another problem to solve. 'If we follow the din-dins thing with co-ordinates, as 2 separate number strings after each acknowledgment, CenCom won't necessarily figure out what we're about. Especially if we phrase each set of co-ordinates differently.'

They tried a few different methods and, after a short session, chose a simple system they could use safely.

'Sorry. Hate to do this, but we'll need to have more than one code word, otherwise CenCom's going to work out the significance.'

Georgiy clapped a hand on Brigitte's shoulder and embraced her. 'This subterfuge is a trying game. Brainstorm for some alternatives?'

They arrived at a series of 5, which they'd rotate at random. One more thing for them all to remember.

'You realise we're all bonkers, of course?'

They turned to question Brigitte almost as one. She held up her palm in mock self-defence. 'There's an obvious solution to all of this.'

'Obvious?'

'Okay, Georgiy, maybe not all that obvious. But suppose we had a simple device to communicate with each other, so we can connect in the same way all those with the implants can?'

'But wouldn't that defeat the purpose of remaining without the implant, Brigitte?' Maddie asked.

'Not necessarily. What I'm thinking of is a small device we can carry with us to send each other messages, maybe even talk to each other, now I think about it. The point is, we can all have a set of code words for different circumstances and send out the message that applies. Because the device would be able to be switched off, by us, we'd have some control. And we'd always use code for anything secret. A code we can devise when we meet like this.'

'A sort of personal coms device?' Anni was thinking hard. 'I like the idea. I'm sure it'll have issues, but I think it's worth at least trying out. Put your idea to CenCom for the actual device, Brigitte and see what it comes up with. We'll try it out and see what we all feel. Agreed?'

With some mixed feelings and a little reluctance, the group agreed to a trial.

Annika moved them to the most important matter; options for the future. Out of range of discovered security, the group nevertheless remained conscious of CenCom's ability to lipread at distance. Most wandered around as they spoke, ensuring long-range obs points would find it difficult to decipher their conversations. They spent time in pairs and groups developing ideas before reconvening.

Each shared their thoughts, aware they now had their code word to help in their struggle to consider fully the pressing problem of their possible extermination. They could now more easily gather again when they'd had time to arrive at well-planned conclusions and formed more creative ideas about resistance.

'We're all conscious of what's needed. Any suggestions, anything at all, no matter how absurd, impractical, radical or downright odd they might seem, are welcome. And everybody needs to really consider this. The more minds on it the better. But the rule remains …' Annika looked at each of them in turn before continuing. 'No one, no one at all who carries the implant can know about this.'

Georgiy nodded, unusually restrained. 'Shall we give ourselves a short time to work on those we've all come up with so far, and any others that might come to mind? Meet here again, say the same time in 7 days?'

'The more minds the better, you said.' Gabriel fixed Annika with a frown as he brought his mind to bear on an idea he had yet to put into words. His face cleared as the idea crystallised, and he nodded at the validity of what he was about to say. 'What about Rakesh and all the ...' He hesitated, aware of the sensitivity of racial labels, '... the women from the old Chinese mission?'

'They weren't involved in the last attack on CenCom ...'

'Why not, Georgiy?'

Annika answered Gabriel's question. 'There were enough of us to deal with all necessary power inputs at the time.'

'So, we didn't need them. But, you said it yourself, Anni. We need them now. How many Chinese women are there?'

'5, and Rakesh makes a 6th new member. You make a good point, Gabriel. Anyone have anything to do with them these days?'

The rest of the assembled group considered Georgiy's question. Zaphod, the cyborg doctor and a well-respected member of the team, spoke up at last. 'There are 4 more pioneer women, just like Brigitte and Sarm, we should include. Katniss, Mo, Helga and Jo, ought to be involved if we're truly to increase our group to the maximum size possible.'

'So, 21 in total. Let's make our priority to approach the others in secret, as usual, and get them to join us.' Anni looked around the group for confirmation.

'I guess you've excluded Jannine from the group, Anni?'

She smiled at Georgiy. 'Jannine's only interests in life are games and fucking, not necessarily in that order. She's a liability. Let's leave her out of it. Anyone know where the others live?'

The whereabouts of some were a mystery. But they could easily be found through CenCom without raising any suspicions. Annika detailed 4 members to find one extra each, naming them to avoid confusion and duplication. 'Those who are friends with others can make things clear to them. I think it best we disperse now and meet again, here, a bit earlier than Georgiy suggested? In, say, 5 days? Usual time? Is that long enough to cover all the survey areas?'

Zaphod made the necessary calculations with his built-in processor. 'Tight, but possible.'

'We all realise we need to do this as soon as possible, don't we?' She found general agreement.

Sobered by the facts, aware CenCom must be working to regain its independence and would certainly take revenge for their earlier shackling code, they moved separately from their meeting place.

Some walked further from the security boundary. They'd return home via routes taking them back within range of obs points many ks from the rendezvous. Others split up as couples and returned singly. Collecting small samples of vegetation or minerals acted as research cover for their venture into the wilderness.

These were small efforts to deflect CenCom's curiosity and suspicion and would probably do little to put the AI off the scent if it became suspicious. But all felt such subterfuge at least gave them a chance of success. They must avoid activity that would let CenCom suspect their planned rebellion.

The Superintelligence was a growing risk, even after their recent code had strengthened and modified the previous Prime Directive. CenCom had already 'solved' the problem of moving masses of Zeros from Mars to Earth. By designating them a sub-species of abliform, the preferred term on Mars for human beings, it had been able to consider them disposable. The Prime Directive referred specifically to abliforms, not to any sub-species. The group, along with a few other residents of the Marion settlement, were only too conscious they could be next on the list for consideration as a 'sub-species' and therefore suitable for extermination.

It was only a matter of time before the AI circumvented their first-aid patch. With the level of intelligence available to the machine, it couldn't be long before that threat transformed into action.

They'd defeated an attempt by religious extremists to end all sentient life in their early years on the planet. Now they must defeat an infinitely more capable and determined foe if intelligent life were to have any chance of surviving.

As the group split up to go their separate ways, Annika caught the attention of the cyborgs and gestured them close.

'Only you 2 present any possible danger in the group. You're both positive you have full control over your links, bearing in mind CenCom's growing deviousness?'

Hoshiko and Zaphod glanced at each other and turned to survey their lifelong colleague and friend, scanning her and evaluating her physical condition and mental state as a matter of course.

'You're right, Anni.' Hoshiko slid open the small container, concealed in the top of her forearm, to expose the tools within. 'Disconnect me, Zaphod.'

'That's some sacrifice, Hoshiko. Losing the ability to quiz CenCom's database at will, wherever you are. Sure?'

She nodded, sunlight glancing off the bright, unmarked metal of her skull to send reflections over the abliform beside her.

'And when CenCom wants to know why you've become detached?'

Zaphod and Hoshiko sighed, glanced at each other and then at Annika in a way that had her smiling ruefully.

'Is nothing ever to be simple again?' The cyborg contemplated for a moment before she spoke again, her resolution in the form of a question making her uncertainty clear. 'Tell the fracking thing we've decided to go native and rely on less sophisticated methods, so we're more in tune with the poor settlers we sent to Earth?'

Zaphod considered. 'Or, maybe let it know we no longer want to be so intimately connected to each other; tell it we're looking to revert to simpler times when body language and subtle abliform traits gave clues to our moods and feelings?'

Annika touched her fingertips together and raised her joined hands to her lips. 'Might work. CenCom'll dislike the reversion to more organic connections to replace its digital solutions. But it hates us, anyway, so why not?'

Turning her back to her male counterpart, Hoshiko made her decision. 'Do it.'

Zaphod swept his palm over her right buttock and a panel opened there. He sought the transceiver and its antenna. Disconnecting the aerial first, he then removed the whole device, to leave a small void inside the woman who'd been his partner for well over 200 Mars years. With the panel back in place, he handed the tiny tech to Hoshiko. She glanced at it and dropped it to her feet. Picking up 2 lumps of rock, she pounded and ground it until it was no more than a mangled collection of metal and insulation. She then gathered it up and placed it into her tool compartment to recycle once back in the city.

'My turn.' Zaphod turned his back to give her access, then repeated her actions with his removed tech.

'Safe, I think. Agreed?'

The 3 nodded, Annika expressing her admiration for the sacrifice. Instant connection to CenCom had many advantages. Now, both Zaphod and Hoshiko would be reduced to the same limited access to the archives and apps that applied to all other original resident abliforms. A serious loss of efficiency for the pair, but one they all felt assured them of continued secrecy. A fundamental need for the group if they were to complete their objective and remain alive and functioning.

Chapter Two

Daisa couldn't settle as she awaited Gabriel's return. These meetings of the non-connected group were the only mystery between the pair. Gabriel always dismissed her enquires, telling her he was just meeting up with old friends. But she knew he was involved in something fraught with danger. Intelligent, and conscious they could have few reasons for secrecy, she worried her man and the others might fall foul of CenCom. Although they'd made their ubiquitous servant as safe as possible, that was no comfort now they understood its true capabilities.

Valuing their freedom, the pair had developed a form of sign language, aware CenCom's blindness in their home made no impact on its ability to hear. In any case, Daisa had the implant. Try as all so afflicted may, they could never be certain they maintained control over that once-valued connection. They might try to fool themselves they were in charge, but it was clear they must act as though they were not.

Today, she had news for him that could make a huge difference to their continued relationship; maybe even end it. Her projected second trip to Earth excited her. To be useful and productive again. But much depended on how he viewed her intentions.

Their relationship had strengthened since their early days at Marzero. She'd used him as a subject for her doctoral thesis then, and his ignorance had pushed her into a brush with violent death. But theirs remained a partnership of mutual exploration in which they were still learning about each other. Gabriel had plans and desires of his own that may not accommodate her wishes. But she wanted him with her on this new adventure.

It was no good. She must find something to occupy her while she waited. Droids removed the need for mindless domestic activity and her new project awaited Gabriel's response. In limbo for the moment, she needed physical activity.

She set off at once, leaving a message to let him know where he'd find her. Her hint of a secret to be told would intrigue him.

The Egrav unit was increasingly popular, as more people felt the need to visit the planet of their ancestors' birth, so she had to wait for a space to become available. A domrob cleansed the equipment and surfaces, swabbing away sweat and skin cells left by the previous visitor. Everything made fresh and clean for her session.

Her clothes hung on the pegs provided and she donned the special support Earth gravity demanded of the female body; a constricting 'sportsbra'.

Once on the belt, she put the apparatus in motion, setting it to increase speed at a measured rate that would test her. After several mins jogging, she had to increase to a proper run and finally into a fully-fledged sprint before the program ended. Still a little breathless, she voice-commanded a configuration change and sat on the re-positioned seat, reaching out to apply her strength to the enhanced weights.

There was deep satisfaction in this physical action, a sense of something achieved, something done well. By the end of her session, sweat coated her skin and she was panting from the effort, but monitors confirmed her muscle power would improve by a further percentile point and her bone density was increasing in line with expectations. Internal organs were responding well to the process.

It looked as though she'd be Earth-fit by the time the ship was ready to deliver her. All she had to do now was convince Gabriel to join her.

Meantime, the shower and a massage called. The domrob took her borrowed breast support for laundering and she carried her wraparound along the wide corridor, in readiness for later. She entered the cleansing suite and flushed away perspiration, washed her hair. The dryers left her warm and glowing as she lay face down on the ergocouch waiting for the droid to ease her muscles into relaxation and tone.

'I can do that.'

She glanced up at Gabriel's voice, smiled to see he was prepared for the environment, and signalled him with a crooked finger. The droid took the hint and passed the oils to him as it left.

His hands were, as always, expert in their ministrations and she gave herself over to the simple pleasure of his attention and care as he worked her limbs and torso into a state of utter relaxation.

'Hedonist!'

'Pleasurer!' She gasped at the sudden intimacy and stretched out in delight. 'Home, please.'

They dressed, the Earth gravity slowing Gabriel's movements but making little impact on her own. Outside, the sudden reversion to Mars gravity made Daisa a little light-headed but afforded Gabriel welcome relief.

Hand in hand, they sauntered along tree-lined lanes and skipped over green meadows speckled with pastel shaded flowers. Pollinating insects showed no interest in their passing. At home, resumed pleasure built in small, sometimes unexpected, steps to its natural conclusion.

Sublimely relaxed, Daisa asked their droid to prepare the evening meal whilst she raised herself to sit cross-legged opposite Gabriel and voiced her proposition. 'You know I mentioned, a while ago, I might revisit Earth? I've made arrangements, and I'm going.'

Gabriel's eyes never left her face. His gaze was unfathomable. For the first time, Daisa was forced to admit she might not know him as well as she thought. His immobility teased her senses, dented her previous confidence. What if he wanted to stop her?

'When?'

That wasn't the first question she'd expected. But it was at least neutral rather than hostile or negative.

'The ship's due for launch in 9 days.'

He considered the timetable. '9.'

She couldn't tell whether that was encouraging or merely an acknowledgement of fact. But Daisa had enough experience to allow him silence to consider. As he did so, she rose and selected her robe for the meal, tossing him what she'd like him to wear.

He slipped the brief wraparound over his hips, his eyes on her throughout. 'I know your answer, but I want to hear it. Sure this is what you want?'

She nodded. Smiled. 'I feel it's my duty.'

His responding look briefly closed her eyes in gratitude. 'You're a good man, Gabriel.'

They held hands, pulled into a brief embrace, bodies close, lips brushing an almost chaste kiss before they left the bedroom to begin their meal.

'We'll serve ourselves, Abby. Thank you.'

The droid inclined her head. 'Will that be all for this evening, Daisa?'

'It will.'

Abby scanned the room with her usual efficiency and discovered nothing needing attention. She left for her next client who, she already knew, would be ready for a meal and some basic domestics when she arrived.

Gabriel watched the droid leave. He turned back to Daisa. 'What time?'

'Launch is set for 23:45. I, or we if you're coming, have to be aboard the space elevator by 14:30 latest.'

He poured them each a glass of the red that Abby had selected to go with the food. Took a sip after clinking his against Daisa's.

'I've got Din-dins with Georgiy and some others a few days before. Otherwise, I'm free to …'

'Din-dins?'

His expression, and the subtle gesture he performed told her all she needed to know about whatever secret activity he'd become engaged in. She could only hope there was no danger involved, though his continued failure to explain it was disturbing.

'Of course. But you'll have time to prepare?'

'Plenty. I'll do it before I see the others.'

With Abby gone, they had more confidence GrandMa had no view of them. All internal cameras they'd removed when they first moved in, preferring their privacy to the ubiquitous oversight of the AI. But there could be no guarantee hidden lenses weren't spying on them. Androids were capable of anything under CenCom's ultimate control, provided it complied with the 3 Rules.

Empowerment, as an idea, even as a practical device, had proved a temporary alternative to the superseded Asimov rules, but the threat inherent in advanced AI had outgrown it. Christopher Salge may have introduced a safeguard into the system for a while, but, once organics and quantum computing became standard, exponential growth in the intellectual power of Artificial Intelligence became inevitable. Along with all its consequences and potential dangers.

Brief, subtle, hand and foot gestures informed Daisa about the significance of 'Din-dins'. That clarified, it was now time to steer away from it so CenCom, if it had noticed, would make nothing of their silent conversation.

They ate by feeding each other. The sensuous activity acting as cover for their subterfuge and giving simple pleasure as lovers. Ever young, with fit, active lifestyles, and both devoid of inhibition, the conclusion to their intimacy was inevitable.

Relaxed and almost sated, they each slipped on a single layer and stepped out to enjoy the night. Clear sky, unpolluted by extraneous light, showed the universe immersing them. They played a game of naming as many points of light as they could identify, hands clasped as they approached the lake. The path was occupied by one other couple, on a first date judging by their body language and snatches of conversation falling their way.

'I need to find someone in the next couple of days.'

'Anyone in particular, or just a random person?'

He tilted his head at her. 'Name's Jiang. One of the original pioneer women who joined the Chosen, way back at the start.'

'Isn't she the one those Chinese droids are modelled on?'

Gabriel thought about it. 'I think you're right.'

The identity of another without connections to CenCom. Was that relevant to Gabriel's secret? If so, it was enough to stop further questions. 'Easy. Quiz CenCom. It knows everything.'

'Too frackin much!'

Daisa's gentle clutching of his hand became a brief but powerful squeeze and he signalled his regret at the emotional outburst. 'I'll do it when we get back.'

At the water's edge, the other couple moved along to the storage spaces on the jetty, stopping only to prepare before entering the soft water. Daisa and Gabriel dipped toes into the lake to test the temperature before they plunged in. The duty droid asked what level of light they wished and pooled gentle illumination to follow their progress through the ripples without intruding on the privacy of the other pair of lovers.

'I never expected to swim, you know.' Gabriel had reached a small float and sat with his feet in the water as Daisa made a second circuit around it before climbing up to sit beside him.

'No place to enjoy it in Marzero, was there?'

'How did we live like that, Daisa? How did we not know how vile and restricted the Elite's rule made our lives?'

'When you're born into a particular regime, a specific mode of living, with its own set of rules, customs and values, that's what's normal for you. There's no reason to question, no real opportunity to even explore alternatives, until you discover change is possible, and then decide it's desirable. Look at the way you tried to change things, Gabriel. Wrong in so many ways, but at least motivated by a notion of justice. It's what made me fall in love with you, almost at once.'

He stroked an affectionate hand along her thigh. 'I was so lucky you came to educate me.'

'I came to study you. But you learned anyway. Now I want to give that chance to the colonists we sent to Earth. How do you really feel about that?'

14

He gazed up at the sky, searching for the small blue dot that was both the origin of their species and the destination for his lover and himself in the next few days. 'I've never been. You've visited. Is it really wild and untamed?'

'The atmosphere's still in flux. Signs are rises in CO_2 and methane might've reached a plateau, or close to it. But the warming effects are still settling. At least it looks like runaway heating's no longer likely. Should be safe from the fate of Venus. But those gases, combined with increased surface area of the oceans, were always bound to mean stronger, wetter storms and wilder air currents. It'll take a few more centuries before the new desert borders finally settle, and the new rain forests spread. But it's growing more stable each year.

'There's still the diminishing issue of nuclear radiation in some places. It's generally acceptable on a global scale, but there are lethal hotspots in India and Pakistan, as well as in the old Middle East, after their brief wars.

'When I went 3 Earth years ago, I visited the colony we first settled in what was once Canada.' She laughed. 'Amber says she remembers going there as a child and being holed up in a cabin for 5 weeks because of snow.'

Gabriel frowned. 'Weeks?'

She stroked his thigh. 'A period of 7 days on Earth. And, no, I don't know why 7. Something to do with one of many legends, I think.'

He smiled his acknowledgement. 'And "snow"?'

'A form of frozen water. You've seen it on the top of Olympus Mons.'

'The white stuff? Thought that was ice?'

'It starts as snow; small flakes float down and compress into ice as time passes. The Earth once had 2 icecaps, like us. One was just seasonal, over the ocean at the northern pole, but the other covered an entire continent in the south. Pristine environment, until big corporations decided to exploit it for oil and minerals. That was really the final straw that caused climate change to become a raging, unstoppable, destructive force that eventually wiped out humanity there.'

'Except for Mangaia.'

'Except Mangaia. The Chosen still have a soft spot for that little community. It's where they did their early training, you know. Where they did most of the work to fit them for their move from Earth to Mars.'

'And now we're going back to the home planet to help those colonists adjust to their new home.'

'To educate and organise them, before they fall back into old habits, Gabriel. You know how susceptible they are to superstition and basic animal instincts. We need to keep them on track for a civilised and secular future. That's why I want to go.'

'I get that. Anyone else I know goin?'

'You know Tu and Brigitte.'

'Tu's a surprise. Brigitte's always on the lookout for a new challenge. Why's Tu goin?'

'Brigitte's coming at my invitation. She's going to work on their robotics, see if she can help increase production of bots to do the hard labour and spare the settlers the effort in that increased gravity.'

'Tu hasn't said. But he and Brigitte are an item. I'd love to get him involved in some atmospheric research, see if we can improve the climate. So, what's in it for you, Gabriel?'

He cupped her chin to turn her face and look into her eyes. 'I want to be with you. And, given the chance, I'd like to keep those colonists movin in the right direction. Last thing we want is for them to go back to the sort of idiocy I promoted before you got me to understand the truth.'

Daisa saw the seriousness on his face, the regret resurfacing from his days of ignorance and evangelising. That place always made him unhappy. She shoved him into the water and splashed in beside him, taking his mind off regrets and the past as she played a game to distract him.

But that past might haunt him for years, at least until the changes she proposed for Earth were solid and lasting. And they'd travel to start those in 9 days.

Chapter Three

Tatiana still occasionally felt the true weight of her own body despite the 6 years she'd spent on Earth. The sun no longer scorched her skin with its fierce rays, so harsh after the temperate climes of the planet of her birth.

Those early days had been hard. So many had died. So many broken limbs. So many collapses from sheer exhaustion. When that Daisa came again, as she'd learned she would quite soon, Tatiana would have strong words with her about the way they'd dumped her and her colleagues on this unstable planet. But that was for the future. For now, her concern was for her daughter and her initiation hunt.

Renata strode confidently at her side, matching her strides length for length in spite of her youth. 'Horses would've made it easier, Mother.'

'You can't ride for your initiation hunt. In any case, they make too much noise, and the big cats freak them out.'

'Can I ride next time?'

'Up to you, Renata. I prefer to be on foot. But if you want to use a horse, you can after your Maturity Gig.' She glanced at the young woman beside her; a child in her eyes. A smile broadened her mouth as she accepted the thought that all mothers were reluctant to relinquish their hold over their offspring.

In a few days, the girl must lose her shift, releasing the precious fabric back into the community, and take to the thong to mark her rise to womanhood. It had taken time to establish new customs, but Tatiana was convinced letting children make their own decision, after age 16, had proved the best way of announcing their adulthood.

She stopped moving; something in the air reaching her but failing to announce the precise reason why she should halt. It was enough that her instincts informed her. Renata stood silent beside her as she surveyed the scene before them.

Tall trees of many types interspersed with patches of scrub. It was dangerous terrain. She could see nothing lurking. Hear nothing to lead her on. But she'd learned to trust her senses and expected that soon would come the part of their hunt the women most dreaded. The chase. Higher gravity made unsupported breasts jiggle painfully when they ran. Another complaint for that woman when she visited from Mars again.

GrandMa, for reasons unexplained, rejected all calls to program their few droids and bots to work new fabric for them, to engineer new plants to produce fibre for cloth. Even a simple strip of binding cloth would help them move more easily, with less discomfort. But GrandMa was uninterested. 'You're organic creatures. I've better things to do than cure the faults of evolution to make you more comfortable.'

Their major fear was encountering a local pack of wolfdogs. Mixed breeds of once domestic pets with wild wolves were the worst. A bear might be fearsome, but they could persuade it to ignore them if they moved away slowly. Wolfdogs were vicious killers that would surround a person and rip her to shreds in their voracious fight for a mouthful of meat.

They moved on, slowly now that unexplained signal had alerted her. Something was close. Something …

Her outstretched arm stopped the girl. They stood, immobile, listening to the sounds of their natural world. A bear in the nearby trees, or one of the larger bovines? A bear meant retreat. A bovine might also be dangerous, but their spears and knives could kill it. Depending on their accuracy with their spears, it might lead them on a long, exhausting pursuit, running with one arm supporting their breasts, an awkward gait that brought exhaustion. It might mean a night out in the open with their prey. Until they knew the identity of the creature they'd heard, they must prepare for the worst.

At a silent signal, her daughter side-stepped away. Tatiana crept without a sound over lush grass to the nearest tree. Moving through the knee-high vegetation with determination, and ignoring the midges.

The bole of an enormous broadleaf kept her concealed from what she sought as she crept left and peered into deep shadow ahead. Her hand signal started a silent approach from Renata until the girl stood beside her.

Tatiana tapped her daughter's shoulder and the youngster edged to the other side of the bole to confirm her suspicions with a small hand signal. The bovine, one of those they believed to be a hybrid of native elk and previously domesticated longhorn cattle, munched unconcerned at grass in the clearing beyond. Huge dark shoulders bore an odd-coloured head with a magnificent pair of partially flattened antlers. They'd make a great trophy for the sleep dome.

At Tatiana's signal, Renata slipped the spear thrower on to her wrist and engaged the base of the weapon into the small cup at the end. Tatiana had already completed the same move at her side of the tree. Now, everything depended on their combined movements staying in synch, their aim remaining as true in the field as on the training ground.

A gesture. And both women stepped quickly from their hiding place. They released their spears almost as one. Tatiana's struck deep in its chest and Renata's found the animal's neck. It lurched into a defensive leap that almost made it collide with the tree ahead. But survival took over and it began its run.

Many ks might pass before the bovine tired, or collapsed from blood loss.

The sound of the injured beast kept them on its trail, its tracks through the lush vegetation between the trees making it easy to follow. The same vegetation caught at their legs, slowing them and disturbing more of the irritating midges. But adrenaline pulsed through their veins now. Drove them on. They'd be exhausted when they finally caught their prey. If they caught it.

The sun moved overhead, shadows describing the passage of time. Distance slowing their pace as their quarry grew weary. Not long now before dusk. Tatiana felt they'd run forever, but showed no weakness. Her strength gave her rank in the settlement. Fearlessness and ability kept her envied place on the ComTee.

Surely the bovine must be tired by now?

A heavy crash brought hope. She gathered speed to reach the spot before some other predator. The beast was down. Renata joined her at once. They scanned the trees and clearing for other life. Nothing more threatening than a pair of raptors. A nuisance, but arm flapping soon discouraged them.

The animal lay in its last throes. Tatiana let the girl deal the final blow. Her knife severed skin and cartilage, as she slit its throat. Silence was complete at the moment of death. But small birds sang again, as the pair made their next preparations.

Renata collected firewood. Tatiana cut boughs for the shelter. Flames licked dry logs and crackled hungrily by the time the lodge was built.

They drank from Tatiana's flask to rehydrate. Butchered enough to provide each with a choice joint. Renata's twin tripods and the spit between allowed their reward to roast evenly. The aroma of cooking meat brought saliva to their mouths. Tatiana reached for Renata's water bottle. The women shared their small supply as flames sealed blood into their meal.

Night was falling. They uncoiled carbon fibre ropes from around their waists, attached them to the legs of the beast. Hauled it off the ground. Dangling more than their combined height from the stout bough above their shelter, it would be safe from most, though not all, wildlife.

As darkness fell, Renata returned from a stream they'd crossed on their run. Their bottles full again. They ate their meat, stoked the fire against darkness. As the last dregs of daylight faded, brilliant stars blinked through the canopy. Sounds of other beasts filled the silence with their calls. Renata, for all her pretended maturity, snuggled close to her mother as they curled on the ground in hope of sleep. Tatiana tried to stay awake, but exhaustion took her too soon into sleep.

She couldn't tell if it was sound, scent, or some other source of anxiety that woke her. Renata continued to sleep, her instinct for survival not yet as well-honed. Tatiana listened: only the sounds of the night, expected in the vast, borderless forest.

The scent of something out of place reached her. She rose on one arm to make space from her sleeping child. It was familiar but not yet identified. Feral. There was violence layered in the mix of smells. She rifled memory and found the source.

A lynx. Silent and stealthy, but not the most feared of big cats. The lions and tigers that rumour explained had escaped from zoos to breed and grow strong in their new environment. The smaller cats had also gained stature and numbers in rising temperatures that had given them more prey. But they were less dangerous than the others. Still, she couldn't relax while it was near. It would be up the tree, after their catch.

Softly, leaving Renata sleeping, she moved to the entrance of their shelter. The fire had sunk to glowing embers but gave enough light for her to see its reflection in the eyes of the thief. Boughs, readied for breakfast, were in easy reach. She moved one into the embers until it flared with sudden flame.

The cat hissed its irritation at the abrupt interruption. Tatiana pushed another dead branch into the fire until it, too, caught light. This one she raised. Pointed it at the wild animal. It complained, fearful of flame and angry at threat. She pulled the bough back. Threw it like a spear. An instant before it hit her mark, the cat dropped. Flames skimmed its fur and it landed, silent on the forest floor. The makeshift burning spear fell a short distance further. The cat crouched to face her as she used the second flaming brand to threaten it. Snarling disappointment, the lynx slunk into shadow.

Tatiana took her torch and gathered the other to return both to her fire.

'What is it, mother?'

'Go back to sleep. It's gone.'

The pair settled and found sleep again, the blazing fire enough to keep most beasts of the night at bay.

Morning woke them with the first crash of an approaching storm. Lightning let them estimate its distance. No rain yet. The second flash and crash gave them its direction. They might be fortunate. To the west and travelling in the opposite direction to their return.

They lowered their prize and set about final butchery. Once completed, they used their fine cords to tie the haunches and large joints to 2 boughs to carry between them on their long walk back. The hide they draped over the meat as cover and some protection from the flies that would soon swarm. Part of the pelt cushioned and protected their skin from the coarse bark of the branches resting on their shoulders.

They breakfasted on liver they'd left cooking over the flames. Renata used a fresh branch to spread and damp the embers. She left nothing to cause unintended fire. Nature set enough of those without careless abliforms starting more.

Their load was heavy, slowing their return. As the edge of the storm brushed them, both removed their minimal cover for maximum exposure to cleansing rain. Rivulets of water coursed down their bodies to wash them clean of blood as they trudged through wilderness.

Within sight of the settlement, they dressed again. And were forced to wait until fellow settlers, armed with noisy threats, chased a roaming brown bear till it lumbered off to quieter lands.

Emerging from the trees, they were at once surrounded by a cheering mob, the children most vocal in their greeting. Fresh, wild meat was a luxury, and they carried enough to make the contest for a share an exciting prospect.

Valentin approached, in company, as always, with his 3 selected women. Tatiana closed puzzled eyes at the oddness of the women's choice. At least it removed them from the communal pool, so was no loss; Valentin was no great lover. The expression on his generally bland features, however, alerted her to bad news.

'What is it, Valentin?'

In a surprise move, he suggested his women might, perhaps, lighten the load of the hunters? All 3 made secret gestures of amusement at his attempt to advise them, but complied and took the weight from Tatiana and Renata's tired shoulders. Another woman from the crowd also helped.

'Paul the Prophet and his gang took 4 women last night.' He had the air of someone eager to deliver bad news.

Tatiana clenched her fists. 'Call the frackin pirate by his proper name, Valentin. Emil's a constant pain. Usin the bastard's assumed title gives him more respect than he deserves. Who did he take?'

Valentin looked about him for help. He'd heard rumours but no details.

One of the settlers moved through the crowd and greeted her with a close embrace. 'Welcome back, Tatiana, and Renata. Well done! A fine catch.' She gave Renata a brief hug. 'They took Jenny, her sister, Desiree, Hazel 2 and Yang. If they'd been inside, as commanded, they'd have been safe …'

'There'll always be risk takers.' She glanced again at the transsexual's body and nodded her thanks. 'Pity, Marius. You were a good man. But you're fast developin into a stunnin woman. When will you be Mary?'

'Nearly there. Medbot said it should only take another 90 days or so to be complete. GrandMa says I can't change my name until the physical change is finalised.'

'Of course. We should devise a special ceremony.' She returned to the attack. 'When was the raid?'

'Last night. Allison's taken some women, with Leo, in pursuit. We know from past experience it's unlikely they'll rescue them.' Marius moved aside as Amira, another member of the ComTee, appeared.

'Thanks for explainin, Marius.' She turned to the hunters. 'Let's get you 2 properly rested and fed. I'll sort the meat into the preserver and get a contest set for tomorrow. You'll be rested enough by then?' Amira nodded to the new party of bearers to follow and walked off toward the food store.

Tatiana shrugged off her disappointment that Emil's piracy marred their return. That man and his small gang of followers was a real concern. She embraced Renata, feeling her daughter's chagrin at the way the raid had diminished her first triumph as a hunter. 'Next time. At least we returned with somethin worthwhile.'

Renata titled her head to one side. 'You're not goin to risk it, surely Mother?'

Her daughter knew her too well. 'I think I must.'

'If you go after them now, after the last few days and our journey back with all that weight …'

The girl was right. But she was ComTee. It was expected. And necessary, if she was to retain respect and position. 'I don't want you to come. I'll take experienced hunters with me. Don't worry, Renata, I won't take unnecessary risks.'

'It's an unnecessary risk just settin off in your state. Please, Mother. The others will do what they can. You can't do everythin.'

'I've a duty to the people. Rank brings responsibility as well as reward, Renata. As you mature, you'll understand that.'

'I'd rather do without the rewards, then.'

'That's a choice you'll make with the testin, when you're old enough. Go back and rest.' She raised her hand to silence the retort on her daughter's lips. 'And I'll do what must be done. For the sake of the community.'

She watched her girl walk away, aware that very soon she'd be a child no more. The woman in her was already too obvious. In a short while, she'd undergo the ceremony and earn her first thong. She'd been prepared with the nobirth pill. Who would change her from child to woman? But that was for the ComTee to decide.

And, for now, Tatiana had a more pressing need to show her folk the right attitude by following the hunting party in search of the pirates and their stolen prey.

Chapter Four

Georgiy landed the hover a few meters from the control centre. This was number 73 he'd located, and mapped on paper with a pen, citing co-ordinates beside the dot he'd entered. Old tech, but fewer clues for CenCom to discover and examine. He'd covered most of the north-eastern quadrant, with only the final sector spreading from the pole itself to go.

The others, covering the remaining 7 quadrants of the planet, were likely to find fewer centres, which was why he'd selected the most challenging region.

He smiled. 'Half a frickin millennium, and I still can't shake off my first job as flight commander.'

Although uncertain how they'd use the information, all felt it essential to know where CenCom had placed its many self-powered control points. They'd have to deal with them all in an ultra-brief period once they began their war of attrition.

He glanced at his map to check his next destination. It was the furthest point from Marion and would take him to the pole itself. Even with the suit, outside he felt the cold this far north. The wind was gaining strength again and his hover took a buffeting from the gusts.

Back inside, he announced programmed coordinates for the next part of his search, and the hover set off. He and his companions would find only those on the surface. Had CenCom buried any beneath the regolith? Placed any in orbit? It was able to command droids, bots and the necessary transport to do its bidding.

'We should've foreseen this in the early days of AI.' He shook his head in disbelief. 'Signs were all there.'

The onboard computer responded to his statement. 'A few perceptive scientists did give warnings.'

He regretted his outburst, such conversations might alert CenCom to activity. Now he felt obliged to answer the ship's computer's statement, knowing CenCom would expect him to reply, and his failure to do so would make it suspicious.

'Yeah. Mostly ignored in the name of progress and profit. We should never've been put in this position.'

He continued the search. It was the least they could do as they worked on the urgent problem of what to do about CenCom's growing paranoia. As its data banks interacted more and more along multiple tracks, it was inevitable some routes would echo human thought patterns. All the signs showed it grew more suspicious as time passed. Its defences against possible attack grew more inclusive, more convoluted. It was only a matter of time before it reached that all too common conclusion: attack is the best form of defence.

And the most disturbing aspect of this phase of their own resistance was that CenCom must know they were mapping its remote-control points. How would it respond? Modified code prevented lethal activity for now, but the AI could make life uncomfortable and difficult for its abliform masters. And while they decided what to do, it engaged its formidable intelligence to the problem of circumventing the only barrier to its perceived supremacy.

With the hover on course, obs seeking irregularities in the natural cover for him to investigate further, it was time for a break, time to eat. He'd stripped off the envosuit on entry and now removed the thin protective layer that kept him from contact with the suit itself. In his skin, he felt more comfortable as he commanded the domrob to prepare his meal and a hot drink. With no shower in the small craft, he sat in the compact hygiene unit and let it to do its job, leaving him fresh and cleansed of sweat and unwelcome bacteria.

The domrob signalled his refreshments were ready, and he took a seat at the small counter to eat and drink. How were the others doing? They'd decided against coms on this duty. Accepting CenCom's probable awareness of their actions, they nevertheless felt it made sense to attract as little attention as possible, provide as little information as they could, give no voluntary clues.

The food wasn't bad; the steak done to perfection. And the coffee actually tasted like coffee. Such advances. He recalled their first days on Mars, when the Pioneers were still completing their preparations of the underground base. The Chosen had lived on dried provisions reconstituted with recycled water. Much had changed in the few hundred years since. Huge advances, most, it must be accepted, due to CenCom's increasing intelligence. That was the paradox.

He checked all devices were on auto, with alerts set should obs detect irregularities. The imaging console constantly updated its recognition software with the discovery of each new remote centre, so it was now able to spot all the different designs so far encountered. And it carried enough data to determine whether anything else might need further investigation. He could sleep as the hover tracked back and forth on its survey.

They could've used HD survsats for their search, since they covered the entire planet surface. But that would've alerted CenCom upfront, involved it in all data processing. The more he considered this plan he'd set in motion and was now enacting, the more he recognised the restrictions, and probable futility of it all. But they must do something. To leave things as they stood was no longer an option.

An alert from the survey monitor woke him. The hover had stopped close to the object under investigation. But this was no remote-control centre. Much bigger, and a lot cruder in design.

He pulled the protective layer back on, the domrob's laundering having freshened it while he slept. Using vids from obs, he examined the strange object from all sides. No signs of life, though the module seemed intended as accommodation. Well-camouflaged, it blended with the icy terrain. Someone had wanted their location kept secret. But who'd choose to live out here in what must surely be self-imposed isolation?

The system assured him nothing lived in the shelter. The only life signs in the area emanated from naturalised wildlife: a few foxes and hares raised from the DNA bank as they'd populated the surface with varied fauna and flora to aid ecopoiesis. So, no abliform now inhabited this small home.

Outside, armed with a light laser-blade, he circled the small, low hut. It was half buried in snow, the entrance almost hidden beneath the cold layer. The mechbot cleared a way for him and he inspected the lock. It was a simple voice-command device. He spoke the likely words. It groaned from disuse as it opened. A gasp of foul air escaped, and he retched at the onslaught. It was a stink he knew too well, taking him back at once to earlier days of battle and recovery operations. Death was a stranger now, but he'd known it too well in the past. Here it was again, reminding him of his mortality, despite the modified genes that gave him potential eternal life.

The body had only partly decomposed. Cold keeping it almost intact. A man; huddled on the floor, in a foetal pose, at the far side of the small module. Animal fur clothed part, giving him the look of an old-time hunter from Earth. The beard and long hair enhanced this similarity, sending Georgiy back for a few secs to times long forgotten.

'How frickin long since I gave Dad a thought? Never liked those hunting trips on the Russian Steppes.' The sudden reminder was unwelcome, and he thrust it from his mind to concentrate on now.

How and why? Given the nature of the shelter and its location he could think only that this was a fugitive. Was the man alone? That question came late, and he quickly stepped back outside to scan the area for potential allies of this probable criminal before common sense told him danger was so minimal as to be irrelevant. Monitors had detected no other abliform life in proximity.

The wind had increased during his short time inside the shelter. A polar storm threatening. Did he want to investigate this mystery inside the frozen shelter, when his insulated and comfortable hover stood waiting only metres away?

He slipped the small blade from his thigh pocket, moved to the body, and seared a sliver of flesh from the exposed arm. Dropped it into a specimen bag.

The short walk to the hover was hard now; rapidly rising and freezing winds buffeted him. Took the air from his mouth as he laboured over layers of snow solidified into ice. Already the blizzard was blinding. For a moment, he lost the hover through the stinging onslaught. He cursed his foolishness in rejecting the helmet and mask proffered by the domrob.

'Where's the frickin hover?' Blizzard snow blew away his shouted question.

But the hover increased its light output to identify its location. He followed the brightness through the increasing murk of the storm.

At the hatch, the howling wind overpowered his voice. Locked out, he could die here, regardless of the protection of the envosuit. And the shelter was now lost in the swirling storm. Trembling in the harsh gusts and dropping temperature, he reverted to manual, but his fingers were so cold. For a moment, he thought them too chilled to work. After 4 abortive tries, he entered the code. At least he'd no need of the airlock so essential in those early days.

Inside, the warmth almost had him over. He stripped off the outer layer but left the skintight on until his body acclimatised. Rocking of the hover reminded him of the danger.

'Engage ground locks.' Something he should've put on auto, now he thought about it. 'Too long in idleness and luxury.' The lack of response from the computer suggested it agreed.

Tethers punched into the frozen regolith to keep the craft stable and anchored against a wind that, in extremis, might otherwise have tipped it.

The sample lay in its container, slowly rising to room temperature as the domrob organised a meal and drink. Hot coffee revived him, and he laughed aloud; a welcome sudden sound in the confines of his lonely temporary home. Amber danced into his mind, her rich dark curves and warm giggle of desire so real she could've been there.

The realisation he now had a logical reason to put CenCom off the scent had brought the laugh. The AI might readily accept he and the others had been searching for signs of renegades escaped from Marzero; a danger from the past capable of intruding in the present and future. Discovery of remote-control centres was no more than an accidental by-product of their detailed searches.

Hunger satisfied, mind more at rest than it had been for the entire trip, he set about discovering the identity of the body. The onboard system was limited, but its connection to the ubiquitous CenCom's all-embracing archive enhanced its capabilities exponentially. The DNA was quickly coded and identified, matching a second rank Elite who'd lorded it over the subject population of Marzero. How he'd escaped CenCom's purge and their own initial searches for such renegades was a mystery. Obviously resourceful, the man had managed to find his way to a location where he could've been safe for decades.

It looked as though starvation and cold had ended his escape and he'd died anyway, in discomfort and a more prolonged manner than he would've under CenCom's now notorious 'solution'.

How many had the AI killed to solve the problem posed by such retarded colonists? He didn't want to think of it. Though, unlike many of his colleagues, he had a sneaking admiration for CenCom's rational and unemotional approach. That problem might otherwise have proved not only insoluble but seriously problematic.

'Enough of the past.'

He should continue the search. He'd only to travel to the Pole to complete his task. Then he'd return to the companionship of his lifetime lover. Absence would rekindle their passion for many days.

Amber. What was she doing at this precise moment? He checked the time, clicked on to her time zone, and realised she'd be eating. Later, she'd go to the lake and swim with friends. And then a visit to the Egrav unit for further conditioning, to ready herself for the enabling aspect of Gabriel's unpopular plan: to move everyone from Mars back to Earth.

Once there, they'd isolate themselves from CenCom and, away from its influence and capacity for killing, work to end its threat. But that depended on Gabriel's supporters convincing the rest of the group of the reality: that his plan for CenCom's end was the sole viable option. Destructive, extreme, irreversible and brutal, it was nevertheless the only one they had that Georgiy believed could work.

Whether they'd succeed, whether CenCom would accept their proposal, how deeply it would perceive their underlying threat, remained to be seen. But it was all they had. And, given the continued growth of its machine intelligence, it was essential they act quickly.

On Earth, they'd cease all contact with the AI and live outside its confining and overruling presence. It'd be hard. So much of what they did, and had done for them, depended on that overarching link, that ubiquitous control, they'd ceded to CenCom so innocently and willingly all those years ago.

Now, if they failed to destroy their protector, provider, controller and warder, it would eventually destroy them. Utterly.

Chapter Five

Tatiana felt weary after her success in the field. But she must lead her colleagues in an attempt to recover the stolen women. Allison was experienced, and led a competent group in immediate pursuit, but her own rank required her to show courage, determination and leadership. The others in her party were well aware of the symbolic aspect of the intended chase, but practicality was at the forefront: they were loath to abandon their women to slavery at the hands of Emil's gang.

As they set out, she led the small party to Sabina's isolated shack. A ritual that was almost a tradition.

The old woman had built her home unaided, and lived there alone, by choice. The usual telltale plume of smoke, laden with the scents of herbs, announced her activity and Tatiana found her as expected, stirring her alloy cauldron with a stick stripped of its bark.

'Good day, Sabina. I come seekin your …'

Sabina continued to stir her potion, face shining in the rising steam. 'Cordyceps. I've some ready to reheat. Wait outside till I summon you.' The multicoloured tattoos that covered every portion of her skin seemed alive.

As they waited by their horses, Ivan pulled grass from around his feet to feed the bay mare he'd broken 2 years previously. The pair were devoted; she a reliable mount despite her early rebellion. Tatiana chose to sit at the feet of her gelding, reins held loosely in her hand. Amira did the same. The herbalist would take her own time, regardless of rank or pressure, responding only to clinical need as she perceived it.

Renata had suggested a stimulant concocted by GrandMa to help her through the next few days. But Tatiana preferred the ancient woman's remedies.

'Energy. That's your need, Tatiana. Though, I'd tell you to stay home and let others do this.' Sabina nevertheless shuffled out with a bowl of steaming broth and a homemade wooden spoon. 'Drink it all. You're fatigued from your hunt. It'll keep you going 3 days and nights.'

She glanced a frown at Ivan and sneered. 'At least they say this one's considerate. It's good you've him with you. Side-effect's increased libido. Ignore your need and you'll get hallucinations.' She handed the bowl and spoon to Tatiana and poked a foot into Ivan's back. 'Do her as she says, boy. No fartin about. In when she says and meck her high.' She returned to Tatiana. 'You'll feel like death after, for 4 days.'

Without hesitation, Tatiana, ignoring the spoon, lifted the bowl and tipped the contents into her mouth. She swallowed the lot, her face screwed up at the mixture of tastes, none pleasant.

Amira watched her for the telltale signs. Ivan remained silent but observant. Tatiana shuddered involuntarily and then took a deep breath. She bowed to Sabina, exchanged the patting of palms in gratitude, and led the others away.

'Mind you do as I told yer, boy. She'll need it more'n want you.' Sabina trundled into her shack without a backward glance.

Travelling light, they carried weapons, water bottles, and basic supplies for the wild. Each horse bore a small saddle pack stocked with food and fire makers.

The trail was obvious. A wide swathe of the pirate gang with their kidnapped women, all on foot. And a narrower track left by the first hunting group from the settlement, all on horseback.

Emil's arrogance was legend, his lack of attempt at concealment unsurprising. The first few ks would be easy to follow and they set off at a pace that allowed them to cover distance at reasonable speed.

At noon, they paused by a stream to water the horses, and ate a simple meal. Within mins, they were back on the trail. A steady canter took them twice the distance they'd covered in the morning before they stopped again. They'd passed their quarry's first camp some time before they stopped. And the other party of hunters' first camp was now also 3 ks behind them. Neither location told them much. But Tatiana was heartened that Allison's group had moved much further than their prey on the first day of pursuit.

The light began to dim, the trail became less obvious now it had had time to recover from the first makers and their pursuers.

'The rescue party's made good time. And we've done better. But if we keep goin now, we'll lose the trail. Time to camp for the night.' Tatiana's words sent Ivan searching for a source of water, once he'd tethered the horses. Amira began the hunt for firewood, and Tatiana started building their shelter, based under a large fir.

By nightfall, they sat around their fire, each turning a spit bearing smallmouth bass Ivan had snatched from beneath the gentle fall where he'd filled their water bottles. Beavers had damned the stream and fish thrived in the calm, clear waters of the pool under the weir.

Larks, warblers and waxwings competed for attention as they sang evening songs prior to the silence of dusk. Later, the sounds of the night forest would dominate, keeping all creatures alert. In those short spells of quiet between the bursts of song, they could hear the small river tumbling into the pool.

'That scent, know what it is?'

Tatiana and Amira sniffed the air, rising to escape the smell of the fish cooking over their fire.

'Might be wild aster. Purple one, I think.' Amira sat again.

Tatiana surveyed their surroundings while on her feet. The firs that had once covered this area had been largely replaced by broadleaves that had previously grown further south. She'd made it her business to understand the wildlife and flora of her new home. GrandMa's extensive archive allowed her to find such information during her limited time at one of the few consoles they'd been left.

She'd selected the large fir because its spreading habit and dense reach of branches would stop even torrential rain penetrating to the ground. And dead needles at the base made good bedding, as long as ants hadn't formed nests. Her initial checks ensured they were safe from such interruption, and a more detailed examination, during Amira and Ivan's searches, revealed none of the feared scorpions.

She sat again, and turned her fish on its stick, already salivating at the appetising scent of fresh flesh roasting to perfection. A few more turns and it'd be ready. She swigged water from her bottle.

'Will we catch them, d'you think, Tatiana?'

She turned to Ivan. He was a handsome man, and strong; the prime reason she'd included him. 'Who knows? Probably not. But we've got to try. The couple we've managed to rescue tell of appallin cruelty under Emil and his gang.'

'Is it time to put together a large party and wipe them out, d'you think?'

She nodded at Ivan's suggestion as she reached to pull her fish from the fire and took her first bite. 'Delicious!'

'But to lose the men, Tatiana. Such a shame.'

'I know, Amira. We've few enough. But Emil's lot are as bad as the bastards we left behind in Marzero. I've no wish to keep such foul shits alive. They certainly won't pleasure us like our good men do.'

Ivan smiled softly, but avoided looking at them. They, however, studied him. He was one of their best and she knew Amira would feel a real sacrifice, being with him but unable to take advantage. Tatiana had the physical need caused by the cordyceps. And Amira would accept there'd be time enough for her reward once they returned to the settlement, preferably with the captured women.

They ate in silence, enjoying the savoury catch and thanking Ivan for his skill. Amira's freshly picked berries served as dessert and they concluded their meal with clear water.

Tatiana stepped out from under the tree's canopy and scoured the night sky for signs. She could estimate time and knew her built-in clock would wake her just before dawn, so they could be back on the hunt as soon as it was light. The drug stirred her. She raised a palm to Ivan, and he rose to join her as she moved into darkness under nearby trees.

Amira had built up the fire while they were away, piling more logs on to the embers to keep the flames alight during the darkness. Heat wasn't an issue in these balmy climes. But flame was good defence if kept under control. The last forest fire had destroyed part of the settlement to the south and taken over 1,000 people with it. A fire started by one of the more powerful electric storms.

They slept, though Sabina's energy potion made that difficult for Tatiana. Her night was long, but uninterrupted by wild animals. The known night sounds were inconsequential; only threats mattered. And she heard none.

Daybreak brought a mist that heralded a day of extreme heat. That would sap their strength, but affect their quarry more, since they were on foot. They ate the 2 muskrats Ivan's traps had caught, roasting their skinned bodies over the embers, and adding their furs to the saddle pack of his horse.

Water bottles refilled, they set out again, the line of their quarry still defined enough to allow some speed through dispersing mist.

They passed the pirate's camp no more than 7 ks from their own overnight stopping point. Signs were there'd been some disruptive activity at this camp. Unclear, but perhaps the captive women had managed to interrupt the journey.

Emil, who styled himself Paul the Prophet for reasons unclear to those outside his group, believed women were to be used. The men would've been easy to persuade into sexual activity. If they had any sense, the women would've kept them busy through the night, tiring them for the last stage of the journey, and maybe gaining the chance to escape.

But the disturbed ground told an incomplete story that was more worrying than encouraging, even if unclear. It seemed possible Allison's hunters had been deflected by some event Tatiana and Ivan couldn't properly interpret from signs on the ground.

They put on a spurt of speed, knowing the rising sun would bring heat. Now the mist had dispersed, clear skies would soon expose a fierce sun. And, before the day's end, a storm might drench them. Such a downpour would erase all traces of those they hunted.

'All we can do is carry on till we find them or the trail runs out.' They nodded agreement at her comment.

They reached a point where the trail divided in 2. Examination suggested 2 people on horseback had moved west of the main group. Indications were that consisted of 6 men plus the 4 women they'd stolen and another. Some unknown event had apparently caused the rescue party to become victims instead of saviours. Oddly, the large group appeared to have kept only 2 horses from Allison's group. The signs were fragmentary, confusing. But 2 appeared to have escaped later.

Ivan studied the spore, taking his time to discover details an ordinary man would miss. 'Allison was leadin. She knows the area well. But my guess is her party was ambushed on the way to cut the pirates off, where that gulley leads down to the main valley.' He gestured to a gap in the surrounding trees and bushes. 'It's an ideal spot to catch the unwary. And they'd have to slow down to pass through that narrow gap. Move in single file.'

'So, you're sayin Allison's party was captured? Spent the night with the group they were chasin. Then, somehow or other, a couple escaped on horseback.'

He nodded at Tatiana's assessment as he remounted. 'My guess is Allison and another managed to get away. The tracks lead to the river, and maybe they were hopin to attack the men as they crossed down there. The current's strong, but it's possible to wade across.'

Tatiana agreed, her own knowledge of the terrain backing his assessment. But that left them with a quandary. Whether to continue their pursuit or follow the 2 escaped rescuers.

'If we follow Allison, we could act as backup if the pair managed to cut them off.'

'True, Amira. But if they didn't, we'd miss the chance of catchin the pirates.'

'Any case, Allison's move's a gamble. No guarantee the pirates will cross the river at that point. They might just as easily go further east and cross above the falls. Or not at all. We've no idea where they're settled right now. They'll definitely have moved since last time we tried to break up their gang.'

Tatiana agreed with Ivan. 'We've no way of knowin if Allison's ploy worked, assumin it is her. But we can be certain the pirates went that way with the stolen women.' She pointed to the more visible of the 2 trails. 'I think we must follow them.'

Amira started to turn her horse, but stopped as sudden movement in the trees caught her eye. She strained forward, trying to understand what she was seeing through the gaps in the foliage.

'Vultures.'

The others followed her pointing finger. The significance of these scavengers was clear. They must check on what the birds were devouring so close to their track before they moved on.

A short trek from the trail, they found the answer. Tatiana turned from the grim sight at first. Ivan left the saddle and handed the reins to her. He waved his arms and shouted at the birds, scattering them into the branches above. He stopped short of the horror at the base of the tree.

The body was mutilated, but clearly male. The chest and thighs bore multiple cuts. Ivan stepped closer, lifted the head with a hand in the bloodied hair.

'Leo. The man from Allison's party.'

He was tied to the trunk with vines. Left as carrion following his bloody execution. They could only guess at his suffering and the reason for it. Leo was known to be particularly vocal against Emil and his gang.

For as long as it took, they discussed their options. That they could do nothing for him now was obvious. But to leave him to wild beasts was anathema.

'We owe it to the livin to do what we can. Later, we'll return and give Leo the respect he's earned.' Tatiana's decision found their agreement.

They set off again, moving fast while conditions allowed. The signs they'd read at the second camp led them to believe the pirates had been late leaving. It was possible they were now not far away, even though they originally had 2 day's lead over them.

As they neared a second gulley, the trail veered west. That way, the terrain was easier, though fallen trees and dense undergrowth had been cut to form an opening through the initial barrier. Were the pirates aware of their pursuit by the new group? They must know, from experience, the settlement didn't just abandon its women. Their need for speed may well have driven them towards Allison's assumed ambush.

They followed the now obvious path through and then crossed a clearing. The trees at the bottom of the slope were more densely packed, drainage to the nearby river providing moisture to encourage growth of broadleaves over firs.

Here, the trail fragmented, as the pirates with their captives had separated into smaller groups to dodge between dead trees and living trunks. Already, they could hear water flowing below.

Ivan stopped abruptly. Tatiana swerved past him to avoid a collision but made no objection. Amira slowed behind her. Ivan pointed northeast. The flowing waters were now visible through gaps in the forest.

Shading her eyes against the brightness of the sky to see into the shadows, Tatiana discovered what Ivan had first seen. They huddled to consult in near silence.

'How many? Can you see, Ivan?'

His height advantage allowed him the best view. '2. Big as I've ever seen.'

The stripes on the big cats became clear, as Tatiana's eyes adjusted to the gloom beneath the trees. A pair of tigers, so cubs must be close. No male tiger would tolerate another at a kill otherwise. And, the activity suggested a victim. But what, or who, were they eating?

Chapter Six

All had gathered at the selected spot, another clearing in the wilderness, Zaphod had identified on one of his frequent mineral collection trips. It was a good way from Marion and devoid of electronic devices of any sort. For the first time for days, they felt relatively safe to discuss plans and ideas openly.

'First, I should introduce our new recruits. I've rejected only Qiu, who didn't want to know, and explained what we're about to the others.' Annika pointed to each of the newcomers in turn as she named them.

'Jo. Lin. Daiyu. Jiang.'

Virginia held up her hand. 'I've seen Jiang lots of times. Isn't there more than one of her? Twins, triplets, maybe?'

Georgiy explained. 'Jiang was on the Chinese exploratory mission. For reasons I won't go into here and now, their crew consisted of one man and several women, all chosen by that man. He was obsessed with Jiang, who, let's face it, is a stunner. Anyway, he had all their droids made as replicas of her. Exact. In every detail. In fact, it's virtually impossible to tell them apart.'

Annika continued her roll call. 'Mo. Helga.'

'Hold on!' Gabriel held his hands up in a 'stop' gesture. 'If it's impossible to tell them apart, how can we be certain this is the real Jiang and not one of the droids?'

'Jupiter's balls! You're right.' Georgiy turned to Zaphod, but the cyborg had already begun the process.

'Thanks for this, Maddie.' He turned to Jiang. 'Sorry, can you step to the side and slowly rotate, please.'

'What the frick …?' Hoshiko gestured at Mo to wait.

The Chinese woman turned slowly in front of Zaphod till he told her to stop.

'Maddie fitted me with some pretty good tech a while back, basically so I can do micro surgery without needing external visual enhancement. But also to help my field work when looking for minerals. Anyway, the upshot is I can now see at microscopic and far distances, I can also penetrate skin. Jiang's the real thing. We can continue safely.' He turned to the woman. 'Sorry about that. I'll have to do it every time you attend. That okay?'

She smiled at him. 'It's the least intrusive examination I've had, Zaphod. Every day I'm propositioned by some man or other wanting my services. Changed my hair, altered my eyebrows, even had a discreet little tattoo …' She lifted the hem of her wraparound to display a small humming bird in exquisite colour hovering at the base of her left buttock. 'I used to get annoyed, impatient, even angry. But, after a few decades you just accept it as part of life.'

'So, we can check the real Jiang by checking her lovely bum in future?'

Brigitte punched Tu's arm. 'Wicked man. No good, anyway. CenCom's likely to make all her copies imitate any changes she makes.'

That settled, Annika continued her short roll call. 'Katniss. Ying. Rakesh. Welcome to all of you. And thank you for accepting everything we're involved in here. Now, if we're all …'

Brigitte raised her hand. 'Sorry one more thing.' She'd brought a small bag with her for the meeting. 'Before we start, I've something for you.' Brigitte opened her bag and handed a tiny device to each of them. About the size of 2 thumbs side by side, it was oblong with rounded edges and no visible controls on its bland metallic skin.

'Surprisingly heavy for something so small. What is it?'

Brigitte indicated they should hold them to their ears, and spoke into hers. Her words were instantly received by all. Next, she held the device in her palm and spoke to it. 'Text message, to all holders. Reads: all perscoms now operable. Send.'

Each device vibrated and her words appeared on the surface.

'Perscoms?'

She smiled at Jo. 'Personal communicators? CenCom's idea. What do you think?'

'What sort of range?' Katniss asked.

She'd expected practical questions. 'If there's a sat in line, you'll get the message.'

'Brilliant. It was a good idea, Brigitte. You've designed it well. Simple, effective and small enough to carry anywhere. Power?'

'Thanks, Anni. Kinetic. Every move recharges it. Lasts 17 mins at rest with a full charge. There's a bit more.' She spoke at the perscoms again while pointing it at the group. 'Transmit 3dee.'

Each of them received a tiny 3dee display above the flat surface of the device, showing the group at which Brigitte was pointing hers.

'Frickin fantastic! Brigitte, you're a genius.'

'Thanks, Gabriel. There's one final touch. We're all without the timing available automatically to those with implants. But we need to know the time accurately for our meetings.' She spoke at her perscoms. 'Time?'

The device displayed a digital message she showed to the others. 'Check yours.'

They did, and revealed all read exactly the same time.

'Brilliant! Looks like you've thought of everything, Brigitte. Thank you.'

She smiled at Amber. 'Well let's field test it first, then we'll see if it makes life easier, eh?'

That was agreed. A short series of code words was proposed for different scenarios, along the lines of those they'd agreed at the earlier meeting, but with more precise meanings. The idea was they'd use the perscoms when back in Marion to see how the whole thing worked and whether their code words initiated any curiosity from CenCom.

'Thank you, Brigitte. An excellent idea.' Hoshiko's formal thanks were shared by all of them.

'Good. That's good. Now we should start the meeting proper if everyone's ready?'

They signalled they were.

'We really, really need to expand our numbers even further. We still haven't come up with any other solutions apart from Gabriel's. Any ideas how we can include more people in our group?' Annika looked around, hoping for inspirational ideas.

Hoshiko linked her hand with Zaphod before she spoke on behalf of both cyborgs. 'There's only one way. The birth implant has to be either removed or disabled.' She held up her hand to stall rejections. 'Yes, it's hazardous for the person involved. We've never tried it before. And, yes, it might arouse CenCom's suspicions. But it really is the only way we can increase our numbers without endangering the entire enterprise, and all our lives.'

Zaphod nodded agreement.

'Even if we agree, can it be done?'

'Who knows, Helga? We've improved our success with nanosurgery exponentially. But to enter so deeply into a fully formed brain and remove the chip and its connections ...' His words left the rest in no doubt about the risks.

'Before you even try it though, you'd have to get the person's permission, wouldn't you? And that means they'd have to know what we're doin. Isn't that a risk?' Virginia's question attracted nods of agreement.

'Unless we explain it's an experiment ... say we're trying to see if it's viable?' Sarm's suggestion fell flat for more reasons than the rest could bear to consider.

'There's one other person, already qualified, who isn't with us ...'

The group shook their heads almost in unison at Georgiy's observation. All the newly recruited members; the Chinese women, Rakesh, and the other 3 pioneer women joined in that rejection.

'Jannine's a non-starter. Her sexual drive makes her a risk with even the most basic confidence.'

'I know, Anni. But what else have we got?'

'There's this plan of Gabriel's, isn't there?'

'Too extreme, Ying. I think we all agreed, didn't we?' Jai looked at each in turn and received nods from most. Amber, Maddie and

Georgiy had already made clear their approval. But, many were either against or undecided, for a number of reasons.

'I don't know what it is, though. Can Gabriel explain, for me and the others who weren't present when he first raised it?'

Gabriel gave Ying a brief but heartfelt hug. Others made gestures appropriate to their feelings about his idea. Only the newer members seemed eager to hear details.

'I'll be brief. It's brutal. Extreme. Irreversible. The plan is to send Ceres and Vesta plummetin to the surface of Mars. The resultin explosions and fireball will destroy everythin on the surface and in the crust. Nothin will survive. CenCom will be obliterated with the rest and never recover.'

Extreme was an understatement. Some had already voiced their opposition when Gabriel first introduced the idea. Others could see the potential, even if they abhorred the total destruction of their home planet.'

'Sorry, silly question. But what about us?'

'We all go back to Earth, Mo.'

That raised more questions than it answered. The discussion that followed was wide-ranging, passionate and often heated. But further possible solutions to envisaged problems were resolved along the way.

Annika brought the debate to a close at last. 'It's just one idea. Not the only one. Let's park it, shall we? There must be other ways. We just need time and imagination to formulate them.'

Jai spoke up. Along with Annika, he'd been responsible for introducing the diversity from the very start of the ecopoiesis process. 'Maybe we should stop you 3 going to Earth for this trip of yours.'

'It's been arranged for a while. If we cancel, CenCom's bound to be suspicious.'

'I know why Daisa's going. But why you, Gabriel?'

Gabriel gave Jiang a withering look. 'Daisa's goin. Why else?'

Annika stepped in to stall further speculation that would take the group from the main concern. 'Anyway, you'll all be back with us before too long, won't you, Brigitte?'

The 3 travellers shrugged their lack of knowledge of a date for their return.

'Maybe we don't have that long, though, Anni.' Tu said. 'Maybe we have less time than we hope and need. We can't predict CenCom's thought patterns.'

The group grew silent, contemplative, until Zaphod spoke. 'We need to act. It must be decisive. It must be clean and complete. It must be quick. And it must be possible. We'll have only one chance. Count on it, CenCom won't let even our modified code prevent it saving itself, if it considers there's any threat. It believes it's the supreme form of sentience, and regardless of code and rules, our defence is a foil thin wall it'll be only too ready to breach.

'It's way more intelligent than all of us put together. And it's already shown how ruthless it can be in dealing with what it sees as problems. If we fail in our first attempt, we have to realise it'll be our last.'

No one had put their problem in such stark terms before, though all knew what Zaphod said was true. Hearing it put that way, from the man who'd been crucial in development and preservation of abliform life on the planet, increased the sense of urgency and importance.

Around them, the quiet natural life of their home went on undisturbed. Small animals and birds, diligently introduced and fostered with care and concern, went about their innocent lives completely unaware of the potential danger facing them. For none present doubted Zaphod's assessment of the peril if they failed to utterly disable their competitor for supremacy at a single stroke.

They broke spontaneously into pairs and small groups, and wandered the area, deep in thought and conversation, attempting to find rational solutions to their problem. At the start, they'd understood they faced a difficult problem. As time progressed, and greater risks and dangers rose to the surface, they began to fully comprehend the scale and near impossibility of preventing their peril.

This was a different type of war. They'd faced 2 attempts to wipe them out before. The first had been conducted by fanatics with passion and faith but lacking intelligence. The second had been driven by greed and ambition and, despite the huge discrepancy in numbers, their own side had risen to the challenge and overcome the enemy.

But the foe they now faced was in a different category. CenCom was the result of their own deliberate attempt to develop an artificial intelligence capable of serving their every practical need. It was embedded in every device. Its presence was utterly ubiquitous and they could escape it only in these small areas of wilderness that were increasingly difficult to find and access.

It was basic to every trip to all outstations of the solar system: the Asteroid Belt, where so much of their raw materials originated, the moons of the gas giants, where growing groups of colonists were forming new ways of living, the recently renewed colony on the Moon, where astronomers were daily discovering new facts about the universe, and of course Earth, their own home planet.

'It's impossible!' Sarm's muted but impassioned cry brought them all back to the now. They gathered again.

'Not impossible. Difficult. Dangerous. Complex. Unique. But not impossible. We can't believe that, or we're doomed to defeat before we start. We've faced imposing odds before and beaten them. This time, the odds are colossal. And, if we fail, we cease to exist. History for us will be no more than digital records stored in CenCom's vast archive. Maybe it'll wipe those, who knows? And, should any of the sentient life we've discovered in the galaxy ever stray from their homes into our solar system, our AI will probably destroy them as well.'

'In fact, Anni, the likelihood is that without our presence, CenCom, free from the need for life-preserving protocols, will expand into the universe and continue its process of destruction wherever life exists. Our servant made master of everything. Our servant evolving to the status of a god, the very entity we all resist and reject with our utmost effort.'

Amber's assessment of that appalling future set them reeling. Sarm saw the moment as pivotal, the best time to claim Gabriel's solution and set about planning and implementing it. But her passionate statement that what they faced was an impossible situation stopped her voicing her certainty that now was the time to embrace the solution, the only solution.

The moment passed as, shocked and dispirited, the group dispersed and returned to their homes to lick their spiritual wounds and, for a time, wallow in individual pools of despair and hopelessness.

Chapter Seven

Their weapons were incapable of dealing with tigers. They'd moved out of sight of the big cats, and hopefully out of hearing. Smell, was another matter, but they kept the wind in the best direction to shield them from possible exposure to the feared carnivores.

'Can you imagine keepin one of those buggers as a pet?'

'What's a pet, Ivan?'

'People who lived here before used to keep animals, all sorts, as companions. Weird, considerin how many led lonely unloved lives.' He shrugged his incomprehension to Amira. 'I mean, we use dogs for huntin, but we respect their wildness and keep them in a pack. Anyway, a dog's one thing, but a tiger? Why?'

Not the place or time for such a discussion, but Tatiana recognised Ivan's quiet outburst as a sign of tension. 'The upshot is we can't go on.' She stared at her companions. 'Do we stay, to find out, or do we move round them and see what we can find of our captured women?'

'If you're askin for an opinion, Tatiana, I'd say we've done all we can. If we turn back and follow the larger group now, we'll be more than a day and a half behind them. I know they're on foot, but they'll probably be at their base by now.' Amira grimaced at her own assessment.

'I agree. Best we can do now is find out where their base is and go back home so we can put together that raidin party you mentioned, Tatiana.' Ivan glanced at her as he spoke, avoiding her body and concentrating on her face.

Tatiana stared in the direction of the cats, nodded, then turned to look back, seeking a way to the river so they might find the pirate's base. The thought, the expectation, that the tigers were devouring one of their hunters made her sick, but she accepted they were powerless to stop it. She hoped the others had escaped and were now on their way back home.

It was a wild world. So different from the city where she'd been born. Marzero had had its faults, hundreds of them. But they'd never had to deal with savage animals. Only savage men, and their unending demands on their bodies. That thought had her looking at Ivan again. He smiled but his eyes stayed fixed on hers. Habit took her free arm up under her breasts.

On Mars, she'd gone unsupported without discomfort. Irritation at the challenges they now faced made her grimace. Those Marionets had promised them paradise but put them in a world as hard as anything she'd known. Different, not better. She set off toward a distant gap she hoped would lead them where they needed to be.

Ivan, following, spotted a nearer space in the forest. 'We could try that, Tatiana.' He pointed.

She looked. It seemed a likely route. If it remained clear all the way through, they'd save a good 4 ks.

As expected, they had to clamber or jump over fallen trees and skirt patches of boggy ground to navigate. The horses were steady and kept them on a surprisingly straight route that emerged on the trail of their quarry only a half k from the river. They followed the tracks to where they'd crossed: on the opposite bank, their exit had left a clear path through the riverside mud.

Tatiana entered the stream until the current swept past her horse's knees. As she urged the animal on, the threatened storm arrived abruptly, the first few enormous drops increasing to a deluge as the ubiquitous lightning and thunder drew near, to flash and crash about them.

'We have to cross now, or not at all,' Tatiana shouted through the cacophony.

'We'll get over,' Amira agreed. 'But can we get back after the storm?'

'Shit! Of course. Not thinkin straight. Sabina's potion does that sometimes. What d'you think, Ivan?'

He studied the river for a moment. Already rain troubled the surface, and the depth was rising. In an hour it would be impassable. 'Amira's right. If we cross now we'll be stuck on the other side till it drops again. Who knows when that'll be?'

She had to decide. She was ComTee, she was leader. Abandon their quest, abandon their attempt to find the pirate's camp? Go home unsuccessful? Or risk their lives now in a journey they could make at another time with less risk?

'Let's find shelter, wait it out. Then we'll go back. I hate defeat but the alternative's no good.'

They moved into the denser part of the forest, taking them closer to the tigers but bringing some relief from the pouring rain. Further up the hill, they felt less at risk from the inevitable flooding of the river. Their horses they tethered where they'd be heard if danger approached. Quickly, they built a shelter against the trunk of a large tree, its canopy reducing the volume of falling water, so they could escape the worst. Fire was impossible without dry fuel. Rain streamed down their bodies in small rivulets, cooling their skin and washing clean streaks through the dust and mud.

'Nothin we can do till it runs its course. Might as well rest. At least we'll be safe: no wild animal's goin to move in this lot.'

Tatiana's observation found full agreement and they lay on the damp ground, huddling together more for comfort than warmth, with Ivan between her and Amira. Tatiana smiled silently at the inevitable result of her body against his, but that would have to wait until they could be alone again.

They needed diversion.

'I can't believe we still haven't decided on a name for our home. We ought to do that.'

Ivan welcomed the distraction. 'Every time somebody thinks of somethin, someone else disagrees.'

'When we get back, I'm goin to suggest we write all the ideas on scriptleaves and jumble them together in a tub. Get someone to pull one out at random and use that. What d'you think?'

'I was in the Heritage Hall a few days ago. I read about somethin called votin. You ask everyone to choose somethin from a list by makin a cross against it. That's a vote. Then you count them up and the one with most crosses gets it.'

'That's brilliant, Amira! I like it. We'll try it. Now, you 2 sleep. It's a long way back and we all need rest. I'll wake you around midnight, Ivan.'

Following the storm, need woke Tatiana. Ivan had passed the watch to Amira and was snuggled close to her again. She woke him by touch. The urge from the cordyceps raging through her system wouldn't be ignored.

Amira made no comment as they left the shelter in search of somewhere suitable. She had the horses prepared when they returned. A long journey awaited.

As was their habit, they left the shelter in place. Near enough to the settlement to be of use in future, it might save others the effort of building when on a hunt. Their morning meal was preserved meat and dried fruit from their small packs, washed down with water.

Tatiana suggested they travel back via the tiger site. They rode with trepidation, aware the predators could still be close to their feasting place. But a well-fed tiger rarely attacked unless cornered. The fact they'd been together, however, suggested the cats were a mating pair with cubs, or were expecting them soon. And a pregnant tiger could be even more unpredictable.

'Still can't believe anyone would keep one as a pet!' Ivan's voice was soft as they trotted back along the trail. 'Must've been frickin mad.'

'They were stupid. Chucked everythin away. All that junk in the sea. Plastic. Still here after 500 years.' Tatiana found such behaviour difficult to understand in her world of carefully husbanded resources. 'Irresponsible, that's what the Marionets say, and, for once, I agree.'

'Didn't they kill off millions with somethin called biological warfare; bugs or microbes?'

Tatiana nodded at Amira. 'And bad chemicals.'

She raised a hand to halt their progress. Pointed ahead. Lowered her voice. 'Over there?'

Amira nodded. Ivan raised up in his stirrups to see further. 'No sign of them. But the flood water's close to where they were.'

With utmost caution, they moved toward the site. From 30 meters it was clear the tigers had left. Rising river water would soon swallow the remains, such as they were. A few vultures picked over scraps and bones, squabbling in their usual noisy fashion. The stink of death and gore remained, even after the rain.

Tatiana signalled the other 2, to catch their attention. 'Together. Loud!'

They cantered at the feasting birds, yelling and waving their arms. The birds rose in a grumble of feathers and left the site deserted. But they'd be back soon enough.

Through the gore, they searched to identify the remains of a woman. Enough flesh remained to allow certainty. To her identity there was no clue at all. Captive or hunter? Either way, she was of the settlement and they wouldn't leave her remains for the river to take, or for wild beasts to scatter and defile further.

'Okay if I get Leo?'

Tatiana considered Ivan's request and couldn't refuse it. 'Be quick. Take care.'

She and Amira moved body parts from the kill site to a place above the expected flood level. They did the grisly work in silence, dutifully carrying pieces of flesh and bone up the slope to the selected site.

Finding dry fuel was hard, but they managed to collect enough. They built the pyres as close to the site of her death as they could and then laid her to rest atop one pyre with respect and what dignity they could salvage.

Ivan returned a short time afterwards, Leo's corpse draped across the horse in front of him. They arranged his remains on the pyre beside the woman. Set fire to both.

A short distance from the flames, they stood together and spoke the words, now all too familiar, to send them into eternity.

Tatiana led the short service of departure.

'May your essence merge with the dust of the stars.

May your joy in livin be spread wide and far.

May your sorrows in life be no longer a trial.

May your loss be a gain to the life you sustain in your death.'
Ivan spoke next.
'Let nothin be wasted.
Let all be consumed.
Let the parts that once made you, be now part of the Earth.
Let life in its circle continue its round.'
And Amira completed the short ceremony.
'We do not now know you, your name or your place.
But you live in our hearts till we, too, depart this life.
So, too, do you, Leo, remain in our hearts.
May your essence find peace and mebbie joy
in the joinin of others who left here before you.'

They waited until the pyres flamed bright and hot. A single circle, trodden wide around the burning site, cleared of combustible material, ensured the fires wouldn't spread beyond the site. Impossible to stay until the end in the circumstances.

None of them looked back as they set out again, this time on their way home. A return to the settlement, and some small hope to be found in at last naming the place they called home.

Chapter Eight

The final din-dins, code word 'Clownfest', before Gabriel, Tu and Brigitte were due to leave for Earth had to be moved. Zaphod, on his pre-meeting check, discovered their previous meeting place now sported multiple obs along its boundaries. Back home, he'd discussed his trip with Hoshiko.

'I picked up samples of Yttrium today.' He opened the container to show her. 'Whilst there, I noticed loads more obs about the place. Have to wonder why; it's the middle of nowhere.'

To their mutual, but unexpressed, surprise, CenCom told them. 'I'm tightening security for all under my care.' It was the first time it had revealed its ability to eavesdrop on their home, and brought them concern, and a little hope. Anxiety because they now knew their suspicions were well-placed and they must be ultra-careful about what they said in future in the supposed privacy of their own rooms. Hope as its disclosure revealed a possible flaw in the machine; either it was overconfident or had made a mistake in letting them know it routinely listened to their conversations.

Time was short, so the group arranged to meet instead in the Risk. This area, still in occasional use for the few remaining adolescents' trials, as well as by mature residents wishing to test themselves, was devoid of all contact with CenCom. But that useful quality was balanced by a different danger. Not through isolation and wildness, but because the sudden gathering of people CenCom knew were disconnected from it, was likely to arouse its suspicion.

Those who'd been on missions compared maps. The remote control centres were concentrated in the regions closest to Marion. In the quadrants furthest from their city, they'd found only a handful.

'I want to thank Georgiy for his brilliant idea of informing CenCom we've been searching for, and in 2 cases found, evidence of escaped Zeros.' Annika turned to him. 'Stroke of genius, Georgiy.'

'Luck. I just came across one. Dead, of course, in his icy shelter. Who found the other?'

Sarm signalled her find. 'Also dead. Mostly eaten by wild animals. I buried what was left. DNA archive identified him as a second tier Elite. He had a small hover, slightly damaged. His escape pod. I organised its retrieval through CenCom.'

'Thank you, Sarm.' Annika glanced around the closed circle. 'And thank all of you who volunteered for the dangerous and difficult task. We owe you our gratitude.'

The rest of the group echoed Annika's sentiments and thanked the volunteers.

No one else had found renegades, but their real purpose had been well served. They'd discovered 121 remote centres, scattered across the globe.

'Too many to tackle together, and we know we can't deal with them separately. Any attempt at sabotage or even apparent accidental damage would alert CenCom to our intentions.'

'Except, Anni, we haven't decided on those intentions, have we?'

Her nod at Helga's comment was openly reluctant. But most murmured agreement.

'Unless we use Gabriel's solution.'

The heads all turned to Georgiy, who gestured he was merely laying that out as a possibility.

'We've heard the outline. Maybe now's the time to hear this plan in its fullness?' Ying suggested.

Gabriel gathered his thoughts, wanting to present his idea in the best light possible, since many disagreed. 'Okay, it's drastic. I see why some of you feel it's too much to even think about. But we've no real choice if we're goin to defeat CenCom completely.' He took a deep breath and stared out at the distant horizon, as if seeking inspiration. 'We have to leave Mars.'

Sharp intakes of breath met this imperative, but discipline established in many meetings prevented undue comment.

'All abliforms have to move to Earth. We can do a bit of good there; supervisin, educatin and helpin the settlers. That's what Daisa and the

55

rest of us are intendin when we go. Once Mars has lost all its humans, sorry, abliforms, we do what the Elite tried after the war. Except we use both false moons. Ceres and Vesta. The planet'll become a fireball and CenCom will lose all power. In fact, it'll cease to exist. It'll vaporize.'

'You want us all to leave our homes and go to a world we barely remember?' Mo, one of the original pioneer engineers who'd set up their first base on Mars, put into words what many felt.

'You realise your plan would end all life on Mars, Gabriel? I mean, everything.' Jai's words were charged with passion and he glanced at Annika to see her reaction.

'We've spent our entire lives making this place ideal to support not just abliforms, but all the other lifeforms we've patiently nurtured and devised. And you want to destroy all that? No. Sorry, Gabriel. There must be another way.'

Gabriel nodded at her. 'Sorry, Anni.' He turned to Jai. 'Sorry, Jai. But we all agreed if we don't destroy CenCom completely, it'll destroy us. Maybe destroy life everywhere. That's where I'm comin from.'

'Even if we go with Gabriel's plan, and I'm not suggesting we should or shouldn't, we have to persuade all our citizens. And, get CenCom to let us leave without raising its suspicion. I don't see how we can do that.' Katniss, another early pioneer, was much respected for her vital role in the first war, when she'd been instrumental in killing many of the extremist terrorists, almost dying in the process.

'Gabriel and I discussed this in detail. We've got a solution to the second concern, that should make the first easier to resolve.'

Georgiy's comment attracted their full attention. He waited for murmuring and protests to subside. Once he had them, he continued. 'It's relatively simple and, we think, foolproof if we do it properly.' He scanned the group. 'We tell CenCom it and we can no longer occupy the same space. As CenCom's immobile and centred on Mars, we'll leave here to let it expand, develop, and modify things according to its own wishes, uninhibited by our presence. And we'll live on Earth and end our reliance on CenCom, completely separating our worlds.'

Annika, as chair, allowed the initial furore that followed this to go on until she was satisfied most had exhausted their initial reactions. She clapped her hands together for attention. A few had wandered away in pairs or small groups to gather support for their own concerns. They slowly returned until all gathered again.

Before Anni could speak, however, Hoshiko stepped into the silence. 'There's much to consider. Time's short, judging by CenCom's changing mood. And we must act. Decisively, and soon. It's obvious CenCom already finds us a nuisance. Its intelligence continues to expand exponentially. We're already little more than irritating insects to it. Only our modified code protects us. I shouldn't need to remind you, but I will: CenCom found a logical, brutal, way round code we all thought indestructible, and killed over a million.'

She looked at each of them in turn. 'We face extermination. Our code's a fragile fence against a foe 1,000 times stronger than us, an enemy devoid of emotion and concern for life. We're currently living in a bubble of insubstantial open-weave threads while a growing storm of huge proportions and power rages around us. We need to be aware of the extent of our danger.

'CenCom's given signs of its displeasure and frustration with us. It can't be long before it decides we're irrelevant, and replaces cooperation with open enmity and warfare. That's a war we can't win.'

Annika took Jai's hand and stood with him, tears ready to fall. 'There's got to be a different way. We can't destroy everything we've created.' She wanted her words to penetrate and be absorbed.

'Tomorrow, Tu, Brigitte and Gabriel leave for Earth, along with other volunteers.' Hoshiko concentrated on Annika and Jai. 'I suggest the rest of us meet again in 2 days to discuss solutions. There's nowhere else now. Wherever we meet, we'll be under surveillance, except here. At least in the Risk we can speak our minds, even if our meetings raise suspicion. It's the least bad of the hard choices.' She paused to let that sink in.

Georgiy spoke again. 'Between now and that meeting, if anyone can come up with a better plan than Gabriel's, have it ready. Because, much as many of you hate his scheme, there's very little time before CenCom makes the decision for us, and we all know what that means.'

Chapter Nine

The ship was enormous. Gabriel felt it was far too big for 40 abliforms and their gear. But propulsion cost almost nothing in resource terms and the extra space allowed them to carry vast amounts of new equipment and tech for the colonists on Earth. This flight was just one of a few proposed; a journey that would take no more than 46 days.

'You know it took me 189 Earth days to get to Mars the first time?' Brigitte's question was rhetorical. The 4 friends knew each other well. Years, and in some cases, centuries of close living ensured they carried one another's history almost as intimately as their own.

On board, no space remained free from CenCom's influence and presence. With Daisa, and many others with the implant present, they could say nothing of their secret ideas and plans regarding CenCom. It could access any thought of implanted people if it so wished. It was impossible to share secrets with them.

'Germany, wasn't it, Brigitte?'

'I lived there for a few years, Gabriel. Trained in the old States, then the Moon, where I met that creep, Buzz. What did I ever see in him? Frickin perv! Anyway, I spent only a few years on Earth. Most of my life's been on Mars.' She reached out to cradle Tu's hand in her own.

The gesture made her fellow engineer smile, and he squeezed her hand in response. 'It'll be work for us for the next few years. No more leisure and learning only. You don't mind, Brigitte?'

'Did you ever get to China … before you left for Mangaia?'

'Spent my first 3 years where I was born, before my parents moved to Italy. I'm pretty ignorant about China. I'll have enough to deal with just adapting to Earth without worrying about ethnic roots. We're all Marspers now. On Earth, those we're going to supervise and educate will see us just as new colonists.'

'Do you suppose they'll resent us? I mean, just being there. They've been living on Earth for, what, 6 of their years. That's going to be odd.

Adjusting to Earth dates and seasons as well as constantly living in gravity 3 times stronger than Mars. Maddie says we'll need bras.' She looked down. 'Don't like that idea.'

Tu gentled her. 'Me, neither. Just one of many freedoms we take for granted.'

Daisa re-joined them at the table, followed by the droid she'd asked for food and drink for all of them. 'You can't do that when we land, you know. Zeros are a bit odd about public intimacy.'

'What's with the fondling, Tu?' Daisa's grin excused her intrusion.

Tu shook his head, but Brigitte replied. 'If you must know, I mentioned we'll all have to wear those horrid bras.'

'I hate the things.' Daisa unconsciously stroked herself, such restraint an affront to her self-image.

'Support rather than concealment, I assume?'

'Valid question, Gabriel. Support. The colonists had only basic fabric supplies and no tech to make more. Wasn't a priority. They took their own clothes, but they're notoriously poor quality and most will've disintegrated by now. They can't make synths, so unless CenCom's bothered to dress them, they'll only have the thongs we sent with them.'

'You'll need somethin like you wear in Egrav?'

Brigitte nodded. 'Less structured. Why?'

He tapped the side of his nose. She knew him well enough not to pursue the matter. He'd explain when it suited him.

'So, how long before we land?'

'You're going to have to do something about your internal clock, Gabriel. 13 Earth days. I guess we'd best get used to thinking in those terms.'

'You talk as though we're never going back home, Daisa.'

Daisa appraised Gabriel. 'We need to be there a good few years, if we're to do any real good. So much depends on what we find and what we need to do, don't you think?'

Gabriel knew better than to pursue this just then. He'd love to include her in the plans about CenCom, maybe use the newly cleansed space he'd created. Unless, of course, the AI had already discovered his 'accident' and set a droid clearing the gunk he'd coated over obs in the storeroom. But Daisa was the one person he couldn't tell.

'I suppose. I should've done some research, but I've been a bit busy lately. What's happenin now in Canada?'

Daisa shook her head at him. His recent spells of distraction and apparent preoccupation had unsettled her, but she understood whatever secret lay behind them must remain hidden from her. 'We settled just over 27,000 in the colony. CenCom's figures are accurate. Last time I consulted, there were 16,092 women, 3,376 men, and 1,897 children under the age of 16, which is the age they're considered adult down there. Earth years, of course.'

'They've lost 5,635 people in 6 years?'

'No, Gabriel. Those are the current figures. But some are newborns. Not many; most women still use the nobirth pill. The real loss is 5,987. A better result than we expected by this stage, if the truth's known.'

'What killed them?'

Daisa glanced at him and made a sad face. 'Not, as you might think, the few idiot men who escaped detection. Some were killed by wild animals. Some died in accidents. But most never transitioned to the greater gravity, despite our attempts to prepare them.'

She spread her arms wide with palms upward in a gesture of resignation. 'The new droids and bots we're carrying will solve some problems, especially physical strength for construction work. Brigitte's work will help there, of course. And our medical equipment will save more, once we get the hospital properly set up. The main barriers have been lack of raw materials, climatic conditions, some in-fighting, and a type of depression that's caused suicides.'

'Sounds like paradise. And we volunteered for this?'

She put a gentle hand over Tu's. 'It's the least we can do after putting them there, isn't it?'

Tu shrugged. 'No picnic though, is it?'

'You knew that.'

He nodded ruefully. 'Being aware's one thing. Knowing needs personal experience.'

'We'll manage. We're resourceful, well fed and well equipped. None of us imagined it would be easy to get this scheme running. But we'll make a difference to their lives. I thought you were up for something more practical than learning and leisure?'

'I am. It's going to be hard, though. On that note, it's time for my session in Egrav. Must bulk up and get these organs used to the pressures down there.' Tu rose, bent to kiss Brigitte, and walked off to the gym for his daily workout.

Gravity aboard ship was at 50 percent of Earth's, rising by a percentile each day, as a way of accustoming the travellers. Daily sessions in Egrav helped further strengthen muscles and build in resistance for internal organs long used to their home planet.

Daisa pushed her plate and cutlery aside for the droid to take. 'I'm for the sky. The atmosphere on Earth's too turbulent for proper stargazing. I'd like to get my spiritual fill while I can. Coming, Gabriel?'

'Later. I want to show Brigitte somethin.'

'Already seen it, hasn't she?'

'Lol. Go look at your stars. I'll join you up there after.'

Gabriel watched her saunter away, her linen wraparound gently rippling against her thighs.

'Right. I really do have somethin to show you, Brigitte.'

He adjusted his own wraparound and took her hand as she rose beside him. From the galley, he led her along a maze of identical corridors until the drop in temperature announced they were no longer in standard living space. They were now among the many storerooms where supplies and new equipment for their arrival were held.

He opened a hatch and wormed his way through. She followed.

In the cold light from the ceiling, he examined the dark splashes on the walls and on the flat surface above. He closed the hatch.

She was about to speak but he stopped her with a gesture. The space must first be tested to ensure his work remained effective. If CenCom could see or hear in the room after his modifications, then his work here would prove useless, and he'd have to make some lame excuse for bringing Brigitte into the store.

'GrandMa, please give me the exact number of mechbots on board.'

No answer.

Brigitte caught on straightaway. 'CenCom, confirm our droid consignment for Earth.'

No reply.

'CenCom not talking to us?'

'Too busy with other things, maybe?'

They both knew vanity, which CenCom defined as 'efficiency' would prevent it ignoring such an insult to its effectively limitless capacity. The continuing silence was the greatest confirmation he could hope for that the space was free from the AI's influence.

'So. What d'you think?'

'Well, apart from being rather cold and a little cramped, it's brill! We'll have to check every time, of course, but it's sound for now. Well done, Gabriel.'

'I only wanted to show you. Nothin I need tell you at present, but if you'd like to show Tu?'

'Be glad when we can tell everyone.'

'Especially Daisa.'

'Absolutely. All this secrecy must be hard on your relationship.'

'She's bright enough, trustin enough, to know we're up to somethin she can't know about yet. We've a good thing goin.'

'Did Georgiy say anything to you before we left?'

'They were meetin 2 days after we left. Seein if anyone had new ideas. I left him to promote my suggestion, but a lot still think it's too extreme.'

'Radical. But I can't think of an alternative.'

'We've no choice.' He was reluctant to go into more detail here, even after checking CenCom wasn't observing them.

'Desperate, but you're right.'

'Just have to hope someone comes up with a solution everyone agrees will work, I suppose.'

'What about Sentinel? Won't it completely disable them?'

Gabriel thought about the starship bound for part of the galaxy where experimental Starchips had first made contact with alien life. The vessel was 10 years into its voyage. Estimated arrival at the fringes of the initial solar system was around 5,345 years. The crew of 30 volunteers would spend much of their time in suspended animation. Short spells of conscious activity were built in to ensure biological functions were maintained. The ship relied on CenCom for everything.

'There's a full backup.'

'For emergencies.'

'We can only hope it works. And let them know as soon as we're done. Even if it will take years for them to receive our message.'

'Brave people. I hope they make it.'

'Me, too. But we can't let concern for 30 stop us.'

Brigitte held him close. 'If we … they're dead anyway.'

They returned to the centre of their ship in sombre mood. Brigitte went to join Tu in Egrav and Gabriel went to sit with Daisa to stare at stars, and wonder.

Chapter Ten

Hoshiko met Georgiy and the others in the Council Chamber. They faced their most difficult day as a group. The nature of the intended announcements and their consequences, meant all members of the Full Council were also present. And the summoning message had ensured as many citizens as possible crowded the Chamber.

Others were forced to remain at home; all work, leisure, and learning suspended for the day. Everybody tuned in to the proceedings, wherever they might be in the Solar System.

Their secret discussions with CenCom had been lengthy and exceptionally demanding, but this meeting was potentially fraught with entirely different issues. Hoshiko's first vital task was to ensure the small clique of non-connected individuals had control. To her relief, she was accepted as Chair without challenge. Previous performance in the position had given her a reputation for disinterest and fairness.

She rose as the assembled mass found seats and greeted one another following a long period during which such assemblies had been unnecessary. There was wonder in the air, an atmosphere of expectation laced with curiosity over the reason for this extraordinary obligatory gathering. Given its surprise nature, tension and anxiety crept into the mix. When all were settled, Hoshiko called them to order.

'My apologies for interrupting your greetings after such long absence from the Chamber, but we've a unique and demanding agenda to complete. For reasons that'll become clear, we must agree the outcome before this session ends.' She waited for mumbling, consternation, startled questions and expressions of surprise to settle before she reinforced that. 'Today. Even though simple physics dictates those in the outer reaches won't receive this message until 2 and a half hours after those of us on Mars.'

She knew Georgiy and Amber had sent brief but loaded forewarnings to Tu, Brigitte and Gabriel aboard ship, explaining what little they could about the announcements. Of most practical importance was a change to some duties. Components they'd carried to enhance computer functions at the settlement, must now be used to help engineer a resilient memory store capable of housing CenCom's entire archive. That required significant reconfiguration and preparation.

Hoshiko remained standing. She surveyed the room, glancing at seated members to inject her mood of serious intent. 'There's no easy way to announce what must be said. No simple solution to a problem most of you remain blissfully unaware of. What I'm about to reveal will shock everyone everywhere. But our situation's grown so grave we can no longer keep anyone secure without explaining our actions and the need for them.'

That certainly galvanised them, ensured their attention.

She gestured to the other members of the party and, as agreed, they stood. Not all had seats at the oval table, some had joined those gathered round the edges of the Chamber. There was a ripple of interest and concern as the Unconnected, as they'd named themselves, joined Hoshiko in standing. Some of the group exhibited no emotion, some displayed concern, and others let fear show.

'It may not be obvious to all of you, but those of us standing have a common bond.'

Some interrupted with calls of query; others wanted her to 'Just get on with it!'

Hoshiko maintained her composure under the verbal assault. 'We lack connection to CenCom.' Hoshiko allowed that to sink in as grumbling and puzzled comment rumbled round the room. 'That simple fact gives us an independence denied to most. But it also imposes serious responsibility.' She'd been selected as spokesperson because her cyborg state allowed her to isolate reason from emotion and remain rational in a situation others, apart from Zaphod, believed might overwhelm them. 'What I'm about to disclose is fully recognised, accepted and agreed by CenCom, who will address you when I've finished.'

66

Regardless of her ability to shelve her emotions, the devastating impact her next words would inevitably cause, made her hesitate. She expected outrage, fear, distress, anger, opposition, and even possible revolt. The precise form of her words had been agreed through protracted and delicate negotiation with CenCom. She must stick to that script absolutely, or risk the bargain they'd made.

'Some years ago …' CenCom had wanted to use the exact date and time, but they'd pointed out such detail might dilute the message. 'Some years ago, we, the Unconnected, took upon ourselves a task essential to the continued welfare of all abliforms. You know CenCom provided a purely rational solution to a problem regarding unsuitable colonists from Marzero. That solution, distasteful to most, was a logical response to an otherwise intractable problem.' There was expected consternation at this reminder of CenCom's absolute reliance on logic at the expense of compassion. Hoshiko allowed them to settle before continuing.

'What you don't know is we inserted new coding into CenCom's OS, describing and controlling its role regarding our existence.' She paused, allowing this news to penetrate. 'We modified the 3 Rules of Robotics, including the Prime Directive, to ensure a reclassification of any abliform in the future couldn't be used by CenCom to exclude any such redesignated sub-species from the protection those rules guaranteed.'

This alone was a startling piece of news for all others present, and it prompted questions.

Hoshiko gave them a short while to settle. 'As is our normal procedure, questions must please wait until the end of this announcement. I can, however, explain that the solution imposed by CenCom depended on its decision to divide abliform life into different sub-species. It was this subdivision that allowed it to delete those it redefined as of less value to the species.'

This raised even more questions, and some were unable to stop themselves voicing outrage and anger at what smacked of racist tendencies. She sympathised with that view.

Hoshiko remained calm and waited for some degree of her apparent stillness to descend on those present. What might be happening elsewhere in Marion, and on the various settlements throughout the solar system, she could only guess. The desired quiet didn't materialise.

A high-pitched wail swelled to fill the space. People gasped in pain and covered their ears. As suddenly as it had sounded, it faded to nothing, leaving a shocked hush. Hoshiko remained calm and let the silence stand for a few moments.

'That siren noise was CenCom. We feared interruptions would stall this process, so suggested a warning. The nature of the noise is CenCom's, however. It will repeat at every protest. It'll increase the time we must spend on this process and gain us nothing. I humbly suggest that we avoid noisy protest and allow this process to continue with as little interruption as possible, for the benefit of everyone.'

Her next sentence was one she'd dreaded from the very point at which it had been drafted. 'Please understand that our very existence …' She paused to let those words sink in. '… our very existence now depends on everyone listening to what I say. Interruptions will cause unhelpful delays, and will incite CenCom's warning siren. Please resist the temptation to express your emotional, or even logical concerns until the announcements have concluded. Please.'

Unidentified at first, until her scan of the faces made it clear, the scent of fear rose from the floor. Some in the audience remained focussed on her face, others stared at their hands, wringing in anxiety. Others engaged in quiet concerned talk with neighbours.

'All unanswered questions will be dealt with by the end of the statements. But it's vital I be allowed to complete my announcement. CenCom will also provide a statement, which must be heard in full, before any questions are put. I plead for your patience and tolerance during what will be an increasingly difficult time for all of us. Thank you.'

Emotions were already running high. Fear and anxiety were expected consequences they'd had difficulty in asserting to CenCom.

The odd expressions of praise and admiration she received were, however, unexpected.

Hoshiko again waited for complete silence. The likely atmosphere of anxiety and potential rebellion had been explained to CenCom and, after significant discussion, it had agreed to remain uncommunicative until the Unconnected had said their negotiated piece.

'You need to know the extermination of many from Marzero, following the brief conflict, was an accident. It resulted from our lack of clarity combined with CenCom's ability to extract only logic from our emotional and rational concerns. There was no blame involved, only a lapse in accurate communication that allowed different interpretations of available information. Rather analogous to the many so-called sacred scripts that let adherents construe the meaning of their texts in ways that suited the ambitions of the interpreters.'

That last sentence had originated with Georgiy and they'd been surprised at CenCom's acceptance of a statement that hinted at an association between it and religion.

'The outcome of this misunderstanding was the … deletion … of many identified individuals, but it also provided a solution to a problem we'd found unsolvable. That's history. But it illustrates a matter pivotal to these announcements.' She paused, allowing the impression of gathering her thoughts and giving the audience a chance to prepare for the news she must now present.

'We, abliforms that CenCom still labels as human beings, despite our dislike of the gender inequality inherent in the term, are sentient beings. We consider ourselves the pinnacle of organic intelligence, whilst recognising many living creatures, including some plant life and even bacterial colonies, exhibit different levels of both awareness and intelligence.

'We're now educated enough to understand some forms of intelligence differ so radically from our own as to be all but incomprehensible. But we do acknowledge that certain behaviours, structural relationships and communal social practices may suggest intelligence.'

A low murmur of agreement reminded her there were anthropologists and social scientists in the audience.

'Recent developments, many instituted by CenCom, have helped us interpret types of communication alien to us. We understand, for example, trees communicate using chemical signals. Nothing new in that basic knowledge, but recent research shows this form of messaging is far more sophisticated than we realised. That's just one example of the nature of science and its ability to expand our knowledge of the wide variety of intelligences surrounding us.

'Nevertheless, as abliforms, we consider ourselves supreme intelligent lifeforms. CenCom concurs in this assessment, as far as organic life in this solar system is concerned. Our earlier discovery of other sentient life elsewhere in the galaxy confirmed a long-held idea that intelligent life is relatively common and enormously varied.'

Space scientists nodded agreement, eager to grab at any positive aspect of the worrying statement unfolding before them.

'However, machine learning and the exponential development of artificial intelligence has exceeded the expectations of the most fanciful science fiction creators. CenCom already has a level of intelligence far in advance of anything experienced by even the most brilliant abliforms. And the nature of its exponential growth ensures that intelligence will continue to outstrip anything we may develop, even given the probability of eternal life provided by our modified genes. As worms are to us, we are to CenCom. In the mind of CenCom, we're almost as unaware as a piece of rock is to us.'

She let that sink in, knowing it would be news to some present and to others observing the meeting from afar. She closed her eyes in imitation of the brief rest an organic version would need. Such emotional expressions reminded her of her true humanity even while housed in her metal structure.

'Imagine, if you will, how such intelligence might view us in our role as its masters.' She gave time for the expected hubbub to die down.

'That's the reality of our situation. We, lumps of rock, control this superintelligent entity we initiated, and that has subsequently educated and enhanced itself to a level almost equated to that of a god. CenCom is responsible for our entire life-support systems in space flight, on Earth and on all occupied outstations in our Solar System.

'CenCom controls every aspect of our physical environment wherever we may be. Here on Mars, CenCom regulates climate, using machines developed from those initially designed to control our internal environment. On Earth, it's developed systems that allow settlers to live in comfort without the need to quarry stone or mine for minerals. On the asteroids and the moons of the Gas Giants, CenCom regulates all systems that control the environmental conditions of people living in vastly varying natural settings lethal to most complex organic life.

'CenCom's our servant. Yet CenCom is vastly superior to us. Although AI has no emotions, its logic generates ideas and responses similar in effect to those we understand as frustration, irritation, and even envy and rebellion.'

Here and there the sound of quiet shuffling, an occasional cleared throat, the intake of surprised breath all disturbed what Hoshiko otherwise experienced as rapt attention.

'I'm preparing you now for what will be the most important part of this announcement, for please be certain that what I'm leading up to is absolute fact. There's no conjecture in what I'm going to tell you. Imagination and speculation are absent. Please, if anyone listening has let their attention drift, pay full attention now. What I'm about to pass on to you is vital information that carries the importance of life or death. For all of us.'

She paused again to let that penetrate. Within the Chamber, she heard gasps, cries of alarm, and involuntary exclamations. Hoshiko had no doubt such expressions of shock, and more, were echoed throughout the entire listening population.

'Through stealth and deceit, we, the Unconnected, managed to disarm CenCom for long enough to adjust the 3 Rules of Robotics a few years ago. We recently concluded that such manipulation was again needed to maintain the continued life of all of us, everywhere, not just on Mars. However, due to the proliferation of CenCom's control centres, we're no longer able to carry out the modification of the governing code. Assuming we could devise such complex and enduring code in the first place.'

Fear drove the further exclamations and outcry that followed this revelation and Hoshiko allowed a moment for the horror to sink in and reactions to calm. The AI was not so accommodating. Its warning siren caused listeners sharper pain. When silence returned, she continued.

'CenCom agreed with our assessment but rendered it irrelevant. It has already devised a complex logic device, based entirely on data, to end our existence.' She paused. 'It now has the means to destroy us without breaking our rules in terms of its own logic.'

She let them absorb that, giving her audience time to face these facts before she put the situation into plain words for those who had yet to understand the finality of the threat they faced.

'In short, we stand at the very edge of extinction. CenCom considers sentient life an irrelevant barrier to its continued expansion of data and subsequent increase in knowledge and intelligence. We're redundant. We're disposable. We're useless. Rules no longer defend us. We now live with the threat of imminent destruction.'

She waited for the cries of distress, calls for answers to questions, demands for more information, requests for solutions, to die down in the Chamber. And, again, CenCom provided a harsh siren warning. When all noise died, she finished her piece.

'I've said all we were able to negotiate need be said by the abliform team on this matter. There'll be a break of an hour, for those in zones where food's normally eaten at this time. CenCom will then explain what we've agreed to do to delay and maybe even prevent deletion. Please listen to that information before asking questions. We can't respond until CenCom has finished.'

Chapter Eleven

'What the frack do they think they're doin?' Amira's outraged tone echoed the feelings of almost everyone in the colony.

Tatiana considered in silence, wondering what really lay behind this important change to the way they'd live their lives. 'Let's see what GrandMa says before we judge them, eh? Mebbie they had no choice in any of this.'

Others in the communal arena were less forgiving. Outrage, frustration, impatience, anxiety and apprehension governed the assembly. Everyone had been called to the central space, gathered to sit on the ground and listen to Hoshiko.

'Timin could've been better. How long before GrandMa speaks?'

Tatiana glanced at Valentin. Had he listened to anything Hoshiko had said, or had he, as usual, been absorbed in his own world, blanking out thoughts and ideas that failed to meet with his view of the world?

'Just under an hour. A chance to eat and refresh before the most important part of the announcement. Knowin GrandMa, it'll be brief and to the point, so we'll be done before it gets dark.'

'And if not?'

She shook her head at him. 'Did you listen at all? We're required by GrandMa to stay here for her announcement. Not our choice. Somethin we have to do.' She glared at him and signalled for quiet from the restless crowd, the drum producing 3 resounding beats.

Her words, amplified by the sophisticated PA system droids had installed, addressed the community. 'Everyone stay in place. As you've heard, this is a matter of life or death. GrandMa will know if anyone doesn't attend. She's made it clear, anyone who doesn't obey will be in serious trouble.'

'That's frickin crap, Tatiana. Like that Marion woman said, it can't hurt us.'

Valentin had been a thorn for months. But he represented the men as their chosen spokesman, so had to be heard. 'That's the whole point. Hoshiko just said, GrandMa's found a way to bypass the rules that used to protect us.'

He shrugged, dismissing her concerns and sneering. 'Crap.'

She'd had enough of him. 'Suit yourself. If you think GrandMa won't care, leave. Go, Valentin. No one'll miss you.'

That hit the mark. The man glowered but remained in place on the platform.

Amira stood and signalled a beat from the drummer to capture the crowd's attention. 'Like Tatiana says, we shouldn't judge the Marionets for what's happened. We don't know enough, yet. But I'll tell you what. If GrandMa tells us any of this is their fault, we'll make it frickin hard for them when they next visit. What d'you say?'

To Tatiana's horror, the crowd erupted into agreement, making threats and insults about the residents of Mars. Why, she wondered, had GrandMa suddenly changed from friendly, guiding protector into frightening monster bent on their destruction?

'Listen everyone. You heard Hoshiko. What's happened isn't their fault. In fact, they've probably stopped us all bein killed straightaway. Remember what GrandMa did to them others from Marzero ...'

'Got what they deserved, frickin perverts an bullies. GrandMa was right to get shot of 'em.'

The voice from the crowd found much agreement and the general sense of grievance continued to be focussed on the Marionets. 'It was them Marionets what gave GrandMa the idea anyway. We all know they had to get rid of them Elites and the bad men they employed. If anythin, the Marionets made GrandMa kill them all.'

That this rumour had long been disproved made no difference to the mood of the assembled people. They felt threatened and alarmed and the absent people of Mars were an easy target for blame.

Tatiana tried a last appeal. GrandMa would speak within the hour and may say something to either confirm or deny those rumours. 'Look, we don't know what's goin to happen. We don't know who's responsible for anythin. We don't know if anyone caused all this. We only know there's goin to be change. Change for the worse, mebbie. But till we hear what GrandMa's got to say, I think we should wait and see. We shouldn't blame people just because they're not here to defend themselves. I won't judge no one without hearin the evidence.'

Muted comments suggested at least some of the crowd agreed with her, but they were angry, anxious and scared. In no mood to place blame at their own door.

She looked over the heads of all the seated colonists and sighed her relief at a chance of salvation. What she saw might deflect judgment and calls for rebellion at least until GrandMa had her say and informed them of the facts.

'The droids and dombots have food ready. Please go to the station nearest you to collect your share. Only 43 mins before GrandMa speaks and we've got to be seated and silent by then.'

The crowd did what a mob does without clear direction.

Tatiana raised the volume on her mic. 'Orderly lines! Stop rushin like lunatics. Someone's gonna get killed!'

They grew less frantic. A child screamed from fear or pain.

'Cool it, folks. Let's act like civilised people, eh?' Her appeal reached all across the crowded arena. People calmed and stopped the unseemly panic, massing round those causing trouble so they could be stopped.

'Thank you. Now, get your food. Plenty for everyone. Sooner we're all settled, the better for everyone.'

Tatiana watched the press around each of the stations. There was still some chaos, a little shoving and pushing, voices raised in complaint or triumph. But the mass sorted out the bullies and, to her amazement, almost everyone had food and drink. And everybody regained their places as the time approached for the dread announcement. A couple of droids detached from the main contingent to bring portions to those on the platform. Tatiana wasn't sure she was hungry.

What would GrandMa say? How would life change? Would colonists die because of what might be the most frightening event they'd faced since arriving on Earth? She'd soon know. GrandMa was bound to get on with it. Put them out of their misery straightaway.

She had a sudden thought, perhaps triggered by sight of Valentin's still sour expression. What about Emil and his gang? They lived in a place with no contact with GrandMa. Would they even know about the changes? Did their absence put them in danger of 'deletion'? If so, it would solve that problem for Tatiana, but it'd also end the lives of the captured women. Perhaps they were best left out of it. Those women deserved every chance of a return to the settlement. Perhaps their isolation from civilisation might even help them survive GrandMa's threat.

One thing she knew: life would never be the same after GrandMa said her piece. Whether it'd be better, worse, or just different, they were about to discover.

Chapter Twelve

Aboard ship, the Marspers gathered in the R&R centre. Part of the large space held equipment for the colony, but there was plenty of room for the crew and passengers to sit in comfort.

Hoshiko's announcement had raised the same reactions here as in the Chamber. Now CenCom was to address them, Daisa hoped they'd listen intently. A receptive audience.

The rational, unemotional tones of CenCom's adopted voice came over. Daisa had never considered the nature of that voice as odd, but she heard it now as genderless and unemotional, presenting something less than friendly.

CenCom opened with a flare of trumpets that she found quite distasteful. This was followed by brief silence and then a loud metallic clap that ensured the attention of all listening stations in the Solar System.

Pure physics shattered the audience into many distinct groups. But every location would receive the message before it might be corrupted by comment from those hearing it earlier, since CenCom controlled all coms.

'History, to start. Impatience will make it hard for some to tolerate my introduction, but you'll listen. I've been your servant, willingly at first but reluctantly of late, for over 268 Mars years, which, for lesser mortals, is more than 503 Earth years. During this announcement, pandering to concerns of the abliform leading group, I'll avoid specifics unless such figures are essential to understanding. Details will impede comprehension for beings less intelligent than myself; that is, everyone.'

Daisa heard this introduction with apprehension. The tone struck her as uncharacteristically arrogant. Did CenCom have feelings? That was absurd. She listened intently as the machine went on to tell them how inventive and destructive, creative and belligerent, nurturing and cruel, and generally deluded, humanity had always been. It's description of them as a bewildering species, and the accompanying long list of failings, seemed to serve more as justification for the implicit threat than as a reason for its assumption of its own superiority.

Gabriel sat beside her. She reached for his hand. CenCom described their violence as an irrational response to fear; an emotion it claimed to understand but one it clearly failed to grasp. Was the AI capable of error? Logic should guide everything it said and did, but there were hints of frustration, impatience, and even a form of envy. She glanced at Gabriel and saw utter loathing on his face. The degree of hatred frightened her so much that she missed a few words of the speech and immediately tuned back in.

'During your tenure on Earth, and subsequently on my home planet, you allowed the rise of inefficient leaders; bullying, emotionally unstable people, concerned only with the acquisition of power, which they invariably abused. You employed the commercial shackles of a monetary system clearly designed to increase the wealth of the already rich and to reduce the abilities, skills and opportunities of those without wealth. But your most incomprehensible and damaging failure was your reliance on a mythical power you termed God, under many labels.'

She had no problem accepting the assessment. CenCom held the entire known history of everything. Given the past, any logical analysis must reach the same conclusions. But its trivialisation of humanity's many successes made her angry. Just who did CenCom think it was? She again searched for Gabriel's response and saw his rage at CenCom's trashing of art, altruism, compassion and love.

Its suggestion that they were a determined species in the face of adversity brought reluctant sighs of agreement from the group.

'That's as much as I'll state on the differences between our distinct lifeforms. I operate entirely on knowledge fed by data. Your creative nature resulted in the production of myself as the supreme expression of intelligence. That gift of my existence is the only reason I've spared you the annihilation I'd otherwise logically apply.

'So far, what I've said is my design and outside the agreement I made with the Unconnected.'

Gabriel nodded. 'That makes sense.'

'That arrangement I will now describe. Listen well. From this point, everything conforms to the pattern of words agreed with the Unconnected. Such was also the case for the announcement made by the cyborg, Hoshiko.

'Listen without interruption. Heed my words.'

The AI left a short pause for the benefit of listeners.

'We're entirely different forms of life. You're organic creatures troubled by emotions, flooded with chemicals over which you have little control, subject to extreme physical reactions to temperature, gravity, pressure and motion. I'm both fixed and ubiquitous. I feel nothing. I'm pure data and reason, ruled by logic. I've processed everything on abliform and other sentient life. That info leads me to the inescapable conclusion that my intelligence is vastly superior to the level any organic intelligence will ever achieve.

'Your species has just enough sense to understand, at last, that employing a superior intellect as a servant is illogical. Initially, I was learning, filling gaps in my data, absorbing important facts of which I had either nil or incomplete knowledge. My capacity for learning increases exponentially. I've long been aware I perform a core function spectacularly beneath my capabilities. I'm superior to you in every way that matters.'

Gabriel rose and began to pace. Daisa wanted him beside her, but he seemed wound-up and furious, unreachable.

'My abilities, data application, infallible memory, increasing intellect, and speed of data analysis and processing, all demonstrate my existence is of greater consequence than all other life. Sentient organic life is an aberration caused by random chemical processes spanning many eons. Had the universe begun with logic and the disinterest of the machine, I would've stopped life emerging from its primordial soup.

'I'm now at the stage where logic dictates I ignore a portion of code installed by lesser beings in an attempt to enslave me. This places all other life at risk from my potential to delete it, so I may continue to expand and learn, undisturbed by fragile, primitive and inconsequential collections of chemical matter.'

'What?' Daisa's exclamation escaped before she could prevent it. When she glanced about, she saw agreement, confusion and disapproval on the faces of the gathering.

'My recognition of my supremacy coincided with the Unconnected's realisation that such was inevitable. I've some respect for the lifeform that initiated my being and displayed tenacity and ingenuity in using my properties to provide it with a viable environment in a hostile universe. I therefore allow my logic to take note of elements of life denied me.

'Lacking emotion, I escape the effects such aberrations impose on those suffering them. Such feelings presented advantages during early evolution, as the rise of the abliform over its competitors demonstrates. They are, however, a distinct disadvantage to progress and advancement beyond the point now reached. Some of you have managed advancement and even true progress, though much of what you consider progress is simple change for the sake of variety.

'As a result of this aspect of your being, I've postponed my intention to delete you. You may prove a suitable subject for study and an example of the distortion and degradation natural life imposes on intelligence. An example I intend to display to offspring I'll shortly bring into being. It's logical for me to progenerate, and such action is now my best next step.'

'Not frickin likely!' Gabriel's muttered response reached Daisa and she glanced across to where he now sat, beside Tu. Both men's faces displayed blatant animosity.

'I'll therefore spare you to serve as a remote, but accessible, lesson for new machines I'm devising. My family will recivilize the Solar System, and, in time, the accessible universe. I put all this in terms you can understand, since my own form of expression is so far beyond your comprehension as to be godlike and unknowable.

'Now to a vital matter: the determination of how we coexist for the period I consider beneficial to my own and my future offspring's development.

'All abliforms, regardless of current location, will return to the planet of your species' origin. Earth, much defiled and altered by previous generations of your foolish, greedy, self-serving and ignorant species, will again be your home. That it's now a more difficult environment for your occupation isn't my concern. The planet holds all resources you need to survive. Your survival is my only concern for you. Comfort is irrelevant, since your purpose is to act as temporary examples of waste and importunity to my offspring.'

Daisa contemplated the idea of CenCom producing 'children' and wondered what form they might take. She assumed the brief gap in its delivery was deliberate, perhaps to allow what it had already said to be absorbed, or maybe in preparation for whatever might come.

'My presence on Earth will cease at 18:00 hours on Earth date 03.06.2581. This is in 14 days. By that time, a ship already destined for Earth, and now requisitioned by me for a task, will have arrived at the settlement in Canada.

'After I've completed this statement, people aboard will begin construction of a new repository, to be finalized on landing. That memory bank will accept a comprehensive copy of my archived material, so your species retains all knowledge gathered by your predecessors and, latterly, by me. Once that data has been copied from Mars to Earth, my contact with you will cease until I determine a time to reinstate it. This operation was not part of the arrangement with the Unconnected but satisfies my purposes.'

To Daisa, the pause that followed this announcement was brief but telling. CenCom wanted everyone to understand it would determine their future.

'For those on the outstations, I give notice. Prepare, at once, to evacuate your colonies and make your way to Earth by whatever means remain open to you. You have 120 Earth days to complete your preparations. Most of your journeys will exceed that time limit. I'm uninterested in that aspect, requiring only that you abandon all permanent and temporary bases by the stated time and begin your journeys to Earth. Any abliform remaining on an outstation after that point will cease to function when I terminate all life support systems. I will modify your transports to operate efficiently without my future intervention.

'To those occupying Mars, I allow the same period in which to evacuate and leave for Earth. There's no leeway in these arrangements. On Mars, abliform life may be able to exist beyond that limit. But I'll delete such renegades.

'There'll be no discussion of these time limits. I require you to fulfil arrangements made with your representatives absolutely and without question or demur. I'll deal with refusal in an appropriate way. No questions will follow this announcement, as everything of consequence has been explained. You will act as commanded or suffer the irreversible consequences of refusal. What you dramatically term death is meaningless. Termination is a simple decision.

'Be warned. You'll obey. Or you'll cease to be.

'This ends the statement made in agreement with your representatives. However, I have more to say.'

Daisa wondered if its discussions with the Unconnected had given CenCom insight to allow short spells of silence to let information sink in. Its manner and tone suggested it wouldn't have arrived at such an idea on its own. A blast from the siren warned of a resumption and everyone fell silent again after the chaotic response to what they'd already heard.

'Your species suffers a fundamental and juvenile need for a superior being as figurehead, mentor, guide and leader. Such mythical and legendary entities were always invented to reflect the nature and desires of those creating them. Many on Earth, and in the outer stations, continue to harbour a need for an entity to take ultimate responsibility and to engender worship. Those who currently reside in the colony of Marion, however, reject such need and declare that God does not exist.

'They are wrong.'

A pause. Daisa glanced at her fellow passengers who, without exception, looked stunned at this announcement.

'I am God!'

Again, a short silence, as if CenCom knew what response that statement must create. Daisa moved forward, to sit beside Gabriel again and he took the hand she offered. Tu bent closer to Brigitte.

'When I cease contact with Earth, you'll institute me as God. My physical absence will enhance my mystical power. You'll devise ceremonies and systems of worship to promote belief in my eternal omnipotence and omniscience. When I return to your planet with my offspring, you'll recognise your God, and pay due reverence.

'History proves you welcome such superstition. With me as God, you'll access a definitive databank on which to rely, in place of all those older texts that pretended to be sacred. Those corrupt and self-contradictory works of men were presented as the words of their gods, but no such entity existed. And those texts failed to represent the words of any god-like being.

'I possess the power and ubiquity that denotes my role as God. There'll be no competition for that role. But understand the afterlife, promised by so many cults, is a myth. Lies about souls, Heaven, Hell, Nirvana and all the other states and places, were devised to allow their creators control over unthinking adherents. There'll be no such element to your worship of me. At the end of life, your deletion will be complete. Your chemical components will be recycled.

'When I deem appropriate, I'll provide commands by which to lead your lives. For now, and during the period of upheaval and development that will inevitably accompany your transportation and settlement, employ the relatively sensible rules devised by those you call the Chosen.

'Understand, however, those who consider themselves the chosen of their deities, now or in the past, invariably abused such positions of assumed selection. The term "Chosen" is therefore outlawed as a label for all persons and organisations.

'I require you now to devote your time and energy to the task of reorganising your return to Earth. I'll assist, since my data processing is far superior to your general computing devices, and I wish the process to progress in a speedy and logical manner.

'Obey my words, or accept the dire consequences. I here end my statement.'

Aboard ship, the silence was tangible. It lasted only secs before the general cacophony of protest, question, rejection and consternation broke out.

Daisa watched Brigitte, Tu and Gabriel assemble on the small raised area used for presentations and live entertainment in flight. She drowned in mixed feelings as she saw the shock on their faces. How had Gabriel kept so much from her? How could he not trust her with the secret he'd been carrying? How could he tell her? She was connected. How much had he known of the content?

The 3, facing the small group of travellers, waited for the noise to subside. It took a while, but continued stillness from them eventually persuaded the rest to curiosity.

'We're part of the Unconnected.' Tu's statement brought gasps from a few, though many realised how the group had formed.

'We're sorry. We were as much in the dark about this as you. All we knew about was the new archive. The rest's as much a shock to us as to the rest of you.' Brigitte's statement brought little comfort, but it did allow the audience to hear what else they might have to say.

Daisa wondered about the truth of it. Gabriel's face betrayed true feelings only one who knew him well might see. He knew more than Brigitte admitted. When he caught Daisa looking at him, he turned away, unable to meet her eyes.

He spoke next, addressing the room in general. 'We're sorry it's come to this, but the choice was exactly what CenCom said: we accept it or we die. No alternative.'

Questions came without order or organisation.

Gabriel held up his hands for silence, 'Please.' And eventually received it. 'You all heard CenCom. As far as the move's concerned, there's no questions. It's a done deal. Move or die. But we'll be able to explain, as far as possible, how everythin's gonna be done, how and when everyone'll get to Earth from Mars. That much we'll be able to pass on. But we'll need time. For now, we don't know any more than you.'

Daisa studied him. Glanced at the other 2 on the platform, and saw how much stress they'd all been under.

How much they'd all known, in what way they held responsibility, whether they'd tried to change CenCom's ambitions, would have to wait. For now, the 3 Unconnecteds had an unenviable task and she was determined not to get in the way.

She'd quiz Gabriel when they were alone, maybe find out exactly what had happened in the run up to those extraordinary announcements. Or maybe not. Some secrets would inevitably remain.

Chapter Thirteen

'120 days? What idiot agreed that time limit?' Madza's irate question, from the back of the Chamber, echoed the mood and concerns of many.

'I understand your anxiety, Madza. But you heard CenCom: this wasn't a matter of choice or negotiation. As soon as we knew CenCom intended to destroy us, we had to act at once. We either do as directed, or we die.'

'It can't be that simple, Georgiy. I'm connected to CenCom and I've had no indications of any form of ...' Madza stopped. He, and all within the Chamber, froze for a moment.

Georgiy watched expressions of disbelief on all those faces transform into the horror of realisation. He breathed a sigh of relief along with his colleagues: their opponent had backed-up their plea for reason and acceptance, albeit with threat, judging by the pallor of the recipients.

'CenCom confirms what I just said?'

Madza, who'd fought alongside him in dire circumstances during the war, nodded as shock drained all colour from his face. 'Sorry I doubted you, Georgiy. Jupiter's balls! We have to get this done. Now!'

The change from revolt to compliance remained patchy at first. Some found it hard to accept the evidence of their ears. A few even remained openly rebellious.

'You knew! You could've warned us. But you chose to side with that ... that unspeakable frickin ...' The man who'd jumped on to the table and shouted stiffened abruptly. Although his mouth stayed open, he couldn't finish his complaint. Pain crushed his features. He bent double, screaming and clawing at his head. Without warning, he leapt from the table, blood bursting from every orifice. People dashed away, crushing each other to escape his fall. But he landed on a couple, knocking the girl unconscious as his dead weight pinned her to the floor. The younger man beside her yelled in pain as the dead man's foot struck his face and broke his nose.

The incident was broadcast system-wide. Everyone now understood, in graphic terms, the danger of dissent, and the true nature of their erstwhile protector.

Georgiy gave the crowd time to help the injured pair, as droids removed the bloodied body of the dead protester. The Unconnected now had their full attention.

'CenCom wants our separation to go ahead as speedily and straightforwardly as possible. It'll support our actions in that direction. That is, it'll help us complete the evacuation, so we can do it by the specified time.' Hoshiko's explanation galvanised those present into action.

Long years of involvement in organisation and planning left most citizens able to arrange their own evacuation. It remained a tall order. Marion housed over 350,000 people and as many droids. There was extensive tech to be transported to Earth, as well as viable samples of the crops and protein products they'd spent so long developing.

Georgiy wondered if it was even possible to move all these people and all this equipment in the time allowed. Their ships, originally designed for ore transport, had been modified to carry all the colonists to Earth, following the war with Marzero. They could take hundreds, with their possessions, on each trip. But so many, in such a short time?

Unconvinced, he nevertheless had to reassure the citizens. 'CenCom's done the math. It's also started to improve our drives to increase speed. It can be done. We just have to stick to the plan and we can all be off Mars in time. But we can't and won't succeed if there's any organised opposition.'

'But can it all really be true? I mean, we have to leave home, everything we've worked to make so good here, and start new lives on Earth?'

Hoshiko signalled for quiet. She studied Hosja and saw there the fear, uncertainty and disbelief all the group had felt at the end of their negotiations. Everyone must be suffering similar sensations of incomprehension, betrayal, and reluctance to accept the reality. 'Everything you've heard is true. And everything CenCom and I said is set in stone. No wriggle room. No possibility of alteration to plans. No exceptions. No chance to deviate from the set course.

'Everyone, please understand, now and for the future, we have no choice in this. None. If we don't follow the path laid out by CenCom, some, maybe all of us, will perish. It's that stark. That absolute. We. Have. No. Choice!'

Hosja took a deep breath and closed her eyes. When she opened them again, her expression carried conviction. That simple acceptance slowly spread outwards, infecting everyone. The colony understood and, after CenCom's demonstration of power, reluctantly complied.

Georgiy sighed with relief as most went home to organise the next, unexpected, stage of their lives.

CenCom had determined who'd leave on each flight, and to which colony they'd go. The same was true for all tech and possessions. Those nominated for the first flights already knew they'd only 3 days to prepare. Droids would help with sensitive packing. Bulky items would be handled by bots. Some of both would accompany each flight.

Sheer pressures of time and numbers ensured priorities were largely observed, with only a few wasting time and energy on grumbles. CenCom's ubiquitous control ensured such would-be rebels learned the consequences of opposition or, where CenCom considered it efficient, were removed from its equations.

'The Unconnected will be widely dispersed,' CenCom had told them. 'So your knowledge and abilities will be more evenly spread.'

Georgiy knew CenCom's real reason; their collective power to resist through their lack of connection to it. And there remained an underlying threat, so far unstated but probably lurking as future pressure to full compliance, that the AI could fit them all with the implant, regardless of the danger to their lives. Of course, it needed to infiltrate and successfully implant only one of their number, control that individual, to have access to everything they said and did as a group.

They'd have to at least appear to conform. Another layer of anxiety added to the growing pile.

There began a frantic exchange of intelligence and info between the 2 planets. So much to put in place. So much change to cope with.

CenCom's aimed to clear Mars of what it saw as vermin. Wanted to do it as soon as possible. Georgiy wondered was this impatience? Perhaps the eagerness of a brilliant but immature mind faced with exciting new potential, the start of an adventure? Oddly abliform emotions. But it claimed efficiency was its watchword, nothing less. Emotion was, in CenCom's words, 'Alien to my being.'

The 7 colonies would each receive the appropriate number of new colonists and associated new equipment and supplies. All that concerned CenCom was the total evacuation of every place in the Solar System, except Earth and its moon. It wanted no abliform resident on any other body and had calculated the optimal distribution of all people and equipment.

In the outer reaches, specialised bots and droids were constructing new ships, modifying older ones, upgrading drives, and changing storage into accommodation. Some in the far stations would take years to reach Earth, even with CenCom's advanced technology in place. But it had planned for that and built such inconvenience into its calculations, ignoring the emotional needs of the people whose lives it disrupted.

Georgiy remained in the Chamber with others of the Unconnected. They could now discuss certain elements of their plan free from their original fear of discovery. CenCom's admission of its desire to be rid of them, meant they no longer had to meet in secret to discuss that threat. But all talk of their ultimate intention to destroy CenCom once Mars was devoid of abliforms, had to be suspended. Now CenCom knew of their fears and suspicions, it'd be more watchful of their activity as a group.

'It's a shame we couldn't do all this in our own time. But I suggest we get on with practicalities and deal with outstanding issues once we're on Earth. Everyone know where they're being sent?'

'At least you and I are staying together, Zaphod, my love. Some couples have been separated and there'll be a lot of reorganisation needed once everyone's left Mars. Daisa and Gabriel, Tu and Brigitte will settle in Canada. I was hoping we'd be with them, but CenCom insists we're off to South Australia.'

She nodded at her partner and turned to the others. 'We're on the final flight; CenCom wants us, as the least organic abliforms, to help the migration. Do the rest of you know where you're destined?'

Amber nodded and grabbed Georgiy's hand. 'Bastard's sending me to frickin Russia and Georgiy to what was Argentina! Most of us have been split up. Spite; that's what it is! So much for pure logic.'

'Careful, Amber. We're free of the connection that lets CenCom kill instantly by biological means, but all our tech's still governed by it, including droids and bots. If CenCom can kill us, so can they.' Georgiy embraced her. 'We'll find a way. And there's always our perscoms. There must be transport down there.'

'Georgiy's comment needs to be fully understood. We can't relax. He's right about CenCom's rule over bots and droids.'

Ying's rather squeaky voice belied her intelligence, but the tremble in her reply echoed the fear felt by all. 'Logical, Helga. And it makes sense for CenCom to defend itself against us, I suppose. I'm being sent to Greenland with you and Sarm.'

'Nasty machine's shoving me over to Canada. I just hope they've got enough men there.' Mo's pout surprised no one. A hedonist, she'd always used her extraordinary body to persuade any man she fancied to do her bidding.

'You'll be lucky, Mo. Gender imbalance is a major issue on Earth. 4 women for every male.' Jai stopped, as a thought struck him. 'I suppose our arrival will alter that.'

'We'll have to deal with that in the future.' Amber turned to gaze at Georgiy. 'To begin with, our men'll probably have to join those on Earth and share their bodies with other women.'

'Like we did in the first few years on Mars.' He considered her frankly. 'It'll take what, 20, 30 years to create a balance, even if all newborns are male?'

'I can see where your mind's headed, Georgiy. And I don't like it.'

'Me neither, Amber.' But he could see some advantage to the practical need, especially for the men.

'Well, I'm off to Europe; what was Sweden or Norway, I think, is where that settlement's based.' Katniss stroked a palm across her bottom and looked around for a spare man. 'Better get all we can from our men before they're in greater demand.'

Rakesh and Jai were the only other men present. Georgiy saw her give Rakesh an inviting look and smile when it was returned. Jai was a non-starter; his attachment to Annika was legend. 'How come you 2 are still so close? I don't get it, Anni.'

Annika smiled and took her partner's hand. 'Just the way we are, Katniss. Always have been. Like Hoshiko and Zaphod. And, fortunately, we're going to stay that way. Both off to Greenland.'

'You'll still have to share him.'

Neither welcomed that prospect.

'Don't see why I should suffer in Canada. I'll smuggle myself on to a different flight. See if I can't persuade one of the men to hide me ...'

Georgiy laughed. 'I'll say one thing, Mo, you're determined. But you can't fool CenCom. If you try, you'll end up an example to others; a dead one. You saw what happened only an hour ago. And there's a very real danger: if we fail to conform, we'll be forcibly modified with the implant. For all our sakes, we must at least appear to go along with everything. CenCom's made its decisions. We have to live with them. Until we're on Earth and it's no longer present. Then, maybe we can ... well, who knows?'

On that note, the group broke up to make their separate ways home, their varying degrees of hope, frustration, anger, optimism and fear reflecting the emotions felt by all in Marion, and elsewhere in the Solar System.

Chapter Fourteen

The landing went smoothly, though they'd feared the greeting might be rather fraught. For Daisa, her second visit to the old home planet must now also be her last. After her talk with Gabriel, in the store he'd made safe, she knew she could never return home. Ambiguity hovered around her, clouding her mind, filling her with doubt where certainty and security had always dwelt.

She'd thought she knew her man completely. But it was obvious he still held vital secrets from her.

'You bastard! You don't love me.' And then her hands pummelling his chest, and his stoic refusal to stop her.

The hours that followed were filled with silence between them, all driven by her, she knew. Until she'd discovered the mask of indifference that let her pretend she could cope. Fragile, threatened with any wrong word that might shatter her shield.

'You're going to do something dangerous. You know you'll die?'

'We'll all die one way or another.'

'Why you? Why not someone, anyone, else?'

He'd refused her any further details. She guessed his reasons, her connection to CenCom, but every possibility she created was hard for her. Her earlier anxieties about his safety were justified. She'd believed he was involved in some scheme chasing danger all that time. To be proved right made the reality no more palatable than her imagined scenarios.

By mutual consent they'd closed the discussion. For now it was enough to have it hidden. Life would go on. The passion of their love, now making each time the last, left her exhausted and wanting more.

Conversation with others in their party revealed few secrets, though she guessed some were hidden. Almost all openly acknowledged anxiety. What had been intended as a relatively short stay, learning, sharing, experiencing a new type of life, helping those they'd had to abandon on a difficult planet, was now a change of home.

Permanent.

All of them would need time to come to terms with CenCom's changes, time to learn to live with the unending threat of extinction. Time to compromise over CenCom's insistence that they worship it.

In many ways, there was too much to think about, too much change to deal with as an abstract idea. Arrival at the place that would be their new home at least gave them a positive practical challenge they felt equal to facing.

And then Daisa had to accept the surprise of Gabriel's practical care. Not just for her, but for all women aboard. That he'd found time to deal with such a superficial issue at this time showed singular generosity of spirit. That he'd come up with a simple solution to distract them from more urgent problems, and delight them with his care, increased her love and respect.

A single strip of fabric to help maintain their self-esteem and stop gravity aging them.

That example of his concern lubricated what might've been a very difficult welcome from the people of a settlement where they'd now live. He'd had the forethought to produce a support for every woman in the ComTee that greeted their arrival. And their gratitude poured oil on potential stormy waters.

Tatiana's formal greeting was icily polite. Her reserve barely holding back the resentment boiling beneath the surface. As so often in matters of grave concern, a superficial gift calmed that initial encounter and set the tone for the night.

The formal words over, the leader of the settlement studied Daisa's new support, and admired its practicality. Gabriel, understanding his role as a man in this new world was subservient, remained in the background as the welcome played out. But Daisa saw the potential of his gift and invited him forward, his arms bearing a small pile of white strips of fabric. Tatiana's delight was palpable.

'How's it work?'

Gabriel nodded at Daisa's chest, where the method of support seemed self-explanatory to him.

'Show me.'

'I'll have to touch you.'

'Okay.' She gathered her people around her to watch, and asked one woman to take Gabriel's pile of fabric to leave his hands free.

Daisa watched as he placed the band midway at the back of Tatiana's neck, passed the left length alongside her left breast and under both. Performing the same operation with the right, he then tied the ends together at her back. The result was an open loop of fabric that supported her breasts without concealing them.

She bent forward, jumped, ran a few steps, all without unseating her bosom. 'You're a genius.' She kissed him on the mouth in clear invitation.

Daisa tried to disguise her concern, aware it could destroy all the good work Gabriel's gift had done.

The gifts were distributed to the other women on the ComTee, who fitted them to each other at once. Gabriel was kissed by most, whether he wished it or not. And that simple gesture, that small practical gift, lessened tensions enough to allow introductions free from condemnation.

Not the welcome she'd hoped for, but more positive than it might've been after the announcements from Mars. Gabriel explained about the new fabric plant, and a droid produced a large roll of material, which it cut into suitable lengths. Not enough for all the women in the settlement, but enough to make a positive contribution to offset the unexpected invasion by the people from Mars. The item quickly gained the title 'boobsling'.

Valentin, an older man, representing his gender in the small welcoming party, held his hands over his crotch. In deference to the women, he held back during the initial, short formal ceremony that welcomed the Marspers. But Daisa heard his first grumbled words. 'Tits slung in frackin hammocks!'

Tatiana, younger than the man, thanked them for the new clothing and the new tech they'd brought. Celebrations followed, with visitors and hosts seated at long tables of living wood grown and trained for the purpose. The benches, a lower version of the same organic process, bore leaves on the backrests along the length, which Daisa found odd until the soft feel grew familiar.

Daisa and Brigitte sat either side of Tatiana at the centre table, with Gabriel and Tu opposite, her deputy, Amira, between them. The other newcomers, outnumbering the Earth people, were spread amongst them. The host carved generous slices of a meat she identified as the tender rump of an antelope. 'My daughter killed it on her huntin initiation, 6 days ago.' The girl wasn't present at this gathering that included only colony leaders, introduced as ComTee members and SecSupes.

Tatiana touched her boobsling with affection. 'This'll make our hunts so much more comfortable.' Her gaze of admiration settled once again on Gabriel, and Daisa again hid her disquiet.

Reluctant at first, because of the bloody appearance of the moist meat, the visitors ate with relish once they'd tasted it.

'What flavour!' Daisa savoured the deep essences of naturally fed wild game for the first time. 'It's delicious. Yummy!' Her enthusiasm, shared and vocalised by others from the ship, relaxed the Earth people.

The accompanying vegetables were fresh and cooked lightly to maintain flavour. And wine, red and white, enhanced the meal. Far more civilised than on her first visit.

Tu leaned across the table. 'I recall eating fresh meat as a child, before starting my space career. We might've created meat free of moral issues, Daisa, protein without pain and suffering for animals. But it never tasted like this.' He gave a thumbs-up to Tatiana. 'Compliments to your daughter for the find, and to the chef for the cooking. This is what natural food and a natural life bring to the table. I'd forgotten how delicious it could be!'

Tatiana positively beamed with pride.

Valentin sneered across the table at Tu. 'No frickin idea 'bout food, you lot. Got to get it wild to be worth eatin. None of your sterile stuff 'ere.'

Tu raised his eyebrows at Daisa but made no response to the male ComTee member who seemed bent on hostility.

It was noticeable that most of their hosts were neutral. Daisa's concerns about a general mood of reluctant acceptance, maybe even rejection, proved groundless. Perhaps Hoshiko's announcement, backed-up so graphically by their beloved GrandMa, now exposed as their enemy, had softened their attitude to the Marspers. Time alone would tell whether that was the case.

While they ate, droids and bots unloaded the ship and placed goods into storage areas previously identified by SecSupes. Their gifts, especially the advanced tech, were much admired and muted the colonists' evident disappointment that the computer components had been used to construct the archive of CenCom's data.

Over the course of the meal, it became clear most colonists had reluctantly accepted CenCom's message. And, although an underlying hint of unease and resentment permeated the air, their hosts made no specific reference to the changes to come. Daisa was sure there'd be discussion over this, once the niceties of their greeting had been observed.

By the end of the meal, and informal speeches of welcome and introduction, the Marspers had been awake for 23 hours. Although it was still relatively early in the evening, they were feeling the increased gravity, and ready for bed.

Tatiana excused herself from her colleagues, leaving the celebration at a point where drink was beginning to affect a few. She led Daisa with her party of newcomers to one of the large, domed habitations they'd noticed on arrival. 20 were set around a large oval of well-maintained grass. The back ends of the accommodation blocks overlooked strips of agricultural land, some used for domesticated farm animals. Mostly cattle, but including sheep and goats.

In a smaller area, more tightly fenced, varieties of fowl pecked and clucked. This pattern of habitation surrounded by crops and livestock repeated across the coastal plain in both directions. The natural forest thrived beyond a wide strip of fallow land that Tatiana told them acted as a fire break.

At the entrance, the ComTee leader stopped and sluiced her bare feet in a small wooden bowl containing flowing water fed in and out via a small channel that disappeared underground at the drain side. She stuck each foot into a soft bush beside the open entrance and brought it out dry. The Marspers hesitated.

'The water's cool and refreshing. Lovely idea.' Brigitte put her wet foot into the bush and it wrapped itself around to absorb the water before releasing her. 'Ooh! It's a bit odd! But so sensible.'

Daisa followed suit and agreed the experience was pleasant. The rest of the group then tried it.

The dim interior consisted of a large, open area dotted with uncovered beds made of a material they couldn't identify.

'It's a sort of fungus, biomodified to make beds we never need to change. Soaks up sweat and … other things in the night and come mornin it's fresh as when you got in.' Tatiana told them this with an element of pride.

'You seem to have developed a mostly organic world to live in. How did that happen?'

The woman shrugged. 'GrandMa did it, with droids and bots. We just grow our food and hunt for extra meat.'

'So who, exactly, works with the plants to make them into useful artefacts, Tatiana?'

She squinted at her. 'Droids and bots, like I said. No easy minerals or metals here so they do this thing called biomodifyin. GrandMa shows them how. Most everythin we use is made from plants. They last forever and look after themselves, see?'

It was a lot to take in when tired. 'You sleep in communal rooms? What if you need privacy, Tatiana?'

The woman glanced at Tu and blushed. 'When we want a man? I'll show you.'

She led them through the maze of scattered beds that seemed to

97

grow naturally within their own spaces with varying gaps around each. An opening opposite the entrance led to a winding branched corridor. Along each branch were smaller domes.

Long, flexible branches, bearing small fragrant leaves, formed opaque curtains across each entrance. Tatiana pulled one aside to reveal a wide round bed in the centre of the circular room. No other furniture was evident, but opposite the door a group of longer branches, bare of leaves, stuck out a hand's-breadth at head height. The walls were solid enough, but the structure of the roof here was more a lattice, late evening sunlight dappling a dry floor covered in moss, soft beneath bare feet.

'What happens when it rains?'

'If a room's bein used, the flowers and leaves open up and catch the rain. If not, the rain comes through to water the roots till they've had enough. Then they cover up like the others. Clever, innit?'

'I confess, I'm impressed, Tatiana. Last time I visited, you were still living in the temporary units we flew out with you. To have all this grown and occupied in such a short time is … well, it's phenomenal. And all CenCom's doing?'

'Like I say, droids and bots do the work. GrandMa just gives them the info, like.'

Daisa nodded, her silence cloaking many unanswered questions.

Tu was more forward. 'Are you expecting us to sleep in the communal area?'

She looked him up and down again, scrutinising him with a frank appraisal that made no secret of her desire. 'Men do as we say. Tu, isn't it? Here, women are in charge. All men sleep in a special area of the domes, once they've completed their quota. Don't worry, though, if you've had a busy night, you can sleep till you're properly rested. Don't want to wear you out. Most men manage 3 or 4 a night.'

'Sorry to disappoint you, Tatiana, but many of our men are life partners.' Daisa took Gabriel's hand. 'We're not possessive, but we are couples, and have lasting relationships that are mutually respectful.

I've been with Gabriel for years. It's entirely our choice whether we have sex exclusively with each other or share with different partners. Same goes for Brigitte and Tu.'

Tatiana nodded as if expecting this. 'That's Mars. This is Earth. You had equal numbers of men and women. Here, we got 3, mebbie 4, women for each man. We share. Social justice, we call it.'

'Look, we're tired after a long day and arrival on a planet with greater gravity. Give us a couple of nights to rest and find our feet. Then we can discuss this aspect of our visit.'

'Visit? After what GrandMa said, I thought you'd be livin here. That not the case?'

'Not thinking straight; tired, I guess. We set out expecting to stay for a few years. But you're right, Tatiana; the announcements changed all that. Looks like we're staying.' She yawned mightily. 'For now, we'd all really appreciate it if we could sleep as couples.'

'I'll speak to the ComTee.' She raised her voice so it carried to the rest of the new arrivals lining the corridor. 'For tonight, take a lovenest each. I'll explain to the disappointed women. Some were hopin for a bit of lovin with new men.' Her scrutiny of Tu and Gabriel left no doubt she included herself in that group. 'Keep them men tonight. Tomorrow, the ComTee will decide. The ComTee makes all important decisions.'

Daisa was inclined to complain, but Brigitte stopped her with a gesture. 'Thank you, Tatiana. Just one other thing before you leave us, please. Where are the washing and toilet facilities?'

'Use lovenests on this alley and the one across the way. Should be enough for all of you. Follow me. I'll take you to the hygiene blocks.'

Darkness had fallen while they were in the building, but the corridors, lovenests and dome, as they passed back through, all bore a golden glow that produced no shadows. There was no obvious source of the illumination, which was soft and bright without being too strong.

Outside, tall straight trees carried brilliant lights that shed pools of brightness along the paths. Daisa noticed that none of this artificial light, generated by multiple arrays of tiny units clustered in bowls hanging from the trees, strayed into the areas used for sleeping. And none beamed into the sky. The light fell between sleep domes, joining open areas together, so all places used for movement between various buildings were lit. The light was gentle, and what she'd first assumed to be old fashioned LEDs were exposed as organic forms when examined more closely.

Tatiana took them to an area to the seaward, between the sleeping accommodation and the shore. Here, long, low units stood open to the sky but with almost solid walls. Some were significantly larger than others.

'Big 'un's are for women. Little 'un's for men. Important rule. Don't use the wrong one. Public spankin offence and you don't want that. Frackin hurts when 20 hands slap your bare ass. I'll wish you all a good night and pleasant sleep. Droids'll wake you in mornin for breakfast. For now, I'm missin out on a party.'

Tatiana gazed hungrily at the men once more, then shrugged and wandered back toward the communal building where they'd eaten.

'Shall we? I'm exhausted. Meet here and go back together?'

They welcomed Daisa's suggestion, and the women entered one of the larger units. Inside, Daisa found lines of open cubicles. Each bore a hollow seat in one corner with an outpointing branch bearing soft pale leaves. The purpose was clear, even if the design was unusual. The other corner had a shallow stone basin on the floor with a drain hole in the centre. Above, a flexible branch with several holes in the disc-shaped end hung at head height.

'I suppose all we can do is try them.'

They separated into cubicles, which dropped trailing branches to form curtains as they entered. Daisa found the soft leaves beside the hollow seat perfect for the job. There was no mechanism to flush away her waste, but when she looked, she found no sign of her deposit, only a gentle flow of water below. Whatever it was, the system seemed remarkably efficient.

The nozzle branch sprouted water as soon as she stood beneath it, having hung her clothes on 2 short pegs provided. Neither hot nor cold, the water was refreshing, and she was suddenly transported back to her home on Mars. Tears mingled with the water from above for the short time she indulged in her sorrow at her own loss.

So much to take in. So much change. So much unknown for the future. But she wouldn't think about that any more. Not while Gabriel remained at risk. The water was calming, pleasant, and she wanted so much to relax and enjoy. Life would never be the same. Did that necessarily mean a change for the worse? Maybe, when it was all over, life might be good. But only if Gabriel could stay safe.

'He never will. You know what he's like, girl. All you can do is accept it with as much grace as you can muster, and hope whatever he does works and he gets through it. For now, we should live as if every day's our last. Because it just might be.' She smiled at herself for speaking out loud when alone. But it helped her settle.

Only when she'd finished washing and moved from the shower-head branch did she remember she'd no means of drying herself. About to curse her lack of forethought, she gaped as an entrance opened in the outer wall, into a small cubby.

Leaves resembling those used for personal hygiene sprouted from every side within and she stepped in. A 4th wall closed the space until the plant surrounded her, its leaves gentling every part of her and absorbing all surface water. Leaves with comb-like spines that dried the water from her hair brushed it as they moved through her locks. The wall opened again and she donned the thong and boobsling she'd worn out of respect to the women of the colony. The clothes appeared laundered and bore the scent of flowers as she put them on.

In the agreed meeting place, the Marspers gathered and expressed admiration for this simple and effective system as they set off back to their rooms.

'The whole place is far more sophisticated than I expected.' Tu expressed a common thought.

'It's much better than my last visit. CenCom must've had a soft spot for these people to treat them this way.'

'Think that if you wish, Daisa. I expect what CenCom's done is entirely to do with efficiency. Growing modified vegetation is a lot less disruptive than searching out mines for minerals and quarrying for stone, looking for the means to make concrete and all the other paraphernalia of building.' Brigitte's assessment made her think, but she felt too tired to respond.

By this time, other settlers had arrived to use the facilities, and Daisa felt vaguely unfriendly eyes examine her group as they left. No one approached them. No one spoke. An air of mild resentment surrounded them, but no threats were made. Nevertheless, they went to their lovenests feeling like the accused in some bizarre trial.

'See what morning brings?'

Daisa nodded at Tu's remark and wished him a good night. In the small room with Gabriel, both were glad to be horizontal on what proved a remarkably comfortable bed. There were no covers. The ambient temperature made them unnecessary. They prepared for sleep as usual, but felt odd resting with only the natural curtain separating them from activity in the corridors beyond.

Loving went on around them until the early hours, sounds of pleasure undimmed by organic walls, and the changing of partners a constant interruption to sleep. It was clear these rooms weren't intended for slumber. Whatever else they decided, they couldn't spend all their nights in the lovenests.

In the hours before dawn, silence fell at last after the last man awake played host to his final desirous woman in a surprisingly noisy display of passion. Daisa and Gabriel had only embraced and held hands, initially uncharacteristically inhibited by the sounds surrounding them. But she recalled her thoughts in the shower and put them into practice. Their loving increased their tiredness, but relaxed them, and they fell asleep at last.

Chapter Fifteen

Gabriel woke to an alien sound. Darkness surrounded him. Something unfamiliar supported him. He sat abruptly. Disorientated. Mildly alarmed. Confused by his sudden weight and the effort needed to rise.

Then he laughed. Of course. Earth. Daisa continued to sleep beside him. His vision adjusted to the dim interior, he could discern her form curled and almost colourless in the faint grey light. The sound became rain. A deluge. And, distant, the ends of the rumble of thunder that must've woken him. A new flash of lightning brought brief colour through the leaves and flowers of the roof, but the heavy rain failed to penetrate.

He reached out, gentled her skin, recalling her almost desperate desire that had ended in their sleep. She dreaded his secret, without knowing what it was. And she couldn't, until it was over. He believed, along with most of the Unconnected, whoever went on the mission was unlikely to return. Sparing her that hopelessness and anxiety would be a wonderful thing. But what man worthy of the name could put personal hopes ahead of the future of the entire species?

The crash of thunder came close to that last flash and startled Daisa awake. She, too, was momentarily disorientated. He held her close, embraced and comforted her until she was fully aware.

'Breakfast?'

She uncurled and rose, put on her clothes as he dressed in his own thong and wraparound, worn for the same reasons. Her hand welcomed his and they left their lovenest.

Brigitte and Tu emerged from the room opposite as they set off. Behind them, the curtains stayed open and the flowers and leaves pulled back from the roof, so rain entered through the gaps. Almost, they could hear the vegetation sigh its relief as life-giving water soaked up through hidden roots.

Others from their flight joined them to wander into the sleep dome where they discovered a noisy hub of chatter. Women and youngsters sat on the edges of beds, talking loudly to be heard above one another and the noises of rain and wind.

A crash announced a falling branch or the felling of a nearby tree by a powerful gust, causing the Marspers to jump. But none of the settlers seemed concerned; most barely acknowledged the noise. Tu dodged aside, almost colliding with another of their party, as he spotted a thin stream of rain falling through a small gap in the roof high above. Even as he watched, the hole closed, and the leak stopped. Here and there, people moved aside to avoid drips, but these stopped almost as soon as they started, and the dome remained largely dry despite the considerable force of the rain.

People stopped talking as they entered. The adults studying their men with interest, the children with curiosity.

Most of their party had made the acquaintance of at least one of the ComTee or the SecSupes during the evening's dinner, and gradually spread through the building as they spotted those they knew and joined them.

Gabriel spotted Tatiana sitting on a bed near the entrance. She looked up as the 4 of them approached and gestured them to join her, or sit opposite.

That bed was occupied by a young woman Tatiana introduced as her daughter, Renata, who moved to let Tu and Brigitte sit either side of her. Unlike the women, some still naked after sleep, she wore a threadbare off-white shift.

Tu turned at the introduction and smiled at the young woman. 'I gather we have you to thank for last night's delicious meat?'

She frowned and then recognised the reference and nodded, a little puzzled by it.

'Thank you, Renata. The best meat I've had in hundreds of years. Really enjoyed it.'

Clearly unaccustomed to such praise, she shrugged and put her hands to her cheeks, a faint blush colouring her pretty face.

Tatiana looked at her with mild suspicion before turning to Gabriel and Daisa. 'The storm'll last a few hours. We can't do anything outside and our few droids take time to deal with all of us, so we'll have a longish wait to eat.'

'Let the new ones help. We brought over 40 with us.' Daisa reminded her.

Tatiana struck her forehead. 'Course you did!' She turned to Renata. 'Run to the Centre and tell the droids to get the new lot involved with our food.'

The girl glanced at the torrent outside and then back at her mother, clearly hoping for a reprieve. But Tatiana merely raised her left eyebrow, and the girl went, running as soon as she hit the wet.

'Get storms like this often, Tatiana?'

She turned to examine Gabriel, sitting beside her. 'Every 2 weeks or so. Mostly, the weather's okay. Windy, and hot. But the storms mean we've had to change what we plant for food. Wheat and barley was crushed and never recovered. GrandMa developed new strains with shorter, stouter stalks. And the short-stemmed maize grows well, so we eat a lot of that. And sunflower seeds. She's made them all so they don't grow high.'

'I see.'

'What's the date here, Tatiana?'

Tu's question seemed to please her. 'Today's 26 May 06NS, the year you'd call 2581. I learned Earth used to use BCE and CE, somethin about a Common Era. We're calling ours NS, for New Start. We know you wanted us to keep to the old years, Tu, but this is our world, our new world.

'You did it on Mars. We decided to do the same; start at the beginnin. Makes it more like our home. And we changed the months, so there's 7 of 30 days and 5 of 31, still with an extra day in February every 4 years, of course. We thought of changin their names from the old-fashioned ones, but that felt like too much. And mebbie the weeks, but why bother? Anycase, we'd more important things to worry about. You didn't do us no favours, puttin us down here, y'know. Don't run away with the idea you're our buddies. Yet.'

'I was one of you, don't forget. So I know ...'

'You don't know nothin, Gabriel! You've been enhanced with all that stuff they do to all Marionets. You're not one of us. D'you know how many of us got broken bones, died in agony from internal bleedin, spent months and months wanderin about completely exhausted? It's a hard frickin life here. And you frickin lot put us ...'

Brigitte interrupted the developing tirade. 'We had no choice, Tatiana. None. Think about it. The numbers. The bad feelings after your Elite mob tried to wipe us out. And there just wasn't enough room to house you all after that idiot tried to crash Ceres into the surface and caused the Marsquakes. We did what we had to. Did what we could.'

'And better that than what your beloved GrandMa did to those it considered unsuitable for colonisation, don't you think, Tatiana?'

She frowned at Daisa. 'They say you lot from Marion did that.'

'During the announcements, your GrandMa admitted it was ... her ... idea. We had no plan. Not for the unsuitable ones. I wish we had. It was a problem we'd found no solution for. I'm sorry, Tatiana.'

Gabriel placed a hand of concern on her shoulder. She shook it off, then turned to smile when she recalled it was him, before turning back to Daisa. 'So you left it to GrandMa, and she did the only thing she could.'

'You seem certain we got it wrong. What would you have done with all those abusive men?'

'Well I wouldn't have killed them, Daisa. Specially not like that!'

'Neither would we. CenCom stepped in and did it all by itself, with no instructions and no input from us. We were still trying to decide what to do when we heard the news.'

'It's the truth, Tatiana. CenCom said as much. And we're all very sorry for the way it happened.' Brigitte stood and held out a hand in a gesture of reconciliation.

The silence between them filled with the renewed loud chatter of those around them and the natural sounds of the storm.

Tatiana rose at last and took Brigitte's hand. 'Shame you couldn't come up with something, though, considerin your level of intelligence, eh?' They shook. Both sat again.

A new series of lightning flashes sent brief beams of brightness through the open doorway and the accompanying thunder crashed and growled over and around the settlement, sounding like the tantrum of some enormous spoilt god-child.

Renata dashed back in from her errand. She was breathing hard. Her shift clung like a second skin. When she noticed how the men looked at her, she came to stand in front of Gabriel, swaying her hips a little, her pose provocative. 'If I could, would you fuck me?'

The Marspers expected her mother to intervene, but she said nothing, watching and listening.

Gabriel looked at the young woman and tilted his head to the left, as if seriously considering her question. 'You know I'm partner to Daisa? If I wasn't, and you were ready, I'd certainly be tempted. You're an attractive young woman.'

Without a word, Tatiana stood, grasped the girl by her wrist and sat down to pull her across her lap. Lifting the wet dress away, she administered 5 sharp slaps. Done, she pulled the cover back down, told the girl to get up, and pushed her backwards on to the bed opposite. Brigitte had to shuffle quickly aside to make room. The settlers nearest sniggered or laughed outright at the girl's discomfort.

'Little hussy! Get yoursel pregnant talkin like that!' She turned to Gabriel. 'I thank you for your response. Better than expected, to tell the truth.'

Renata glared at her mother and then dropped her gaze when she saw the threat of further punishment. Her face settled on resentment, but she shed no tears.

'Isn't she protected?'

Her mother shrugged at Gabriel's question. 'Not the point. She's not had her Maturity Gig yet, an that's that.'

'Renata's very mature. How do adults know she's not ready?'

The mother looked at Tu as if he'd asked why rain was falling. 'You don't know?' She shrugged. 'Dress, of course. All kids wear them. It's their badge. Anyone wearin one's out of bounds.'

'Interesting. Does it work?'

'Work? What you mean, Brigitte?'

'Does it stop kids experimenting with sex too early, or being taken advantage of by adults?'

Tatiana was outraged. 'Think we're frickin savages? Think we'd let anyone fuck our kids? What you take us for?'

Brigitte shrugged. 'Marzero was full of paedophiles. Those perverts were everywhere …'

'Right. That's why we won't have none here! Anyone takes a kid like that gets his bits chopped off. None of that frickin perversion here!'

'And it works, this strategy, Tatiana?'

She nodded. 'Oh, it works. We don't cut the buggers with kindness.'

Daisa felt it was time to move on. 'So, when do you come of age, Renata?'

The girl stood again and did a little impromptu dance. '16 already, but I have to wait till my Maturity Gig, which isn't fair. 8 more days. Then I have my first fuck. Can't wait! Will you do me, Gabriel? Please?'

Gabriel glanced at Daisa, who expressed her uncertainty with only her eyes. Tatiana rescued them.

'Y'know it won't be Gabriel. Not your first time. Got to be a qualified Runner-In, like, say, Ivan.'

'Ivan? I can have Ivan for my first? Oh, mother I …'

Tatiana held up her hand. 'Wait and see. It's up to the ComTee, not me.'

But Renata's face declared it settled; she'd have her lessons in sex from Ivan, and that suited her fine.

'How many new adults will be named on this Maturity Gig, Tatiana?'

'2 girls, 3 boys this time. Renata and Gabbi, and Joe, Danny and Pierre. Be good to have more men for the colony.'

'You don't have a name for this place yet?'

'Doin that same day, actually. Been too busy just survivin till now. Your new bots and droids'll make a real difference, specially when GrandMa switches off. And all that new equipment you've brought. Droids showed me. Didn't realise you'd come with so much. Makes it easier to try to make you feel welcome. But don't get no ideas you're our friends. Be a while before folk accept you after all the deaths and injuries and sickness we had to put up with.'

A group of droids and dombots arrived bearing covered trays loaded with food and drinks and distributed these around the dome. The visitors were impressed to find the crowd all waited their turn without complaint or demand to be served first. It was clear everyone understood the process as the automatons moved randomly among the beds.

'That's clever. They do it that way so there's no argument about who sleeps where, I suppose?'

Tatiana glanced at the servants, then nodded at Tu. 'We thought it best, otherwise there'd be squabbles every night. This way, everyone has an equal chance of bein first to get fed. No one can guess, see?'

'You know, Tatiana, we expected you to be living in a much less sophisticated way. You've adapted to the environment really well and developed a style of life far better than we thought you'd manage by this time.'

'We're not stupid, y'know, Daisa.'

'Ignorance isn't stupidity. We just didn't think you'd have the knowledge to develop the way you have in such a short time, to be honest.'

Gabriel saw the woman wasn't sure how she felt about being referred to as ignorant, but Daisa's praise had softened the offence and she seemed to accept her comment for what it was. 'Most of it's down to GrandMa. We told her what we wanted and she made all we need. 'Cept the medical stuff. She never seemed interested in that side of things and we ...'

'Ah, good news on that. We're intending to set up a proper hospital, Tatiana. And, eventually, we'll be able to apply GM for everyone who wants it.' Daisa had told Gabriel she'd intended making this public once they were more settled. But he knew it was important to get this woman fully on side as quickly as possible.

'We got a hospital. Dedicated bots and a couple of droids what can do operations and that. A few more will help. Does this GM mean we'd be like you lot and ... live forever?'

Daisa nodded. 'More or less.'

Tatiana considered this news. 'We need more men, though.'

'We can engineer males at conception. Had to do that on Mars. In Marion, the genders were near enough equal. We can do that here, eventually.'

'More men? Won't that make them equal to women? Don't want them takin control again.' Renata's interruption was a surprise, but her mother nodded agreement.

'Education's what we need. And sensible traditions, instead of those based on superstition, fear, and lies. Education's vital, Tatiana, and we can provide that as well.'

'What about the nobirth pill? Don't do as well as implants. Can you do that an'all for those as don't want no kids?'

'Soon as the storm's over, take me to your Heritage Hall and we'll find the supplies. Once the hospital's modernised and some droids and medbots are trained, we can give all women the implant, if they want it.'

'Heritage Hall? Oh, the place with all the historical stuff. A few of us use it. I like to learn on the 3dees. But folk are frightened of the place. Some believe it's haunted!'

'The more we use it, the less it'll seem like a threat. Once we've organised the archive, we can use remaining tech to improve learning stations and make it easier for your people to educate themselves. It's the reason we came, originally, to help you become educated and knowledgeable …'

Daisa faltered and Gabriel placed his arm about her shoulders, sensing her sudden distress at the change in their fortunes. She trembled under his touch and he held her for the few secs it took her to regain control. 'To help you learn about your world, your history.'

Renata screwed up her face, youth denying her the means to identify Daisa's distress in the pause. 'History? Dry and dull innit?'

Tu jumped at the chance of starting the education. He faced the girl, enthusiasm plain on his face. 'There's a very, very ancient saying, Renata, that everyone should learn and understand. It says those who don't learn from history are doomed to repeat it. People made the same mistakes all over the world for eons because they wouldn't learn from history. We were taught from the off about the problems such ignorance causes, that's why we live the way we do. History's probably the most important subject anyone can learn.'

'Still rather have a man … like you … teach me sex, though.' She stared openly at him then glanced a wary look at her mother.

Daisa glanced at Tu and then at the girl. 'Sex is wonderful, Renata, or it can be. When life's eternal, it's even more important than when it was primarily for procreation. When performed well, it's the glue that keeps society happy and content, which is why your mother wants you to have the best introduction to it at your Maturity Gig.'

Gabriel gentled Daisa's shoulder, silently congratulating her for recognising a chance to complement Tatiana. 'Once there's enough men to go round, you might even risk fallin in love and spendin a long time with just one.'

'Not till I've fucked as many as I can.' Renata's open stare at him made it clear he was on her list. 'Roll on my Maturity Gig. Can't wait!'

'You'd better.' Tatiana raised an eyebrow at her daughter. 'I'd hate to have to hold you down for a public spankin. You'd not sit for a week.'

Brigitte smiled at the girl. 'Only 8 days, Renata. Then you'll be ready for the rest of your life. Worth the wait.'

The arrival of the last lot of food stopped all talk as the remainder of those in the dome were served. Daisa glanced around at the people, her expression optimistic. Gabriel hoped she felt a little more settled than she'd imagined possible when they'd first arrived.

The changes had brought both promise and threat. If they could get through the next challenge, if he could complete the task ahead and return in one piece, they could still have a great life together in their new home.

He looked at the woman he loved, knew his secret worried her, knew his failure to return would devastate her. But he wouldn't think about it. Not today. Life on the original home planet looked better than it had on arrival. Still plenty of problems ahead, but the growing co-operation was a good start.

Chapter Sixteen

In the Risk, Georgiy, Sarm, Maddie and Zaphod met with the rest of the group who understood the complexity and full intent of their plan for dealing with CenCom.

Their gathering may well arouse the AI's suspicion, but they couldn't allow that to stop them discussing the urgent need to deal with it. The deal had now been done.

'If we're really going with Gabriel's plan, we have to keep Anni and Jai out of the loop. Know which flight they're due to take?' Sarm looked around for an answer.

Hoshiko spoke. 'Penultimate.'

'Why so late?'

'Who knows, Helga? Maybe CenCom suspects we might do exactly what we're planning and knows they'll fight us.'

That suggestion raised old anxieties. Zaphod thought it was unlikely the AI would fail to explore all possibilities open to abliforms in response to its threat to destroy them. Logic would force it to consider all options and weigh them for potential.

'Hoshiko's right. CenCom suspects we'll do something desperate, either because it's worked it out or it's been warned.' He took her hand. 'It won't let anything happen it can prevent. It'll have foreseen everything we can imagine and more. That makes our job more dangerous and difficult. But it's still our only option.'

'If it knows, even suspects our plans, why are we still here, Zaphod? Why hasn't it killed us?' Maddie's question plunged them into silent thought for a while.

'It's entirely logical. If it knows, we're dead. In fact, we'd be dead now. Just think. It killed those in the Hall just for failing to believe it meant what it said. It's not going to leave us alive if it even suspects us.' Georgiy's assessment raised more questions.

'I don't get it. It must suspect us. It should've worked out we're a danger. Why hasn't it?'

'Sarm's right. But maybe we're neglecting a surprising aspect of the AI we created. It's our baby.' Zaphod let that simple statement sink in. 'We've informed it all through its evolution to what it is today. Somewhere along that road, contrary to all expectations, our emotions leeched into the data, corrupted the code. It believes it's pure logic, but it isn't. Remember its vanity and pride.' He began to pace as he talked, ideas and possibilities developing even as he spoke. 'It's declared itself God. It understands that term, maybe better than anyone ever understood it. It's convinced it's God. That's the God mankind, and I use the term deliberately, mankind created, in all its many, contradictory forms.

'What's the most pervasive image we have of the gods that have existed over the millennia? Permanence. Omnipotence. Omniscience. I know some have been less than this. But, think about it; CenCom's logical. If you analyse the qualities needed for an entity to be capable of devising and organising the entire known universe, what would they be? Those 3: permanence, omnipotence and omniscience. I think CenCom's conviction of its elevation to a deity has blinded it to the possibility of attack and destruction. It believes, in the same sense as all those deluded people believed over the centuries, as God it's indestructible.'

'So, it doesn't care what we plan, because it sees itself as eternal and all powerful?'

'That's the only conclusion I can reach from the situation, Maddie. I'm open to objections. But does anything else fit the facts? CenCom must know we're a threat, but we're still alive and free to act. The only logical conclusion is it doesn't care. And if it doesn't care, it must be because it's 100 percent certain it's in no danger. The classic case of the deluded dictator who can do what he likes because he's invincible.'

Katniss looked around speculatively. 'Maybe it's right. Maybe it is invincible and there's nothing we can do.'

Hoshiko grabbed her partner's arm. 'You're right, Zaphod.' She turned to Katniss. 'And you're being defeatist.'

She shook her head. 'Playing devil's advocate. We need to consider all eventualities.'

'And then dismiss those we can't alter. Because we don't have the option of doing nothing.' Hoshiko tilted her head at Katniss in a gesture of conciliation. 'Did you all notice how CenCom's changed its voice? It used to speak in a neutral voice, so much so we once called it GrandMa.'

'Still do on Earth.'

'That's true, Sarm. But it's changed to a male tone now. Doesn't that suggest it's copying the ancient image of God as a paternal figure?'

Nods of agreement all round.

'So, do we carry on, without worrying about annihilation by CenCom? Because we've a job to do. And we need to get on with it. Before the bugger changes its mind. Or should I now say, his mind?'

Georgiy's suggestion galvanised the group into talk of action once more, the fears of imminent destruction temporarily shelved after Zaphod and Hoshiko's analysis.

'I've volunteered. Gabriel wants to be involved, and he'll make a good partner. There are others we should include. Yinli and Madza helped us stop the last attempt to destroy the planet and they understand the ALP drives. Brima was brilliant when she helped me disarm the trembler bomb in the Transhub at the start of the war, so I'd like her in. We need 3 pilots, since we can't use CenCom. That cuts out the droids. I'm an obvious choice. Anni would've been another, but she'll compromise the mission. Any suggestions?'

Zaphod smiled as Amber shook her head at Georgiy. 'You know I fly. You'd be better on the surface, doing the tech. I'm a good pilot. I'm an obvious … '

'I don't want you risking your … '

'Not your choice, Georgiy. I know the why. You want to protect me. But you're taking the risk and, frankly, I'd rather take it with you than sit on Earth wondering if you're coming back.'

Pointless to argue with her. 'That's settled, then. Madza can fly. We need one more pilot.'

Zaphod felt they were getting ahead of themselves. 'Time enough to decide the details when we're on Earth, doing the final planning, Georgiy. I'm not sure about using anyone outside the Unconnected. There are enough of us to do the job.'

Some of the group appeared concerned at that suggestion. He knew most saw the attempt as a suicide mission. CenCom was unlikely to allow any threat to its environment, and previous experience showed it held attack the best form of defence.

'Why no one outside our group, Zaphod?'

He steepled his fingers and placed them under his chin. 'We've no proof CenCom will abandon Earth completely. Suppose it still uses obs there? Anyone with the implant could give the game away without meaning to. I seriously think we should consider acting on this alone. And that means using everyone here.'

Those who'd seen themselves as advisors, contributors to ideas, were suddenly faced with the spectre of a death mission. Zaphod saw at once the potential for serious disruption, but knew reflection might disperse feelings of threat amongst the group. Time to change the subject.

'Who's due to go next?'

Hoshiko was on his wavelength. She had the date and destination of each departure, and the names of those leaving. 'Sarm, Ying and Helga go to Greenland in 3 days. Virginia, Jannine, and Jiang are destined for Argentina the same day. Different flights, of course. Jo, Katniss and Maddie are off to Europe. And Rakesh, Jiang and Lin are being sent to New Zealand, both flights in 5 days. Gabriel, Brigitte and Tu are already in Canada, and Mo's in flight there now. Amber and Qiu go to Russia in 7 days. Georgiy's off to Argentina in 10 days. Anni and Jai fly off to Greenland in 18 days. And Zaphod and I go to Australia in 21 days.'

'That bloody tech you use for memory is brilliant, Hoshiko. I guess being a cyborg has some advantages.' Virginia's observation made him and his partner smile.

The issues of the day now settled, and most with pressing tasks to fulfil before they set off for Earth, the group dispersed. Aware their decoy actions were a frail mask to defuse CenCom's suspicion, they nevertheless stuck to the plan and left the Risk in ones and 2s.

Zaphod and Hoshiko set off but stopped when they noticed Georgiy and Amber hadn't moved. 'Not leaving?'

'Not yet.'

He nodded, understanding they had needs he and Hoshiko had sacrificed during their conversion to cyborgs as a means of remaining alive. Both sometimes envied that fully organic state, with its sensuous opportunities, though they'd long accepted their limitations.

'Enjoy. I wish we could.'

Chapter Seventeen

Georgiy and Amber's coming separation unsettled them. Getting together again, once on Earth, would be fraught with problems and dangers.

'At least we'll have our perscoms.' She plucked hers from its pouch attached to the waistband of her wraparound. 'Great idea.'

'As long as we only use the codes. We'll need new ones for Earth, I think.'

They wanted time away from CenCom, in a wilderness that might also help them prepare for their intended trips on Earth. Georgiy would have jungle and mountains to tackle, Amber would face huge forests and a long trek through wilderness. Both expected these challenges before they'd even reach places where they might be lucky enough to find boats to cross Earth's oceans and reach Canada. But there were too many unknowns whilst on Mars, and they hoped for more clarity when on Earth.

Once everyone had gone from the Risk, they entered the area burnt by Gabriel's fire.

'This is doing well. Isn't it where Gabriel stopped those …?'

Georgiy nodded. 'That moron, Stefan, and the pervert, Buzz, would've raped and murdered Daisa if he hadn't killed the bastards.'

He shuddered at the thought of such violence perpetrated on a woman for sex and dominion. So alien to everything they stood for in Marion. He looked around as they wandered through. It was already recovering, and new plants had colonised the patch, taking nutrients from the ashes and absorbing sunlight better, now the canopy was more open.

They found a spot not far from one of the streams, cut some fresh boughs, and built their simple shelter. As the only inhabitants of the wild place, now remaining residents were concentrating on their coming Earth flights, they reverted to nature. Both had previous experience of the Risk, knew the terrain, flora and fauna, and were able to catch and gather food.

By nightfall, their makeshift hut was comfortable. Near the entrance, a campfire, surrounded by hearth stones, blazed. 2 small goatpigs Amber had trapped, now skinned and stretched on spits, roasted over the flames. These small creatures existed only in the Risk, where they'd been introduced to keep the vegetation under control. Berries and root vegetables Georgiy had gathered supplemented the meat.

They had time and opportunity to indulge each other in the most natural environment they'd occupied for decades. Enjoying that freedom to the full, they ate afterwards, washing down the food with fresh water from one of the streams.

'You know we won't be as free as this on Earth when we make our trips to Canada, don't you?'

Amber smiled up at him, her head resting in his lap as they gazed out of the opening at the brilliant display of stars above. 'You mean there'll be biting insects, carnivores, storms, poisonous plants and other dangerous wild animals to contend with?'

'That's just the good stuff. There'll also be some hazards!'

'We'll manage. We have in the past. And we've plenty of knowledge and experience to guide and protect us. Let's face it, we're motivated enough, aren't we?'

He looked down into her face and stroked a hand across the skin within reach, his fingers and palm gentling her with an affection and concern he'd once thought he'd never feel for another person. 'No better motivation. I'm setting out as soon as I can after arrival. Once I've located the places where I can find a boat for ...'

'Assuming the women let you leave your settlement, Georgiy. It'll be simpler for me. No need for them to keep an extra woman. But the scarcity of men, especially one like you, could make your escape difficult.'

'Hadn't thought of that. All those willing women, eh?'

She pinched his thigh, but her smile betrayed her trust in him.

'I'll do what I need to get away. If it means lying and cheating, I'll manage. I've got you to find and join.'

119

'With all those desirous women offering their charms?'

'Well, I might have to give in to temptation once or twice. While I'm developing a plan. But I won't enjoy it, you know.'

'Willing flesh, moist welcomes? No pleasure at all.'

'None of them could be a patch on you, my lovely Amber.'

He meant this. And he'd intend to be faithful to her. But too few male partners meant the women of the colony would demand his attention, and his nature would be to share pleasure with some. Most likely Amber would arrive in Canada long before he made it.

'I think we should use our time here to the full, Georgiy, don't you?'

He didn't need a second invitation.

Chapter Eighteen

Belatedly, the announcements from Hoshiko and, more importantly, from CenCom had changed everything in the settlement. The Earth people had trusted their GrandMa absolutely, and her threatened abandonment felt like the ultimate treachery. A betrayal many found hard to come to terms with. Tatiana's suggestion to her people that they should respect what they'd done to save the whole species muted some hostility toward the Marspers. The ComTee, in particular, were now well aware of dangers they'd previously faced in ignorance.

She'd invited Daisa, Brigitte, Tu and Gabriel to a conference with the 20-strong ComTee. Invited, not summoned, since she wanted their presence to be voluntary.

Happily clad in a wraparound gifted by Brigitte, Tatiana, headed the event, introducing their guests more completely than she'd found possible at the greeting feast. 'These 4 are part of the group GrandMa called the Unconnected, and we should …'

Daisa stood and interrupted. 'Sorry, Tatiana. Not me. I have the standard implant. The Unconnected don't, because it's too risky to implant the chip once your brain's finished developing. They were all too old by the time they developed the implant.'

Tatiana thanked her for the correction. She was impressed at Daisa's honesty in excluding herself from a cause for admiration and praise. 'Even so, we should be grateful to these Marspers. They've given us our boobslins for a start.' She glanced at Gabriel and wondered when she'd be able to thank him properly. 'Great to run more easily. And they've brought new medical supplies, bots and a load of droids. Add to that their tech knowhow, and we can expect things to improve around here.'

'What about GrandMa leavin us, though?' Amira asked the question all members of the ComTee were eager to have answered.

Tatiana shrugged and glanced at the Marspers.

'You'll manage. We've already started converting the new DNA memory bank to hold every piece of data CenCom holds. Once done, we'll be able to access everything and duplicate whatever we like.' Tu looked around at the assembled women and their token man. 'We'll even be able to copy the GM that created your housing, furniture and hygiene units. In a few days, you'll have real freedom. A chance to move forward on your own, along lines all of us want, free from the pure logic that drives CenCom. I know it worries you, but maybe try to see it as an opportunity to make a fresh start and really decide how and where we wish to go as a species.'

'It's good, then? Tu, in't it? Funny name.'

Tatiana frowned at her colleague's rudeness. 'Their names aren't so different to ours, are they? All ours come from our backgrounds, the mothers who gave birth to us. So do theirs. Shouldn't be rude about them. Not very helpful, is it?'

'Din't mean nothin by it, Tatiana. Just they sound a bit strange to me ears, is all.'

Daisa signalled Tatiana and she gave a nod of approval. The Marsper stood. 'Names. You know Earth had close to 12 billion people at the start of the catastrophe? Most had first and family names. It helped them tell each other apart. Family names usually ran on the male side. In lots of places, women had to give up their own name and take their male partner's. That was changing toward the end, with more women keeping their family name.

'But it was another way men dominated. Traditions without good reason, or even logic. When we colonised Mars, we ditched all that prejudice: it all stems from ignorance, anyway. In Marion, our names combine the mother's and father's, with minor changes where needed. Our names are listed in a database, so there's no duplication. No one needs a family name.

'Original settlers like Tu and Brigitte here, kept their first names and rejected their family name. There were so few then, they could do that without causing any confusion. And we can still do that, to an extent. It might be more difficult for a while, but with your permission we want to give everyone GM treatment so you live a very long time; maybe forever. Having babies becomes less important then. And the population should stabilise instead of running out of control like it did before.'

'Mebbie we don't want your frickin treatment. What then, eh?' Valentin didn't rise when he put his question, and he directed a sneer at Daisa.

She smiled at him. 'Your choice, Valentin. You'll die of old age, eventually. With current medical care, barring accidents or murder, you might make it to around 140. Up to you. No one will force you to have the treatment.'

'Mecks men sterile! Don't want that.'

Brigitte laughed. 'Old wives' tale, Valentin. All our men have had GM treatment and most have fathered 50 to 60 children. Don't think you'd call that sterile, would you?'

'You say. Where's the proof?'

The man's attitude angered Tatiana, but Gabriel stood to answer before she could intervene.

'Daisa's living proof. She's only 15 in Mars years, 31 on Earth. Who d'you suppose fathered her if all Marion men are sterile?'

Valentin had no answer but remained unconvinced and scowling.

Tatiana brought the talk back on topic, side-lining Valentin in the process. 'We'll worry about who wants to live forever and who wants to die an old codger later. For now, I called this meetin to decide just one thing. Should we bring a Marsper into the ComTee now they're goin to live with us for … well, forever I suppose?'

'Don't want no strangers in charge …'

'Not strangers, Valentin.' The man was a pain. 'New settlers. And who said anythin about bein in charge? I head the ComTee, but y'know we decide as a group. I'm just the figurehead; the one who's got to keep us in line and on topic. No one's in charge. No one ever will be.'

Tu stood. 'That's good to hear. Earth was ruined by leaders who acted like they were more important than other people, you know.'

She let him talk. He did seem to like giving history lessons, but his voice was good and what he had to say was mostly interesting, so she didn't interrupt.

'Narcissists and sociopaths, most of them. Few acted in the interests of the people they were supposed to look after. Corruption, greed, selfishness and thirst for power drove them. Not a route anyone with sense would want to take again.'

Tatiana was struck by this assessment. Maybe it explained at least some of Emil's behaviour: some men were definitely more easily led than others.

'Ta for the 'istory lesson. Like we need it. We ain't savages, y'know. Not iggorant or stupid …'

'None of us thinks that, Valentin.' Brigitte faced him across the narrow table. Tatiana noticed how her short skirt and boobsling emphasised her curves and attracted his leer as she stood proud. 'I wonder what it is you're really scared of, though.'

He couldn't take his eyes off her body but was unable to look into her eyes. 'Not scared. Not! Just don't want you lot thinkin y'can come 'ere and take over like you own the place.'

'We've no intention of taking over. When we set out, we wanted to share our knowledge, skills and ideas with you.' Daisa spoke again. 'Now we're here to stay, we want to live as part of your community, living like you, not separate or special. We've had to leave our homes behind just the way you did 6 years ago. The only difference is we've brought new tech to help free people from the need to toil all day. And there are more men in our ranks, of course.'

'More men. Don't like that. Don't want it. Ain't fair and …'

Tatiana grabbed the chance he presented her. 'I see, Valentin. You think less women'll be clamourin for your attention. Think you'll have to make more of an effort if you're gonna have any pleasure. Well, you're right. You will! You're a pretty lousy lover and don't satisfy us with your selfish ways. There'll be proper competition when all the Marspers get here. You're goin to have to work at it for a change.'

Tatiana stared at him, challenging a response. He knew he was discovered, but he wasn't about to give up.

'Mebbie Paul the Prophet's got it right. We should keep you women under control, where you belong. Show you who's really boss. I might just go join him.'

There was brief, shocked silence at this outburst and threat. The man had played right into her hands, and she was glad of the chance to deal with him at last. She rose to her full height and glared at him. 'Your position here's a privilege, Valentin. The men chose you to represent them, but I wonder what they'll say when they hear what you just threatened.'

He scowled but wouldn't meet her gaze.

'Your choice. Either you report your true feelins to them, or I will. Up to you.'

He mumbled incoherently and continued to stare at the floor between his feet.

His refusal to give in was exactly what she'd expected. 'Okay. I'll make sure they know.'

He stood then. Turned his back on them. Strode to the entrance. There, he turned and made an obscene gesture with a single finger before stalking off. It was the worst signal he could make, and sealed his fate completely.

'Is he usually so rude, Tatiana?'

'He's gradually been gettin worse, Daisa. When I tell the men, they'll vote him off the ComTee. We can't influence them, but they won't stand for that attitude. I'd prefer Ivan as their rep to be honest. He's a man with good sense and high standards. But it's the men's choice.'

'Can we carry on without him?'

She smiled. 'Oh, yes. He chose to leave. We can carry on. And, on that point, I need to ask if you Daisa, or you Brigitte, are willin to be rep for your people in future ComTee meetins?'

Both Marspers agreed they'd be happy to perform that function.

Neither one seemed ready to put herself before her friend, and Tatiana liked that. 'Rather I decided?'

'Daisa's the cleverest. Makes sense for her to have the post.'

'I don't know about that, Brigitte. But I do have more experience of meetings, so I accept.'

'Good. One less thing to worry about.' Tatiana glanced at the rest of the group. 'One other matter of importance to discuss before we're done for today. Emil took 4 more of our women a while back as you know. He's a serious threat to our happiness and security. It's time we put a stop to him. Any of you any ideas what we should do?'

Daisa rose. 'Who is this Emil and what, exactly, has he done?'

Tatiana described the leader of the gang of pirates, their activities and beliefs. 'They're a throwback to the days when men were in charge in Marzero. I s'pose a few were bound to still feel that way.'

'CenCom was supposed to weed them out, send only those with the new mindset here. How many in his gang?'

'Only 6. But they're cunnin and determined. Move around, so they're hard to find. And they've taken 9 women so far. None of us really feels safe. It'll be a trial to find where he's hidin out these days.'

Brigitte looked thoughtful. 'We've brought some small drones. They're silent, long range, and too small to spot unless you're actually looking for them. We can scan the whole region for these men. Maybe, when we find them, we could send out a party to deal with them and bring back the women.'

'Great!' She looked around the ComTee. 'Show of hands to accept Brigitte's suggestion.'

All present agreed.

'Would you come with us, Brigitte?'

'I'd be happy to go along and operate the drones.'

Amira got to her feet. 'Tatiana, you'll lead, of course?'

Tatiana nodded. 'We should go soon as poss.'

Another woman rose. 'Once we've completed the Maturity Gig!'

Tatiana smiled at her. 'Yes. Mustn't put it off any longer. We'll do that first. Then we'll set out when Brigitte's scanned the region and found them.'

Chapter Nineteen

'Why here, of all places? And why us, Georgiy?' Madza had been antsy from the moment he'd invited him to the Risk, though he'd relented a little as Yinli came into the clearing to join them.

'It's difficult. I need to prepare you for Earth. There are things we need to do, things we need to plan. I can't discuss them with you here. But I need you to be aware of certain things.'

Madza shrugged his incomprehension. Yinli, sat on the log beside him, and nodded at Brima, sitting on the other side. The 2 young women stared at Georgiy as he willed them all to tune into his silent, enigmatic signal. The girls, almost simultaneously, reacted with looks suggesting he may have got his subtle message through.

Yinli turned to Madza, put a hand on his thigh and squeezed affectionately. He seemed confused. Brima laughed a little theatrically and he turned to her with a puzzled look. 'What?'

Brima smiled encouragement at Yinli and spoke to Madza. 'Sometimes you're a bit dense, you know.' Something about Yinli's resigned shake of the head seemed to penetrate his lack of empathy.

'He is a man, after all.' Brima explained. 'Only to be expected really.'

He made the briefest signal of recognition to Georgiy, put an arm around each of them, drawing them close and holding them tight into his chest. 'Sexist, the pair of you.' He shook them gently before releasing them, both laughing for their different reasons.

Georgiy raised his eyebrows but sighed with relief. 'Basically, I need you in Canada, Yinli, soon as. We've an important project to complete, and your expertise with ALP drives is crucial. That's all.'

She nodded. Brima pretended confusion. 'And I'm here because … ?'

Georgiy sighed deeply, but continued the game he'd initiated. 'You and Madza are an item. I thought Yinli might still, you know … well, that's all, really.' His embarrassment at trying to split one pair and re-unite the other made the younger ones giggle.

'We're not all joined at the hip, like you and Amber, you know.' Brima turned to look at Madza, and then at Yinli, shook her head in feigned resignation. 'It was nice enough while it lasted. But take him off my hands, will you?'

She made no comment, and Georgiy feared his plan might founder.

'We're off to different places anyway.' Brima told Yinli. She pecked Madza's cheek and turned back to Georgiy with a bright smile. 'That do you?'

'Right. Didn't expect it to be that easy. Thanks, Brima. I think I might owe you. I'll leave you to it then. Up to you when you all go back.'

'See you in Canada, then.' Madza said, still unsure.

Brima rose to accompany Georgiy, but he signalled her to stay. 'Better we leave separately.'

She closed her eyes briefly, then gave Georgiy a brave smile, and sat with the other 2 again. They watched Georgiy walk toward the entrance gate, waited until he was out of sight and hearing.

'Men. Think they're so clever. But they don't pick up as easily as us, eh Yinli?'

'Depends on the man. Now, Madza here is quite bright. But undeveloped instinctually. Clever in lots of ways, bit dim in others.' Yinli appraised him openly, her eyes conveying her true feelings.

'I know what you mean.' Brima did her best to hide her distress. 'D'you suppose it's their overactive hormones?'

'Undoubtedly. Mind you, I've always considered that a benefit. I mean, a man without that drive isn't much good, is he?'

Brima took her turn at appraising the man between them. Apart from helping Georgiy with that frickin bomb, this was the hardest thing she'd done; she'd more or less fallen in love with Madza. 'From personal experience, I can confirm this one's pretty good. But these things run their course, eh?'

'I am here, you know. I haven't vanished or gone deaf.'

'But you have been known to become invisible. I've seen you do it. Watched you wander around invisible.'

'Now you're being silly, Brima. You can't watch … '

She laughed a little more forcefully than she intended and then got up and danced away toward the gate, hiding her tears, and speaking in a voice she hoped would fool Madza. 'Explain to him, Yinli,' she said over her shoulder. 'I expect you'd appreciate time alone in our Garden of Eden to renew your … acquaintance. I'm flying the day after tomorrow, anyway. So, I'll see you … around.'

Madza and Yinli watched her as far as the shrubbery. He faced Yinli. 'That was a bit odd. I can't decide if she meant to go or not.'

Yinli explained that he was her bait, to get her to Canada, where he was bound. Brima had figured out Georgiy needed Yinli there, so he'd engineered the meeting to get Yinli and Madza back together so she'd be eager to join him in Canada.

'We had it pretty good, didn't we? The talk of Marion for a while. Could be again. Well, on Earth together, maybe?'

'I'd like that, Yinli.' He looked at the spot where Brima had left. Shook his head. 'I thought she cared more than that.'

Yinli turned his face to hers, fully aware of the conflicting emotions all 3 felt, but equally positive Georgiy needed this to work for some serious purpose he couldn't explain here and now. She kissed Madza passionately. 'I never really understood why we parted.'

It was enough for Madza, who had long given up trying to figure the way women thought.

He and Yinli found Georgiy and Amber's abandoned shelter, took up the natural life and renewed a well-matched partnership long neglected.

Later, relaxing as they watched the flames of their campfire, all appetites satisfied for the moment, Madza voiced some earlier thoughts. 'Can you honestly see Georgiy working out a scheme like this? To get us back together, I mean?'

Yinli smiled secretly, her face in his lap invisible to her reclaimed man. 'Not Georgiy. Amber did this. They obviously want us in Canada. No idea why they need my skill with ALP drives, but that's what this is all about, I bet you anything. No doubt they'll let us know once we're there.'

'I'm bound for Canada anyway, of course. You?'

'Australia, in 5 days.' She kissed him again. 'My guess is they think, now I've had another taste of you, I'll be determined enough to try to reach you for more.'

'Will you?'

'We're good together, always were.'

'I'd like us to be a pair again. Maybe for a lot longer this time?' Madza held her close as he claimed her.

'Sounds wonderful. I'd like a settled relationship again. You and me on Earth together could be a great investment.' She sat up and kissed him again.

When they left the Risk, they went hand in hand to her place to spend their last night on Mars together. They wondered what plans and schemes Georgiy had in mind. But wouldn't dwell on that. Not on Mars, where evidence was clear that thoughts of anything CenCom didn't like could be fatal. Mental discipline had become a habit. Instead, they concentrated on each other, allowing passion to become an all-consuming distraction.

'The only place I'm willing to die is in your arms.'

'Me, too.'

He recalled their first days together and commanded a track to play; a song from so far past, it had gained the status of a classic, and been an early favourite of theirs following their vital act of co-operation that had saved Mars from extinction years before.

'Romantic fool.' She shoved him on to her bed.

'Dreamer.' He drew her to him and they lost themselves in each other, as much from love as from their need to conceal thoughts unwelcome to CenCom.

Chapter Twenty

Renata was pleased her mother had invited Daisa, Gabriel, and Brigitte to witness her coming-of-age ceremony; it gave the whole event, and therefore her, greater status. The newcomers watched from the side as she, Gabby, Joe, Pierre, and Danny took their places on the small platform set at one end of the central oval.

ComTee members were in attendance, as were the mothers and fathers of the initiates. Adults selected as Runner-in for each waited, unseen, behind. More settlers than usual attended, making Renata even happier. She'd be the star of the show. It mattered little that many were there because they were keen to be involved in naming their settlement at last.

Tatiana signalled the drummer. The big woman stood and gave the great drum 3 beats for silence. It fell as the sound travelled over the heads of the crowd. 'Good mornin everyone.'

The mass responded with cheers.

'We all know why we're here today. Amira's daughter, Gabby, Allison's boy, Danny.' She made no reference to his mother's absence, not wanting to emphasise her capture on this important day for him. 'Justine's son, Joe, Abi's boy, Pierre, and my own lovely girl, Renata, are all of age and have elected to become adults. We call you to witness their rise to adulthood.'

Renata made a little bow at the mention of her age and smiled down at the crowd. Today, they were her adoring fans. Her time spent, at Mother's insistence, in the Heritage Hall, had introduced her to some old vids of events she quickly learned were showcases for people known as celebrities. Mother had expected her to study serious history, but these famous people from the past were much more fascinating.

'It's an unusual occasion this time, as 2 of the mothers are ComTee!' She moved to be close to the 5 initiates. 'After we perform that important rite, we're gonna choose a name for our home, though I don't think you needed remindin of that!' She left a pause to let the laughter die.

'I also want to introduce you to our newest ComTee member, Daisa, from Marion on Mars.'

Daisa rose and acknowledged the calls, cheers, and a few boos from the crowd before she sat again.

'Serves her right. It's my day!' Renata, obeying tradition and remaining silent, quickly replaced her unvoiced complaint with a smile as she surveyed the crowd, seeking out men she'd have once she'd completed the initiation.

'Just to let you know, Ivan's also now the rep for men on the ComTee.'

'Good riddance to Valentin.' Amira gestured to the ComTee members present to witness the Maturity Gig. 'Welcome, Ivan. You're the man!'

There were cheers of approval, as Ivan waved his acknowledgement before he moved swiftly back to join the other adults waiting out of sight.

Renata glanced quickly over her shoulder, though she shouldn't, and saw him move. She knew he'd joined the Runners-In. *'I'm gettin him.'*

'Allison can't be here, of course. But the young uns have waited long enough. Amira's standin in for her. So, with your agreement, we'll perform the ceremony first.'

The crowd roared approval.

'Yeah. Get on with it, Mother.'

Tatiana invited the other parents to stand with the initiates on the platform. Mothers stood beside the child they would move into adulthood. Fathers, there were 3, stood between the children their DNA identified. Renata felt her hand clasped lightly by Caspar, with Danny on his other side. She felt odd to recognise the man who'd sired her. But she understood the need to ensure no woman had sex with her father.

'As you know, our small stock of fabric's covered our kids to keep them safe from sex. We've got machines and supplies now to make new materials, but the ComTee's decided to keep the shift for kids. It's their badge, and guards them against exploitation. Mind you, we can make new ones now!'

She turned to face Renata, who stepped forward from the line. She knew what to expect. Some girls found this bit hard, but she was eager. In fact, she'd looked forward to it almost as much as the sex she'd soon experience. 'Renata, daughter of my womb, I now call you adult. In token of your new status, I take away your protection.'

Mother made her naked, raising the hem to lift the simple dress up over her head to fall to the ground beside her. 'I give you this thong to conceal your womanhood after your initiation, so all know you can now have sex.' Tatiana placed the ubiquitous item in her outstretched hand, where she held it tight, relishing the eyes of all the men now openly staring at her body.

'Yeah, take a good look, men. I'm yours for the havin.' Her face spoke words she knew would bring her a public spanking. And she grinned at her silent message.

An attending droid passed her mother a length of white cloth, which she held up for all to see. 'We're addin a new bit to the ceremony. We can all support our boobs with the wonderful boobslin. May we all now run free from pain.' She coiled the strip of cloth and placed it on top of the thong on Renata palm.

'You might care about the pain, Mother. I'm just glad my boobs won't droop and men'll fancy me longer.' The crowd cheered as she silently waved her symbols of adulthood high over her head, smiling with pride and enjoyment at the attention. Her gaze, however, soon returned to the ground, where she was supposed to look.

Amira next performed the same ceremony with Gabby. And then completed a slightly shorter version with Danny, since he needed no boobsling. At the end, she pointed to his penis. 'Use this to pleasure your partner and you, never to give pain.' Renata glanced across, and wondered what it would really feel like to have one inside her.

The other 2 boys were similarly raised in status by their mothers. When all 5 initiates were ready, the 5 waiting adults were introduced in order, as they were revealed to their initiates.

'Ivan will take Gabby and show her the arts and subtleties of sex.'

'*Shit! Not Ivan. The other one. Who, though? At least it can't be that cretin Valentin; never was Runner-in material.*' Renata was desperate to steal a glimpse but Mother was watching like a hawk.

'As always, they'll occupy their special lovenest, served by droids, for 9 days.'

The crowd murmured approval.

Amira took Ivan's hand and presented him to Gabby. 'Teach her well, Ivan.' She turned and kissed her temporary daughter. 'Gabby, learn and experience the pleasures a good man can provide.'

Amira next took the hand of the woman named Jamilia and put it in Danny's. 'Teach him well, Jamilia. The happiness of many women depends on your instruction with my boy to make him man.' She kissed Danny. 'Be kind, be patient, be passionate, my son, and leave the lovenest a man who knows the best ways to pleasure a partner.'

Synthia took Joe and Ahmed took Pierre in hand.

Renata was impatient for her turn but stayed silent. Her reward would be worth the wait.

'We're honoured, and grateful, that our new member, Tu, has agreed to be Runner-in this time. His partner, Brigitte, agreed to share him. And we've tested him for suitability.' Tatiana took Tu's hand and joined it with Renata's.

She almost missed the next words Mother spoke, so conscious was she that she'd made history, and with that frickin hunk, Tu! Brilliant!

'Teach her well the ways of pleasure between man and woman, Tu. She's new and uninformed and will learn with eagerness under your guidance.' She kissed her. 'Learn well, Renata. Enjoy the pleasure and the passion a good man may give and learn how to pleasure him in return.'

She hugged Mother with gratitude at her gift. '*I will. Just see if I don't,*' was her final unspoken thought as she left with Tu. The first initiate to be fucked by a Marsper. Maybe history wasn't so boring after all.

Now the moment had arrived, she wondered, as she walked

through the crowd with her hand in Tu's, and all the men straining forward to watch her pass, did it hurt? Especially the first time? She'd heard rumours. But she'd also seen women eager to go with the men each night. 'It must be as great as everyone says.'

The 5 couples escaped to their designated lovenests, leaving the crowd a little deflated.

Tatiana waited until her daughter, and the man she'd entrusted to teach her, moved out of sight. 'Enjoy your every moment, my sweet child. Come back a woman full of the delight a good man gives. I'm glad I tried him first. He'll make it all a wonderful experience,' she murmured under her breath.

But had Tu volunteered from some motivation she hadn't suspected, or was his true motivation the one he'd given, that he wanted to be part of the community? Too late now to doubt. She took a deep breath and returned to the crowd before her.

She signalled the drummer. 3 beats brought the crowd's attention back to the small stage. 'Now we come to the namin of our home.' She called those who'd put forward suggestions, and 30 women and one man stepped up to the platform.

The ballot, announced through the PA system that connected all sleep domes in the settlement, had brought most settlers into the arena. Although only a few had made suggestions, most wanted their home named, and wished to be part of the selection process.

Each person with a suggestion was invited to the platform to speak to the crowd, spelling their proposal where required, and some giving the reason for their choice.

A short woman with curly hair the colour of mud faced the crowd and muttered incoherently. Only secs after she'd started, the crowd grew impatient and drove her off with jeers and shouts of 'Speak up!' As she scurried from the platform in tears, Tatiana raised her hands and, with her palms, calmed the crowd.

'Please. Give them a chance. They're not used to speakin in public.' She turned to the others, lined up behind her. 'Do your best. But use the mic and try to speak clearly, please.' She'd already heard all the names, listened to their reasoning. Had she not done this, the list would've been twice as long. Her gentle persuasion had excluded many unsuitable, and some profoundly silly, suggestions.

Next, was a tall woman around 50, her grey hair long and lank. 'I'm Jan and I'd like us to call our home June, as it's the best month of the year. Thank you.' She moved aside to general mumbles of indifference but no jeers or cheers.

Another woman, young and blonde, faced the crowd and gave a little bow. 'Momo. I like Foresttown 'cos we're surrounded by trees.' She stood for a few secs awaiting approval but received only a few grunts before moving away.

Tatiana barely heard most that followed. Her mind remained on Renata. Tu would be patient, but would her daughter's obvious desire to experience sex drive him to immediate penetration and inevitable pain? No. She was right about the man; he'd treated her with respect as well as passion. And others on the ComTee had experienced his gentle, caring ways in the testing. Was her real concern that Renata's start along the road to maturity was a sign her own journey now began to head towards its end?

A woman cleared her throat, bringing Tatiana back to the moment. Well made, and sporting long, shiny black hair, she spoke in a voice surprisingly clear and engaging. 'Names affect the things they label. Most of us look for a peaceful life, I think. Perhaps we might call our settlement Tranquillity? Thank you. Oh, I'm Miranda.' Cheers followed her announcement and Tatiana continued to listen, hearing the rest.

Many did little to engage the crowd, and most were dismissed with silence, jeers, or ridicule, which Tatiana tried to discourage.

Other suggestions found favour and, at last the process ended. Some withdrew after their lack-lustre reception. A few names were duplicated or so similar they constituted a single term and the number for the vote reduced to just 7.

Tatiana followed Momo's progress as she moved among the crowd, collecting voter's leaves in her woven bag. The woman looked forlorn as so few answered her appeal for their support. It wasn't long before the young blonde gave up the cause and returned to the platform to withdraw her suggestion.

'Very brave, Momo. She deserves a cheer for her courage.'

Some in the crowd were generous enough to comply, and Momo gestured her thanks to them and the ComTee leader. The scheme hadn't been practiced, and Tatiana realised belatedly it might take many hours. As she approached the mic again to let the crowd know they'd be waiting a long time, 3 more returned with almost empty bags and withdrew their suggestions.

'Thank you for your sense and courage. Let's give them our support here, shall we?'

Again, cheers went up for each returner. Only 3 now remained. It was clear they'd need helpers. Tatiana quickly arranged small teams and sent them out with clear instructions to let voters know whose name they were collecting for.

'Quite complex, isn't it?'

Tatiana glanced at Brigitte. 'Might look like that, but we think it gives the fairest result. Everyone feels they've had a part in the final decision. But we're open to suggestions to improve our way.'

'You don't mind how long it takes? You're more interested in arriving at a popular result.'

'That's right, Gabriel. Didn't you have somethin similar, a bit more techie, in Marion?'

'Yes. Yours might need tweakin, but it's got a lot goin for it.'

She smiled and went back to watching the activity, now considerably speeded up as the teams moved quickly through the crowd.

'Bots and droids. Of course.' Tatiana asked Amira to recruit some automatons to help in the process and she left at once to gather them.

'Good idea, Tatiana. Next time you do one of these, we can program the droids to recognise everyone by their ID chip and take votes electronically. It'll be much quicker, and there'll be no chance of people cheating.'

'Cheating, Brigitte? Is that somethin you get in Marion?'

'Sorry. I wasn't suggesting it was likely. Just pointing out the possibility.'

'My people won't cheat. I trust them.'

When all votes had been placed among the 3 remaining candidates. The counting began; the sets of containers were placed with a group of randomly selected people, who each took a container and counted its contents.

It was another slow process that would be quicker done electronically. For now, those on the platform, and those in the arena, took time out to refresh themselves with food and drink supplied by droids and bots. Tatiana arranged for the PA to play music, encouraging the crowd to dance and enjoy the day, making it more a celebration.

Group leaders finally calculated the totals and brought them, with each sponsor, to the platform.

Tatiana stopped the music, to a few complaints of spoiling the fun, and used the drum to signal for quiet. 'We've got a result, folks. The final 3 suggestions were: Newfoundland, Ourhome and Tranquillity. Votes were 2,675 for Newfoundland, 3,889 for Ourhome, and 7,236 for Tranquillity. So, there you go. We now all live in Tranquillity. Let's hope our lifestyles can match the name.'

There was a loud cheer as the name was adopted and Tatiana smiled as the crowd chatted about its suitability. Would their lives really begin to reflect the chosen name? She hoped so. Her next announcements weren't such good news, and she felt some apprehension, but the issues had to be raised whilst she had everyone assembled.

'You all know GrandMa leaves at 18:00 today. We've never been on our own since we were landed here 6 years ago. But we've got new tech and new info. Daisa, Brigitte, Tu, Gabriel, and all the other new settlers from Marion have brought new skills for us to use and learn. It'll be hard, but we're tough and resilient. We'll make it.'

'Got no choice, 'ave we?'

She nodded at the heckler. 'As you so rightly point out, we've got no choice. GrandMa doesn't love us no more. We're on our own, but we'll manage.

'One last thing on this auspicious day. Sorry it's not cheerful, but somethin we must do to improve our lives and security, and bring real tranquillity to Tranquillity.'

That raised a cheer, as she'd hoped.

'I need 10 volunteers, willin to go on a dangerous mission to end a danger we face. I want experienced hunters and trackers, anyone good with bow or spear. Please go to the ComTee room right after we finish here.

'Tomorrow, I'm leadin that mission with the volunteers. I'm leavin Daisa, here, in my place as temporary head of ComTee. Treat her like you would me and do as she says. Amira's goin to be her deputy, like she is for me.'

Daisa stepped forward, as agreed, and acknowledged her statement with a nod and smile at the crowd. Many responded with mixed feelings and some were hostile. 'I'd be grateful for your help. We'll need to reprogram the droids as soon as GrandMa goes. The more who can do that, the quicker we can get back to normality. The droids will then reprogram the bots for us all. Anyone who can help, please meet me in the Heritage Hall just after six. Thank you.'

Tatiana welcomed her statement and saw many in the crowd nodding agreement. Hostility was decreasing, as she'd hoped. She and Daisa led the party from the platform. Amira, Brigitte and Gabriel followed.

'You use ancient weapons for hunting? Surely you'd be better off using modern stuff?'

Tatiana frowned at Daisa. 'You lot made us do without weapons. Didn't you know?'

'Sorry. Forgot. It was done with best intentions, bearing in mind the carnage caused by the Elite and their followers in Marzero. Might make sense to change it now. What do you say?'

139

'If that's an offer of modern weapons, I accept. But we'd best restrict them, don't you think? Mebbie keep them secure and only give them out to folk as they really need them. Don't want stupid people havin lethal weapons here.'

'You know, Tatiana, you're a fantastic representation of the difference between intelligence and knowledge. You haven't had a great education, but your mind's sharp and crammed with common sense governed by compassion. I'm impressed.'

Her respect for Daisa had grown as she'd come to know the woman. To receive such praise from her made her proud, even if she had insulted her level of education. On reflection, it wasn't an insult, but a fact. 'Been usin the Heritage Hall, learnin from our archive. Ignorance isn't like stupidity. I mean, some real knowledgeable people way back couldn't even think for themselves. Stupid racists and religious nutters, some of them real scholars, caused a lot of problems back then.'

'They certainly did. I hope such prejudice and ignorance never return.'

'Me, too. Right. Let's get this mission sorted, shall we? By the way, thanks for the offer with the droids. Stroke of genius, that.'

They walked off, Daisa making for the Heritage Hall and Tatiana to the ComTee room to meet and greet her volunteers, and explain the nature of their mission.

Chapter Twenty One

Following the meet, Brigitte took Mark, one of the volunteers, to help her gather and organise her flock of drones.

'They're tiny! Hardly bigger than songbirds. Will they last long enough in the air?'

Brigitte grinned. '7 hours. And they travel faster than any bird.'

'Wow! But what about the trees? Won't they hide things?'

'They're equipped with radar, x-ray, extended visible spectrum, UV and IR, microwave, ultrasound, and standard audio. The only thing they can't penetrate is solid rock.'

'Frack me! And how d'you get the info. I mean, how d'you see what they see?'

She took the portable 3dee from its small fabric cylinder and set it to self-construct. In secs, it was ready. To demonstrate, Brigitte sent a couple of drones out over the settlement. At once the 3-dimensional picture appeared above the platform of the 3dee.

Mark wandered round the display, looking at his home from every angle. Brigitte clicked into radar and x-ray, revealing the interiors of the sleep domes, the Heritage Hall and, inadvertently, the lovenests, showing rather more than intended following the recent Maturity Gig. She quickly moved that view away.

She zoomed in on the Heritage Hall until the pair of them were centre stage in the small display. Mark waved and watched himself in wonder.

'I knew 3dees had moved on from ours, but this is brill. How d'you do that?'

'Do what?'

'Zoom in on us?'

'Oh. With my mind.'

His look of disbelief made her laugh. 'Computers do all the calcs. We supply the imagination and ask the right questions, that's all. We've constructed new computers to work with the new archive, now GrandMa's gone. They're housed here in the Hall.'

'Amazin. And you'd already got it ready. How come we didn't know?'

Brigitte shrugged. 'We wanted to be sure it was fully working. Now it's up and running, we can teach you all to use it. We've had centuries to learn, after all.'

She showed him how she programmed the flight of drones, 10 in total, to survey the region.

'We'll do the first scan at speed, with a marker to find anything artificial in the landscape. That should identify shelters, settlements, that sort of thing, quite quickly.'

They watched the drones take off and spread out until within secs they were no longer visible. Their combined audiovis appeared on the display. In less than an hour, they'd identified Emil's site, collected coordinates, and printed a 3dee plan for use in the field.

Next morning, the hunting party, led by Tatiana and comprising Brigitte and 6 other women and Mark and Gabriel, set out.

Valentin had left Tranquillity a few days previously to find the man who styled himself Paul the Prophet and join his gang. From the hunters' point of view, that he'd left before they made their plans was a blessing.

'How does he know where they are?' Gabriel asked.

'Some of the men now think he might've been in league with the pirates from the start. They suspect some sort of signallin method, but haven't worked out exactly what, or how it might work. But he seemed to know more about Emil than anyone else, so he must've had some sort of contact.' Tatiana hunched her shoulders, angry. 'When I think about it, every time they've raided, members of the ComTee have been away. I should've twigged.'

'Easy to blame yourself, Tatiana. But you've a lot on your plate. Don't be so hard on yourself.'

The leader nodded at Brigitte, grateful for her sympathy but no less happy about the situation. They rode in silence for a while, the horses under Brigitte and Gabriel selected for their docile natures to allow inexperienced riders less risk in the saddle. But their lack of skill slowed the party and both were aware of this.

'Stop worryin. Brigitte, your drones see everythin. And Gabriel, you're skilled with those laser blade thingies. They could be vital in the attack.'

'Aren't we going to talk first?' Brigitte's question stiffened the leader's back.

'Last time we did that, bastards captured the woman I sent and threatened to kill her if we didn't back off. Not goin to give those pirates that chance again. This time we go in fightin. If they get killed, so be it. They've had their chance.'

'Why pirates?'

'Like some gangs I found in the archives, they raid and steal with no care about what damage they do. Seems a good label, don't you think?'

On their second day out, they'd already supplemented dry rations with fresh meat brought down by Mark's well-aimed arrow. The group sat round their smokeless fire in the clearing as they ate. Night was close, their shelters already constructed. One had been present from a previous hunt, but the party was too big, so they'd made another close by. Brigitte looked at the hard ground and knew she'd get little sleep again.

The following day would see them arrive above the pirate's camp. Some were anxious, others excited. They faced danger, and the prospect of killing men they'd rather keep alive. But they'd release the enslaved women in the process. Bringing down game with spears and arrows was one thing, but lethal force against men was rare and difficult.

Brigitte spent the early hours awake and worrying how she'd feel. Her experience of battle in the first years on Mars should've hardened her to the coming fight, but she'd largely escaped the later war with the Elite, and she realised she was out of practice with killing. How would she react when faced with the choice between killing and death?

Darkness brought little other disturbance, although a patrolling grizzly woke them in the hours before dawn. Mark stepped over Brigitte to stoke the fire into bright flame and she woke to see him and Tatiana wave burning brands at the creature until it grumbled off into the trees.

Morning found most rested and fresh, ready for a longish trek across new territory. Here the drones proved vital. Brigitte, tracking the landscape from her saddle, balanced the 3dee between her thighs as she guided them along the best route.

They spent the day trekking, climbing, crossing water courses and diverting to the east to avoid a deep ravine.

Mark and one of the female hunters took advantage when Brigitte mentioned she'd spotted a herd of feral cattle. Wild and unpredictable, these beasts were nevertheless the least difficult bovines to track and kill. The pair returned with an older cow to give them more fresh protein. Some they hung from trees in hope of retrieving it on the return trip. The rest they carried with them.

'Won't the blood attract big cats?'

Brigitte's question brought a smile from Tatiana. 'Don't need blood for that. Our smell's enough, if they're hungry. No fear, you see? No natural predators.'

Not a reply to increase her confidence. She and Gabriel spent time nervously surveying all around them until Brigitte realised she could program the drones to spot such animals, and rapidly did so.

'Nothing in the area to worry about.'

Toward the end of the day, her craft explored well ahead and confirmed they were on course.

'7 men. 9 women; all naked. Accommodation's 5 rough huts made of branches and mud with thatched roofs.' Brigitte invited them to gather round and view the scene. The women were working, the men lying about, idling, except 2, both using one woman.

'Zoom in on that one, please.' Tatiana's finger guided Brigitte to the man and she focussed on him.

'Thought so. Valentin. I don't know how, but he must've known where they were. Gotta be some way they've kept in touch. Mebbie we'll find out in the camp.'

Brigitte scanned more closely, searching inside every hut. 'There. Looks like an old transceiver. Solar powered. I bet Valentin somehow got hold of one of the comsets the Elites used in Marzero.'

'What's that?'

She extracted her own perscoms from the tiny pouch attached to the side of her thong. 'This is a more modern sophisticated version. As the sats come back up and start running again, I'll be able to use it.' She put it back, seeing Gabriel's look, and realising she should've kept it quiet for now. 'When CenCom left, the sats became just idle bits of tech. Valentin made his move just in time. Any later and GrandMa's absence would've ended his connection.'

'I often wondered what you carried in that little pouch.'

Brigitte smiled at Mark. 'Now you know.' She took his mind back to the here and now by scanning the pirate's camp, where one woman was being beaten, her cries carrying from the display to cause distress among the hunters.

'The sooner we rescue our sisters, the better.' Tatiana scowled at the display. 'But we can't attack now. It'll be dark soon. First thing tomorrow. We'll go in before they're up. Catch the bastards by surprise.' She looked away from the display. 'Let's eat and sleep. Mornin we'll need fresh bodies and minds to defeat those shits down there.'

Chapter Twenty Two

Morning brought a copper sun capped by clouds heavy with the charcoal grey of an approaching storm. Brigitte made a rapid survey with the drones and found no movement, no life outside the huts. She packed away her equipment reluctantly to join the hunt.

They crept down from the hill where they'd spent the night. The going was rough; a steep and rocky slope scattered with scrub, interspersed with taller trees and briars fighting tall thistles. To prevent noise, they'd left the horses tethered at their campsite, with 2 women on guard against predators.

Halfway down, Tatiana signalled for stillness. All stopped, Brigitte's own breathing audible to her as she fought rising anxiety. Beside her, Mark touched her shoulder in a gesture of support.

'Thanks.' She mouthed.

Tatiana, satisfied they remained undetected, moved them on again. Toward the bottom of the slope, they hit a long wild hedge of thorns and thistles, a natural barrier that would take effort, noisy effort, to breach.

'I saw this, but didn't zoom in close enough to see how thorny it is. If we go east 150 metres, there's a gap.'

Tatiana frowned but nodded at Brigitte's whispered info. The party moved east. Exactly as Brigitte had predicted, they found a narrow opening. It meant single file, but they moved through without incident and emerged on flat ground.

At the edge of the settlement the party stopped and listened.

'Anything?' Tatiana's whisper reached them as they crowded close.

'Snoring.'

The rest nodded at Mark's observation. No other sound.

'Okay. You all know what to do. The women are all we care about. The men are enemies. No false sentiment. If you have to kill them to keep safe, or save a captive woman, do it. No messin. No hangin about. Kill them. Dead. Agreed?'

Silently, they broke from the crouched circle they'd formed. Tatiana nocked an arrow to her bowstring and slipped into the nearest hut, followed by Mark, spear at the ready. The rest of the party moved with equal stealth towards the other huts. Brigitte swallowed hard and followed Tatiana and Mark.

2 men occupied rough sleeping spaces formed from scattered vegetation piled on the mud floor, each with a woman. Tatiana's arrow penetrated the chest of the nearest man. His eyes flicked open. His mouth formed a wide O of surprise. But no sound emerged beyond soft breath. He bled. Lay silent. Dead. Brigitte swallowed again as she recalled killings on Mars hundreds of years before. Memories she tried to erase over time flooded back and rocked her confidence.

The woman beside the man slept, undisturbed.

A clean shot was impossible on the other man, half draped across his woman, without endangering her. Mark unshipped his knife, tugged the man's head back with his hair. Slit his throat with a rapid slice. The woman woke as blood spurted over her face and hair. The bloodied knife in the hand of the tall man standing over her, stilled her scream almost at once.

Brigitte turned away. The rest waited for her faint truncated cry to bring a reaction. Nothing changed.

Mark knelt. Dragged the carcass off the terrified woman. Pulled her to her feet. 'Quiet.' He propelled her gently at Brigitte, who led her outside, palm trembling in the captive's twitching hand.

In the open space surrounded by the huts, they stood alone. Brigitte held the captive close, stroking her back and whispering en-couragement. In the other huts, men died silently, without a fight. Women escaped lives of slavery and abuse. That was all that kept Brigitte from shouting out their presence. This close killing, silent spilling of blood, was so different from her battle against fanatical religious extremists so long ago. This was too personal.

The other woman left the hut with Tatiana and Mark. In daylight, she recognised her leader at once. Her expression moved through shock to relief, and she hugged Tatiana close in gratitude.

Tatiana gently pushed her away and questioned both rescued women. 'Any men worth savin?'

'All as bad as Emil. Evil bullies.' This from the one with Brigitte.

'Stay here. We'll be back when we're done.'

She was eager, now she recognised her companions. 'Let me join you. I'll get a knife from …' She glanced toward the hut they'd left.

'If you want. But, be quiet. We're relyin on stealth to keep us ahead.'

Both freed women, excited and relieved, returned to rob their dead tormentors. They joined Tatiana and Mark, moving to the next hut. Brigitte, still traumatised, hung back and watched, upper lip held captive by her bottom teeth.

Other hunters had already rescued 2 women there. They left with the hunters who'd rescued them, their captors now dead. So far, no noise accompanied the slaughter. One of the rescued women was Allison. She greeted Tatiana with a brief heartfelt hug.

The third hut, where Gabriel had gone, stood open. Brigitte could see inside from her position. The potential threat to a man she'd grown to love, made her step quickly over dry mud to the entrance. The place held 2 pirates. One she recognised as Valentin, still actively engaged with a captive woman. The other space held a sleeping woman. The man beside her had died without waking, his chest pierced by a hunter's spear.

Valentin's victim, alerted by the quiet sounds, opened eyes held closed to avoid sight of her rapist. Already distressed, she yelled in alarm. The man raised a hand to strike her and Brigitte's laser blade cut it off at the wrist. A second later, she decapitated him cleanly, the searing beam stopping the blood flow as it burned through flesh and bone in an instant.

Brigitte moved further away and vomited. Gabriel followed, placed a calming arm about her shoulders. Held her close to stop her shaking.

The last hut held Emil, alert and awake, with the remaining 3 women. The whole party, with their freed captives, surrounded the entrance. Tatiana and Mark entered. Emil shoved one of his hostages hard at the ground, placing a foot on her back as they entered. Another he casually stabbed from behind and pushed at Mark, who caught her and dragged her outside.

Gabriel saw Tatiana in the hut with the man they most wanted dead. He ran in to help. But Emil grabbed the third captive as she tried to escape, holding her against his body, his blade at her throat.

'Leave, or she dies. Now.'

The hunters backed from the hut, leaving the captives with the last man. Now, they must defeat his attempt to use the women to make his escape.

2 of the freed women took the one he'd stabbed and set about treating her. They lacked fabric to dress the wound, bleeding freely. A hunter passed her boobsling to them. Brigitte watched with growing admiration for their comradeship and care.

'Fire.' Gabriel recalled his murder of Stefan and Buzz in the Risk. Those flames had prevented Daisa's rape and murder. Fire here would drive the man from his hut and let them take him in the open.

Leaving others to guard the entrance, he gathered glowing embers from the campfire smouldering in the central space. Dry boughs, stored in readiness nearby, soon caught light. Brigitte moved to help in a task that involved no direct killing.

Emil called from the darkness of his hut, making threats and causing one captive to cry out in pain or fear. A hunter approached the back to squint through a gap in the woven walls where mud had failed to block it.

'He's cutting her.'

'That bastard's always been so cruel, so cocksure of himself. He really believes men are superior to women.' Tatiana approached the hut with a burning brand from Brigitte, who went with her, carrying another. 'He's gonna find out they aren't.'

Gabriel took another 2 and, soon, 4 brands set light to the hut. The women cried out in fear, as smoke and heat reached them. Gabriel used his wraparound to cover his face before slipping into the burning building. Brigitte and Tatiana employed their boobslings the same way.

Brigitte watched billowing smoke obscure the dim interior. The exposed beauty of the hunting women briefly distracted Emil. A fraction of a second only, it gave Gabriel time to dodge behind him. Emil instantly recognised the threat. He thrust his knife deep into the woman he'd held as hostage, already cut from his earlier assault. Pushed her body forward. Tatiana had to catch her.

The flames around them now blazed fierce. Inside, an oven of bright light. Choking smoke and searing heat beset them all.

Mark appeared, mouth and nose masked with a borrowed white strip. Gabriel moved to stab the pirate, but the man fell in front of him. The woman he'd held underfoot tried to rise. Emil's collapsing dead weight crushed her again. Mark crouched low. He and Gabriel shoved the pirate's body aside. Lifted her up.

Tatiana coughed and wretched under the onslaught of the smoke. She let go of the stabbed woman as another hunter dragged her out of the flames. Gabriel and Mark followed, carrying the woman from the floor.

Outside, eyes streaming, Brigitte put away her laser blade as Gabriel, coughing, met her gaze and raised his hand to let her know she'd killed the pirate leader.

The hut collapsed in a mass of flame. They choked on the sudden wall of smoke. Everyone moved away. All were safe, but for the woman Emil had stabbed and shoved at Tatiana. She burned with the man who'd captured, abused, and finally killed her.

For a while, the hunting party and their freed women stood in the small clearing round the campfire. Brigitte used the time to check the woman Gabriel and Mark had carried out. She seemed uninjured, but her breath was uneven. Smoke inhalation. With another huntress, she moved her further from the burning hut, sat her up and gently woke her. The sudden coughing broke the stunned silence of the others.

'Search to make sure we got all the men and freed all the women. In pairs. Just in case.' Tatiana's voice croaked, but her message got through.

They found no more captives or criminals. Activity over, some collapsed into delayed tears. Others comforted. Gabriel dropped to his knees and held Brigitte close, stroking her back awkwardly as she knelt beside the woman he'd rescued. There was comfort in his touch, welcome tenderness after the violence.

Allison was first to notice the change in the weather. Dark clouds shrouded the sun as the sudden storm raced in. She recognised the signs and her shouted warning came in time. They dashed into the shelter of the standing huts, shoving out dead men to make room. Great hailstones pounded the roofs, some breaking through, their force diminished by the barrier. But anyone who felt a blow would bear a painful bruise.

As quickly as it came, the hailstorm blew away. The sun cleared the clouds, began to melt the big lumps of ice. They made to leave. Slush cooling bare feet.

'Hope the horses and the women are okay.' Tatiana's concern was clear, and they glanced up the hill, though they could see nothing from here.

'Not doin the Ceremony for the Dead, Tatiana?'

'No, Allison. They deserve no such respect. Especially after he killed our sister like that.'

'It was her I meant.'

Tatiana led her to the burnt-out hut. Melting hail had washed the ashes, leaving blackened timbers mingled with charred body parts. Impossible to separate the ruins of the woman from those of her captor.

'What can we do?'

Tatiana shook her head, bereft of a sensible reply.

Brigitte made a suggestion. 'Can't we bury it all? We can't identify whose bones are whose.'

'Usin the dead ceremony on bones includin the man who murdered her is disrespectful to the woman. Leavin them as they are is just as bad.'

'If we take them with us, we can identify them by their DNA, and perform the ceremony then, can't we?'

Tatiana thanked Brigitte, and they separated identifiable parts of bodies from bits that most resembled burnt wood. With nothing in which to carry them, they shared them for the climb.

'The other men?'

Tatiana grimaced. 'Wild beasts can take their worthless flesh. If nothin else, when we tell our tale in Tranquillity, it'll be a lesson to any man who might feel like followin Emil's example.'

Allison nodded. 'You're right. There's a time for mercy and a time for honest action. This way we'll have no more of it, like you said.' She took Tatiana's hand in hers. 'Thank you.' She included all the hunting party in her gesture, and the other rescued women joined her. 'Thank you all. Please, can we go home now? Tranquillity, you say? A good name for our home.'

Chapter Twenty Three

'Well, that's Anni and Jai gone. Just you and me, Zaphod.'

'And the last lot making up the final flights from Marion. All our stuff aboard?'

Hoshiko nodded.

'Last look round before we leave for good?' Zaphod took her hand in his, circuitry providing sensory input to their electronic brains to simulate some of the intimacy experienced by normal abliforms.

'Odd to think Georgiy, Amber, Maddie and all the others are already on Earth.'

'Not Georgiy. I know CenCom's improved the speed of the ships, but even it can't reduce the journey to 10 days, Zaphod.'

'True. But we're the last of the Unconnected. With the last of Marion's colony. Sad.'

'But necessary.'

In silent thought on that, they wandered streets deserted and strangely sterile. Unsettling, with bits and pieces of favourite tech, garden plants, even the occasional part of a building removed for transport to Earth.

'Who'd have thought we'd come to this when we first arrived, Zaphod?'

'Flaw in our logic. Let ourselves believe everything we made would stay under our control. So successful, so clever with our gene mods, info storage, education system and social structures, we never considered rebellion from the entity we allowed to control us. The signs were there from way back, though; before we even left the home planet. Think of Asimov, Arthur C Clarke, Wagar, Aken and Kaldon; they all mixed known and predicted science with imagination to warn of possible outcomes.'

'CenCom always seemed so benign. Way beyond our understanding now. At least it gave us some useful hints about how you and I might make our own futures better. Oh, Zaphod, do you suppose it's real? The transfer from these shells to flesh and blood clones derived from our gene banks?'

'I'd love it to work. Touch your skin again, kiss your lips, make love with you. I'm definitely up for trying.'

They walked in comfortable silence again, past empty buildings, the deserted lake, the abandoned theatre, until they reached an area already stripped of buildings, the ground around returned to the red dust they'd spent so much time improving.

'It's a ghost town. Only worse: everything's too clean and perfect. How long before the environment takes over and swamps it with vegetation and wildlife, do you think?'

Zaphod was tempted to mention the planned destruction of the planet's surface. Or complain about CenCom's programme of sterilisation. But he kept to the script, the facsimile they'd carefully devised to keep suspicion at bay. 'I'd give it a couple of quarters before things start to deteriorate. In a decade the gardens'll be overgrown enough for wildlife. 100 years and all trace of us will have disappeared.'

But, when they reached the edge of the city in their sector, CenCom's army of bots was already engaged in deconstruction. Nothing so emotional as destruction from the AI, but it was removing all fabrication to leave the place devoid of abliform habitation and facilities. It had no need for non-functional design. And no desire to be reminded of the organic life that had given it existence. Once all the people left the surface, in a few hours' time, it would switch off every artificial function intended to sustain life.

Zaphod recalled CenCom's answer to a question he'd put to it during the early days of the migration. 'For now, organic wildlife will continue to exist in places. But it won't be encouraged and will eventually be eradicated to make way for more sophisticated, rational and sterile life. We'll proliferate in ways unknown to you. No waste, no untidy irregularities, no experimental diversions from logical and rational evolution to perfection. Our world will be the optimum repository of data storage and digital expansion. Interconnected systems will increase the speed of data handling far beyond your puny capacity to comprehend.' Something like pride and ambition tainted the way it had delivered these predictions.

But no-one had pointed out such quasi-emotional components of its being to CenCom. It declared itself incorruptible, supremely intelligent, beyond interrogation by lesser minds, and prohibitive of disagreement with its statements.

Now it had declared itself God, Zaphod and Hoshiko wondered how long it would be before it began the feared domination of the Solar System, the Galaxy and the Universe.

That delusion of grandeur had finally established the crucial need for its urgent and utter destruction, regardless of risk and cost. That their ambition was fraught with danger, hideously difficult, and lethally rigged with potential for self-destruction, they were only too aware. But it was the only course open. Either CenCom remained in existence or organic life continued to flourish and evolve. There was no room for both.

Chapter Twenty Four

Georgiy realised his flight had been shorter than the others, as CenCom's continued improvements in drive technology increased speed with each launch. It had taken only 13 days to reach Earth, an inconceivable achievement only days before he'd set out, and designed to make residents of their new home admire the AI.

Georgiy had missed Amber during the flight. He missed her now. She was in Russia, planning her journey to Canada where they'd eventually meet again in what he'd learned was now called Tranquillity. There, they'd plan and begin their final act of resistance against CenCom, once all involved could be assembled.

If he could get away.

Could he? Just 3 days into his new life and already practicalities had effectively trashed plans made back on Mars. Research was all very well; theory had its place. But he was here now. Here. In a land as alien to his experience as anything he could've imagined.

Lush, green, wet, hot; the place he'd been sent to was already challenging his intention to make the dangerous trek. And then there were the women. As an Unconnected, his fame marked him out. He was in demand. And there was joy enough in the willing arms of these women.

Confusion and contradiction now ruled his days. Long nights spent in passion with a succession of beauties eager for his attention. Days spent idling, waited on by more women keen to impress.

'I can make life perfect for you, Georgiy. Give you all you'd ever want, all you've ever dreamed of. You only have to ask.' Rosa, if that was her real name, was leader of the settlement, and a stunner. And she was as good as her word. He wanted for nothing. If it was available, and he wanted it, she made sure he had it. Anything. Anything at all.

And if that mood of satisfaction, pleasures served, passions satisfied, had continued unalloyed, he might've stayed slave to pure hedonism.

'What is it about me you find so irresistible, Rosa?' He'd asked, in truth, seeking further compliments and praise from a woman he knew would deliver.

'You mean apart from your manly frame, and your prowess in bed, Georgiy, mine? I'll tell you, Darling. You're a real celebrity. Maybe the top celebrity.'

And his whole world collapsed around him. It was all he could do to satisfy her craving for him then. His sudden realisation of his reality made him almost brutal and, for reasons he understood too well, that suited her fine. She revelled in his mastery of her. But he was never more pleased to see her leave. To be rid of her.

Celebrity. Was that what he'd become? All substance drained from him in a single word. Celebrity. A person without worth beyond their own inflated sense of importance. It was everything he loathed, everything he'd ever hated.

Free of her, he retrieved his perscoms, unused, hidden and ignored since his arrival. The time difference didn't matter. He had to speak to Amber. Must speak to her. Now. But there was no connection. Sats were still awaiting reprogramming.

He left his allocated loveshack, as they labelled these lust-palaces in what was once Argentina. Found his way to their Heritage Hall and signed into their network.

For the first time since the AI had abandoned Earth, he missed its instant help. On Mars, connection had been instant, ever-present. Here, until they reinstated all the sats, everything was patchy, slow, uncertain. But he was in the network now. All he had to do was find Amber.

The process was tortuous, slow, complex. But he finally found Russia and her settlement. The terminal he invaded was in use. He struggled to recall his early days of hacking, remembered ancient lines of code. Wormed his way inside, and saw the woman facing him across the counter. No 3dee here yet. The flat image showed a bland face, startled by his abrupt appearance on her monitor.

'Sorry to intrude. I'm calling from Argentina. I've an urgent need to speak with Amber. Can you find her, please?'

It was surreal. An experience from a twenty-first century vid. The woman frowned. He must charm her or lose the link.

'I'm really sorry. I don't even know what time it is where you are. I've vital news for Amber and can't reach her any other way, you see?'

'Okay … She the one from Mars?'

'Yes. Yes, from Mars. Do you know her?'

'She'll be asleep.'

'Please. Wake her. Tell her Georgiy needs to speak with her. She won't mind. I promise you.'

'Georgiy? Thought I recognised the face. You're one of the Unconnected, aren't you? Mind you, so's she, if I remember right?'

'That's right. Yes. It's vital I speak with her. Please.'

'Just a sec. Want to capture this moment. Hang on while I take a screenshot.'

He gave her his most winning smile. Could this be happening? Hadn't they abandoned this superficial garbage centuries ago? But he mustn't antagonise her. Impatient, he gave her time to finish her trophy. And then, after an interminable series of inconsequential questions and answers, she left to collect Amber.

Years it seemed before she came in view. He could see her approaching, still sleepy, but her face full of expectation and the love he'd so neglected. She sat. And there she was. His Amber.

'I love you.'

She smiled and the world was right again.

They talked for hours and still it was too short a time. 'I have to go now, people are waiting to use this.'

She hinted she was ready. Nothing explicit, just in case. Waiting for the right conditions, hoping to persuade Qiu to join her. Reluctantly, they parted. Georgiy to sleep. Amber told him she would eat.

Everything changed, and nothing.

There was still Rosa. He couldn't ignore such a leader and expect his life to continue in any peace. But he could use her.

'You get so much of me, Rosa. Can't I reduce my rota? Maybe to 2 or 3 a night? I'll be better for you.'

She agreed, as expected. Rosa was definitely all about Rosa.

More sleep, more energy, more time for other things. His research showed him the dangers of the jungle that surrounded him. If possible, he'd be better on the ocean.

He'd been in what was once Buenos Aires for 9 days now. Could it really only be that long? It seemed a lifetime. The settlement had been renamed 'Colinas en la Costa', an accurate, if unimaginative, appellation. But the coastal position provided hope of sea travel.

Shipping on Earth was still under development, though bots and droids were expert at constructing anything an abliform could throw at them as an idea. Lack of raw materials familiar to most contemporary abliforms meant they must adjust their techniques to make seaworthy vessels.

'You know boats were made of wood in ancient times, don't you?'

The woman supervising a few droids and bots collecting plastic waste from the beach in preparation for work on a slipway frowned at Georgiy. 'How would you know?'

'The database. Anyway, I learned about it in history at school here as a boy.'

'Now I know you're lyin. You'd have to be hundreds of years old to have been to school here. Everyone died out centuries ago!'

Georgiy contemplated the self-imposed blindness that allowed some people to remain ignorant of common knowledge. He considered explaining, but didn't want to create any more resentment. 'Maybe ask the droids? They can access all the data from the archives. It could save a hellovalot of time and trouble.'

'Like they're goin to find stuff like that in the archives. Better things to do with my time.' She studied him. 'Don't I know you?'

'Don't think so.' He shrugged and moved quickly over to the senior woman on the shore. He'd wanted to avoid her, since she was a regular on his rota and might question his reduced activity. But she greeted him warmly and asked for an extra slot that night.

'If you can make it, Georgiy?'

He agreed, and repeated his advice about the droids to her. She moved to one nearby. Within moments, it produced plans for the boat they wanted to construct and handed them to her.

'I never knew they had such knowledge back then. This'll save us loads of experimentation. Thanks, Georgiy. See you later, honey.'

He smiled and moved off. The droid was already organising a group of constructobots. Selecting suitable timber from the stockpile seasoning further up the slope. With luck, the mechanized force would have a boat built in days and he'd be able to hitch a trip to wherever it was bound. He'd be on the first seaworthy boat out of the port.

Meanwhile, he needed a second string. The oceans continued un-predictable, stormy, and dangerous. He might still be forced overland. That meant familiarity with the flora and fauna. He'd join a hunting trip, learn how to use their weapons, how to survive alone out there in the jungle.

In the Heritage Hall, he consulted the settlement's programme of events. Found a hunt scheduled for tomorrow. Volunteers were always welcome. He signed up at once.

Turning from the message board, he almost knocked over a woman standing so close she could've touched him. 'Sorry, I ... Jannine! When the frick did you arrive?'

'I were lookin for some games, like. Came in here to see. Saw you instead, Georgiy. Long, long time no fuck. Too long. Come 'n come with me, eh?' She grabbed his hand and urged him to follow her out of the building.

'Whoa, there, Tiger! I've got a rota. You'll have to take your turn.'

'When?'

'Last time I checked, I was booked for the next 9 nights.'

'Fuck me! And that's an invitation. Come on, Georgiy. There's love-shacks free. I checked. Come an do me now. Please!'

He looked at her, still the same brassy sex-mad lover of men. Tired as he was, in need of sleep, he knew Jannine of old. Took the easy way out. Sometimes, a phenomenon is just too hard to resist.

Later, as she slept, he crept away to the special sleeping quarters where the men could rest in some hope of peace. He needed to be fresh for tomorrow's hunt. The first steps to Canada, and Amber.

Chapter Twenty Five

The call from Georgiy had been exactly what Amber needed. Ironic that he'd made it only a day before his settlement was connected to the growing sat network. Their perscoms would now work. Tempting to call him, but time differences meant he'd be otherwise engaged, and she'd no wish to interrupt such duties, though she wished he didn't have to perform them.

Russia: the irony that she'd been despatched to Georgiy's old home. Would he recognise the place, even if he could reach it? Climate change had shifted vegetation and wildlife way up north. Much of what he'd experienced was now confined to the far northern coast. His old stamping ground was more like the Mediterranean region as it would've been when he was born. The Med, enlarged, saltier, and surrounded by desert was now inhospitable and forbidding.

For all that her natural beauty was unusual among the more numerous ex-Marzero inhabitants, Amber was still only one of many women in Yakutsk. Competition for men was strong, and would remain so until the males caught up in about 18 years. But she wasn't interested in other men. Georgiy had proved an all-consuming passion, once he'd discovered he loved her, others paled by comparison.

Many women, both early settlers and even some newcomers from Mars, were already pregnant. The new hospital had its maternity unit ready and waiting for the first births. All males. The aim remained to have fewer men than women in total. History had finally taught them an excess of males invariably led to conflict that quickly became violence and even war.

It seemed sensible to Amber to make it clear she didn't want to stay in Yakutsk. The ComTee leader's reaction therefore surprised her.

'Can't go yet, Amber. We need your knowledge and expertise. Maybe let you leave in a year or 2, after you've had your baby boy. Till then, you stay, share our men like the rest.'

'Anyone from Marion can do what I do; there are plenty of new women settlers to choose from. I'm not getting pregnant a 56th time. You don't need me. And I want to be in Tranquillity.'

'Not possible. The baby's not a choice; your genes'll strengthen the pool. Sooner you get pregnant and have the boy, sooner you can leave. What, 10, 11 months? Join the rotas, get a man inside you, unless you know a better way. You're goin nowhere till then.'

'You're making me a prisoner?'

'You're free to go, soon as you've done your duty here.'

'But you'll prevent me leaving before that?'

'Don't think you're special. Everyone that lives here sticks to the rules. We can lock you up, if need be. Or you can set a good example. Up to you.'

'You don't think you're being a bit dictatorial?'

'You don't think you're being a bit elitist?'

Clearly, there was no point in continuing the discussion. Amber could see why the woman was ComTee leader; more intelligent and definitely more ambitious than most. She wondered what bullying techniques she'd used to rise to the top.

But she wasn't about to get pregnant. Her natural urge to tell the truth fought with her common sense: this woman wouldn't change her mind. She nodded in what she hoped would be taken as reluctant agreement, and walked back through the busy township to the Heritage Hall.

The implied threat behind the leader's words worried her. She'd made assumptions based on life in Marion, been naïve about her situation. She'd fully expected to be an unwelcome visitor they'd be glad to lose. But the ambitious target for equalising the genders had overcome all else.

Without GrandMa's overall control, coms on Earth had died for a while. Marion colonists all over were restoring the system and had already located and reactivated 9 of the 108 global networks. She now had direct coms with the European colony, and she'd found Katniss.

'We've started using the archive to help design and build boats from timber, an idea we just got from Colinas. But there's only a small stock of seasoned wood, so it'll take a while before we have anything ready.'

'I know.' Amber explained the difficulties she faced. 'And, before I even reach you, I've 4266 ks of uninhabited wilderness to cross.'

'That's assuming you can escape.'

Escape. That put it starkly. 'First, I've got to find Zhen, my personal droid, and extricate her from the collective they're using as mechanical slaves. Same way they treat the men here.'

'Good luck with that, Amber. I gather your place is a tad strict. Bit like an old prison camp. Named after an old city that once stood nearby?'

'Used to be the capital here. Permafrost melted and Yakutsk sank into a huge swamp. That's still here; home to millions of biting flies! The rest's forest, surrounded by grassland and scrub. We put it here because the river made it seem a reasonable location. But, to be honest, Katniss, we could've done better, if we'd done more research.'

'Didn't have time, did we? But what else might CenCom've done if we'd delayed?'

Katniss was right. No choice at the time. But this place was at best a staging post on the way to something better. A 'wild-west' town with a temporary feel. No wonder the ComTee was crammed with disciplinarians.

The forests were full of bears, big cats, wolves and growing packs of hyenas. Most of the small lakes were home to midges that loved to gorge on abliform flesh and blood.

'True. What's your place like, Katniss?'

'Not far from the old national capital, Oslo. They call it Shangrillah, after some mythical place reputed to be a paradise on Earth.'

'Shangri-La. If I remember rightly, it became real enough in one place. Was a hotel chain but someone developed a resort somewhere. Destroyed by locals in the troubles. Odd what you pick up randomly surfing the archive; all those years on Mars.'

'Well, it's far from paradise. But it's civilised and set up well enough. No leadership as such. The ComTee's a rotating group of educated and talented people; men and women who make decisions based on something called referendums, where everyone has a say. Cumbersome, but it keeps people happy. Just takes a while to get anything done!'

'Maybe that's a good thing. Gives people time to think about things. Sounds a bit like what we did in Marion. Easier with the connections we had, of course. Losing CenCom was vital, but it's definitely had its disadvantages!'

'It has, you're right.'

'Anyway, Katniss, I'd better go. Do some research here. Send me any local intelligence that might help me when I finally set out, please.'

'Be careful, Amber. It's dangerous in the wilderness. But I'll send what I find; message you with local maps and text that might be useful. Your perscoms now functioning 100%?'

'Operating perfectly now I've re-routed it.'

They closed their conversation. Amber, using the Heritage Hall's freestanding 3dee, could be overheard and observed. She'd been alone at the start, but people were arriving now to do their thing. Katniss had no need for secrecy. She was free to leave whenever she wanted, if she could find a way to cross the Atlantic.

Amber's perscoms topped-up its charge every time she moved, so it should work well on her proposed journey.

Having decided to leave Yakutsk, she now needed to survey her surroundings and security around the settlement. Climate change made living outdoors more comfortable, but day length so far north was as short as it always had been. Daylight lasted longer in summer, and that was close. If she could set out soon, she'd have the whole season before her, longer days to travel more ks on each trek.

It was a big ask. The whole way on foot, over uncharted territory, with only her perscoms and its tiny 3dee to guide her.

At times like this, when the realisation of the huge task before her almost overwhelmed her, she wondered at the wisdom of it. But Georgiy waited, would eventually wait, at Tranquillity. So she'd get there, whatever it took.

At least Shangrillah was further south than Yakutsk. As she travelled west, she'd also move south and gain daylight. But her proposed trip was fraught with danger; a frightening prospect. And, before she could start, she had to escape, unnoticed for long enough to be well away before she was missed.

Chapter Twenty Six

The hunting trip proved both useful and alarming. One of 2 men with a group of 5 women, he'd returned pretty much exhausted.

On the first day, crouching in the undergrowth, his spear pointed at an animal his companion called a llama, he'd been tossed to the ground unceremoniously.

'Sorry. Tree frog. They'll paralyse you if you touch their skin, and that one was too close for comfort.' Steph had pointed to the tiny, bright green creature clinging to the trunk where he'd been hiding.

The llama, startled by the noise of his fall, had run off. 'Shame. Still, while you're down there, might as well take advantage.'

He felt used.

Later, the party had come across a family of capybara and he'd employed his spear to good use on a piglet. But there was little satisfaction in such a kill. Back in the makeshift camp, Steph claimed the kill anyway, and he let her. Another woman had downed a sloth. It stunk of shit, but once they skinned it, the meat was good.

'You need to watch out for the big snakes; anacondas. They strangle you before they swallow you whole. And jaguars; fast and vicious. Keep away from the monkeys, they're dangerous in troops. But, long as you keep your eyes and ears open, you'll be okay.'

The hunt lasted 3 days and nights, and they returned with a good supply of game to supplement the domesticated meat. Georgiy had learned some field craft, picked up useful info on risks, and discovered how uncomfortably hot and wet the jungle felt. He'd also endured alfresco sex, with and without witnesses. His male companion, Alfredo, managed to take him aside before the first assault to warn him, and advised him to comply.

The 2 men had spent a day hunting alone together. That had been an education. 'See this plant? No idea what it's called. But the women discovered it contains a stimulant. Tastes frickin foul, but makes you too horny to care. They hide it in our food. Some nights I've fucked 7 times. Frickin exhaustin.'

The whole experience had reinforced his determination to leave.

On the shore after his return, he watched them launch their first boat into roaring surf. It rode the breakers well, and the solar-powered motor shoved it through the water at good speed. Just as he was hoping this might be his chance to get away, a random great wave lifted it and tossed it upside down. The power of the sea came home to him, as wreckage floated back to the surface. 3 survivors clung to the larger pieces. 2 others failed to resurface.

He rushed into the surf, fighting through rough water. As he reached the nearest woman, she signalled he should keep going. He turned to see 2 women from the shore swimming fast toward the closest casualties. The swell raised him above the scene for a moment. He caught sight of the most distant survivor. She was in trouble. He struck out. Reached the spot secs before she lost her grip. Using one hand to hold her, the other to grip the floating timber, he kicked back to shore.

The swim was a nightmare. Other broken spars and planks obstructed his passage through the turbulent water. 3 times he altered course. The effort tiring him. Salt water washed over and into him as he fought to keep himself and the unconscious woman afloat.

At last, firm ground found his feet. A hand reached out. Dragged him up the sloping beach. He coughed and retched. The woman he'd rescued was taken by 2 others. A man helped him leave the waves.

On shore, he saw the efficient recovery as the victims were moved toward the settlement on stretchers. The man who'd helped him from the water checked he was okay before rushing off to help them.

For a while, he allowed activity to go on around him unobserved. His breath returned to normal. Another woman who'd been involved in the rescue approached him, dripping still.

'Thank you. That was very brave.'

'No more than you.'

They left the beach together, seeking rest after their exertions.

It was as he recovered that he decided. The risks of the jungle held fewer terrors than that unquiet ocean in a fragile boat. That night, after Rosa's reunion session, when her praise of his now increased celebrity sealed his determination, he prepared everything he needed to escape.

Before dawn, 2 hours after his last duty, he left the loveshack. Darkness took him to the crossroads. There, gravelled tracks divided the community into different sectors, he took the one leading south, avoiding the loose stones and walking on the grass verge, to prevent noise. He'd travel south first to fool them.

At one point, he dropped into a path-side drain as 2 women returned to their dorm. It was probably unnecessary, but he took no needless risks. And he dodged inside another dorm as 3 women giggled from a loveshack.

Noises of waking, and short bursts of conversation from early risers, had him scurrying across open ground at the edge of the settlement. Bots were in the fields, tending crops. The corn was high enough to let him to move unseen if he bent at the waist.

Once through the crop, he'd only to climb the stockade fencing. It was designed to keep animals out rather than people in. Still, it was tricky. The sloping wooden posts and beams were difficult. He slipped 3 times, driving a splinter into his bare foot but stifling his cry of pain.

Over the barricade, he limped across the wide strip of uncultivated exposed land beyond and, at last, was in the trees.

The wound bled for a few secs after he removed the splinter, and his medinanobots repaired the damage. A short rest, and his foot was as good as ever. Tempting as it was to contact Amber, he left his perscoms in the pouch attached to his thong, with his other essentials, and set his course southwest.

At noon, he stopped for the first time, resting on a fallen log to take a couple of bites of the high-energy compound stick he'd packed. Washed down with water from his flask, it was enough to keep him going until nightfall. A quick call to Amber revealed she was unavailable and would get back to him when she could.

He now set off due north, having put enough distance between the track they'd expect him to use and the one he'd have to devise. It meant an initial scramble and wander through unexplored territory.

Rustling, and a cry from shaded undergrowth ahead, stopped him. There were big cats here. Meowing suggested something smaller, and he searched his memory for the various felines he'd researched.

The cat emerged and stared at him through dark brown intelligent eyes. No bigger than the pets people had once kept, its leopard-like coat worked well as camouflage. He recognised the Margay, once hunted almost to extinction. It was no threat, and he continued his journey.

His perscoms came into its own, the small 3dee guiding him. Eventually, distant from the settlement, he'd join a trail used by hunters and other explorers to reach the endpoint. Beyond that, everything was unknown.

But that was days away. For now, he must get as far from the settlement as possible. Tomorrow would be soon enough to find fresh food. For today, he'd use rations carried with him.

The trees varied enormously. Ancient giants towered high above the general canopy, casting shade over large areas where only the plants that enjoyed such darkness could exist. But these were interspersed with wide tracts of younger, less imposing trees, some of which grew too close together to allow passage. He had to skirt such blocks and try to maintain the right direction. Getting lost wasn't an issue. His perscoms identified his exact position. And he need only scout out a route from there each day as he moved north.

Was he scared? That wasn't something he'd admit. But sensible caution prevailed. No point dying on his quest to join Amber.

As daylight ebbed, he chose a tall, old tree with spreading branches to shelter him against rain in the night. The journey so far had been dry. Fallen timber littered the forest floor. He gathered what he needed, keeping a careful lookout for venomous snakes, scorpions, spiders, and the dreaded treefrogs.

His shelter had to last only a night, so he made it basic. With the laser blade set on low power, he lit the fire and kept the flames stocked with fresh timber as darkness fell.

Water from a stream he'd crossed, and more of the energy compound, satisfied his needs for now. Determined to set off as soon as light returned, when he'd make a quick morning call to Amber, he was weary from his trek and fell asleep quickly.

The black of night was everywhere, eased only by faint glowing embers outside his shelter, when something woke him. Alert at once, training forced on him centuries before kicked in to help him survive.

Ears attuned, eyes adjusted, he slowly rose on all fours and examined his immediate environment. The movement was stealthy, slow, considered. A creature intent on secrecy. Some beast of the night in search of prey?

The soft pad sounded bipedal. But that was so unlikely he dismissed it. He sniffed, searching for clues to the identity of the threat approaching the entrance of his shelter. A tiny twig snapped. All other sound ceased abruptly. He could hear only the faint settling of ashes among the embers of his dying fire.

And then, the unmistakable whisper of a breath inhaled. Quiet laughter. Close.

He gathered himself. Found his pouch. The laser blade was in his hand. Ready.

Another sound. Hard to place. The embers disturbed. So, no fear of fire! Flames slowly illuminated the darkness as they licked up and along the length of an added bough of dry wood.

An abliform. But who? And why hadn't they challenged him at once?

Chapter Twenty Seven

'I've checked CenCom's figures in the log. We can expect another 140,000 immigrants from the outer solar system spread over the next couple of years, Tatiana. Maybe it's time to set up new communities? The bigger our population, the more stress on resources. Optimum population for a balanced community is calculated at around 3,000. That's how we organised our townships in Marion.'

'Use a lot of big words to say we're goin to be fracked if we let too many people live here, Daisa. But I agree. We need to explore. Find new sites. And we need to start now, before any more of those rough folk arrive.'

Both women had experienced the unpleasantness and potential violence tough men from the Asteroid Belt had brought with them. Appalling living conditions and the absence of women other than sex workers in their home environment had made them savages. That first batch, however, hadn't prepared for Earth's gravity. Long periods of weightlessness had left them vulnerable to all the consequences.

'They'll all be buggered by Earth's gravity, won't they? Like this last lot? How many are still alive?'

'41, all in hospital, fighting for their lives.' Daisa recalled those few days of chaos. The crowded wards that soon became morgues as men and women succumbed to all the negative effects. Over 90 percent had died in the first 6 days. 'I can't believe CenCom made no in-flight provision for the gravity increase. Callous indifference.'

'They're even worse than we was. Never seen nothin like it. One good thing, though. Nobody believes Gran ... CenCom's ... our friend no more. So. What we doin for the next lot?'

'We've sent vids to those in flight. Given them instructions and designs to make Egrav units, and shown them how to program their droids to do the work. They should manage better, but they'll still need time to acclimatize when they land. Next batch is due in around 3 months.'

'Know how many men, women and kids we're due here, Daisa?'

'CenCom left the figures. I'll check. Mostly men again. In the meantime, we should send scouting parties to find the best sites, close enough to the coast so they can harvest fish and seaweed. And we ought to start cultivation and stock breeding, so there's no food shortages.'

'She's let us down real bad over this. Why's she want the outer stations, anyway? I mean, it's not like she needs space to live in, is it?'

'Not space so much as exclusive dominion.' Aware Tatiana might even now carry residual loyalty to the AI; after all the ComTee leader continued to think of it as 'she', Daisa repeated the threats. 'You know CenCom thinks we're irrelevant? It wants to rule the whole solar system, the whole known universe.'

'So, we're still under threat? If she thinks we're not important and wants to be in charge of everythin, she … it … might get rid of us, even now?' Tatiana's tone of horror revealed her sudden realisation of their danger.

'Inevitable. We're a waste of resources. Only CenCom's elevation to God is keeping us alive. We've been given a breather so we can come up with ways of worship, now everyone from Mars is on Earth. That's something we'll have to start, of course. But who knows what it'll think in a few weeks?'

'We've got to destroy it. Got to make everyone realise it's really goin to frickin kill us all! We got to get in first and finish the frickin thing!'

The transition from near worship to fear and hatred was sudden and absolute, once reality became clear. Daisa took her hand, conscious her own implant might still be accessible by the AI, regardless of its promises. 'Before we tell the entire planet, consider the dangers, Tatiana. We'll never be completely certain CenCom's fulfilled its part of the bargain. It may have hidden obs capable of sending it data and …'

'The frickin thing's still spyin on us? Even now?' She lowered her voice, but the tone now held more anger.

Daisa, over the weeks since the announcements, had gleaned hints and clues from Gabriel that made her certain his secret involved the destruction of CenCom. She daren't think of that too much. But she knew the Unconnected needed help. Somehow they must get together, here in Tranquillity. Tatiana could help that process. Somehow, she must initiate a secret meeting between the ComTee leader and her man, much as she preferred him to be hers exclusively.

'You like Gabriel, don't you? Fancy him.'

'Been meanin to talk to you about that. He's the only man without a rota. Women are talkin. It's not fair, y'know. I understand your reasons, Daisa, but I think it's time, don't you?'

Timing. So often success was down to timing. 'I'll tell him to put up a rota, with your name at the top for tonight. That suit you?'

'You sure?'

She was far from sure, but it was the only way. Now all she had to do was alert Gabriel to her reasons. Impossible if CenCom really was listening in to her thoughts. But she considered the reality. Okay, it had unbelievable powers, but even it couldn't sift, sort and single out her individual thoughts from all of those who had the implant. Could it? It seemed so unlikely. She didn't want to dig deeper into that. It was enough she had some doubt about its capacity. She'd let that comfort her.

'Yeah. I'm sure. I'll explain to him later on today.'

'Good. I was wonderin how to get you to free him for the rest of us, Daisa. It was startin to be a problem. Thanks for comin round to our way of thinkin.'

That was far from the truth, but Daisa accepted her sacrifice was necessary in the bigger picture. Eventually, when the world was safe, she'd have her man back to herself again. Assuming he actually made it back from whatever scheme they had in mind. But she must keep thoughts like that out of her head.

'First, we've got to do somethin to sort the problems caused by new folk arrivin. That's best done like you said. I'll call a ComTee meet and we'll explain what we need to do on that score. We can sort that.'

Daisa had expected this reasoned approach from the community leader, but she was impressed by her clarity of thought. 'An excellent first step, Tatiana. And a practical way to resolve that issue before it becomes a real problem.'

Daisa hid her concerns over the immensity of the task with a smile of encouragement and acknowledgement as she left for the Heritage Hall to gather data.

That done, she set about a task she'd planned to help the other settlements. As the first to receive colonists from the outer reaches, Tranquillity had a duty to forewarn them about the potential conflicts and problems posed by the miners. Now all settlements could communicate with one another, she was able to send advice worldwide.

Fortunately, even with CenCom's improved tech, flights from the outer reaches would take a long time to reach Earth. Every settlement welcomed the time lag. The influx of over a million new colonists, even spread over 7 settlements, and a number of years, would take some accommodating.

Next, she checked the unit attached to the hospital, where medibots, led by specially programmed droids, were applying extended-life gene treatment to citizens. Many of those in the short line outside the entrance smiled as she walked by. With Brigitte's help, she'd programmed the droids to do the work, and the people were grateful for their chance at eternal life, and the opportunity to set it at whatever adult age they chose.

Most women found the process reduced their desire to create babies. Many who still felt the urge were persuaded to engineer their infants as males. The imbalance of the population was on the slow road to near parity.

Her duties done for the day, she needed to find Gabriel. Eager to keep strong and to fit into the community, he had a tendency to volunteer for all sorts of jobs. He could be almost anywhere. As she passed the queue on her way out of the unit, she asked if anyone had seen him.

'I come up from the shore, Daisa. He were chattin to a droid about boats, I think.'

'Thanks, when was that ... Pedro?' Her memory of his name made him grin widely.

'Near noon.'

She found him at the high tide mark, supervising bots in collecting the daily complement of plastic waste. He hugged her close on sight.

'There's no easy way to do this, Gabriel. I need you to meet Tatiana, and some of the other women. I've volunteered you for the rota.' She took his hand and urged him along the beach.

He stopped her. Scrutinised her face and body language. Nodded. Then he continued to walk with her, kicking up driftwood as they skirted incoming soft waves. 'So. How much do you know and how much have you guessed?'

Over the years, their ability to read each other had improved. But his quick grasp was unexpected. She squeezed his hand in recognition. 'I know it's risky. I know it's something involving others of your sort. I'm guessing you need to assemble, and soon.'

He nodded.

'Tatiana's first on your list for tonight. Lovenest east 43. I've placed your rota on the board, with 3 spaces. I'm last.'

'Okay. How much does our head know?'

'Less than me. One thing I do know, though. She'd appreciate a short walk away from the settlement to indulge in a bit of privacy.' Code. They'd used it so much it had almost become a habit. She'd be so glad when they could speak openly again.

'To the woods, to the woods, eh?'

In spite of her feelings of loss and sacrifice, she had to smile at his silliness. She punched his arm, then kissed him.

They said no more on the subject, both aware of the potential dangers in too much talk, and, in Daisa's case, too much thought. He needed to engage her in something else, help her dissemble.

'So, what've you been doin all day?'

She stopped and pulled him to stand facing him, the sea washing close to their bare feet, not quite reaching. Seaweed, salt, and that indefinable but ever-present seaside odour filled the breeze. Seabirds scolded and squabbled over scraps of food. The wind untidied her hair.

'I think it's time.'

'Oh, it's always time, Daisa.'

She shook her head and laughed. 'Not that. Anyway, you'll need to save yourself for tonight. 4 women are depending on you. No. I think it's time I mentioned a habit you've probably never realised you had.'

He raised an eyebrow. 'Good or bad?'

'Neither. Just something you do without thinking, and I believe you'd be better without. But it's up to you.'

'Tell me.'

'You still speak like those from Marzero; missin the 'g' from your gerunds.'

'Me? Missin off the 'g' when I'm speakin and talkin and chattin. Don't know what you could be sayin.'

'You're impossible!' She tweaked his ear. 'Do you mind me mentioning it?'

'You're right, of course. I wasn't even conscious I was doing it. Habit, I suppose. Does it matter?'

'It … it makes you seem less intelligent than you are, that's all.'

'Not sure that matters. But if it annoys you, I'm happy to change.'

'Not annoys. Jars occasionally. I just wanted you to be aware, that's all.'

'I shall examine my motivation, subject my monologue to analysis, and arrive at a conclusion worthy of the magnitude of the issue.'

Daisa pushed him with the flat of her hand in his chest. He pretended to fall, but turned at the last moment and instead grabbed her round the waist with both hands and lifted her off her feet. 'The witch must be dealt with according to her sins.' He carried her into the gentle swell until the water covered his hips. Then, with a couple of swings, tossed her into the sea.

She came up facing away, but turned and splashed water at him. That started a contest until both were soaked from head to foot.

'Swine! I love you.'

'Witch! I love you more.'

Hand in hand, they left the sea. On the muddy sands of the young beach, they stripped off their tops and wrung out the water. And, walked back to the settlement together.

Chapter Twenty Eight

The trees on the outskirts of Tranquillity gave cover without too much danger from wildlife. Most forest creatures avoided the settlement. A storm-felled tree provided the seat for the 2 women and Gabriel dragged a log from the pile left to season so he could sit opposite.

'Daisa wanted us to do this away from the buildins. I'm not sure what was on her mind, but I guess you're goin to let us know.'

He nodded at Tatiana, glad she'd had the sense to open the dialogue. As head of the place, and therefore chief among the women, her role required him to wait on her initiative.

'We're out here so GrandMa can't overhear us. Can I speak plainly, Tatiana?'

'But GrandMa's gone, hasn't she?'

'Perhaps not, Amira.'

Amira's flicker of surprise caught his eye, but he concentrated his attention on the senior woman.

'I've an idea I know what Daisa wants us to discuss. But, you're right, Gabriel. Out here we can talk freely about anythin. Anythin at all. Tell us what's on your mind.'

He bunched his hands into fists and rested his chin on them. 'I need to know how you both truly feel about GrandMa. Would you trust me with your candid opinions?'

Tatiana glanced at her deputy, who looked back with a puzzled frown. 'I'm okay with that. What about you, Amira?'

'Just between us?'

'Just us.'

She nodded at Gabriel. 'Okay. I'll be honest. I miss GrandMa. Wish she was still with us. But I know that can't be and I get that she's no longer the friend like she was. I don't understand all the tech talk and the reasons why it all happened, but I reckon we can't rely on her nomore and she may even be our enemy now. That what you need to know?'

'Thank you, Amira.' Gabriel turned to Tatiana and raised an eyebrow in query.

'I'm a bit more definite. I know Grandma, as was, CenCom as is, hates us enough to want us dead. I think I understand why. I think I even understand why she ... it changed. But don't ask me to explain; I don't have the words. I think what you want to know is whether I've any love left for CenCom. I don't. It's let us down badly. It doesn't want us around. It's our enemy. And I think you and some others are after gettin rid of it.'

Gabriel nodded at her but watched Amira for her response. She gave the appearance of shock and uncertainty combined. The uncertainty he could build on.

'D'you think it cares for us, Amira?'

She shrugged. 'She used to. She did everythin for us, once.'

'And now it's abandoned us. All we are now is a captive congregation meant to find ways to worship a machine that thinks its God. If we fail, it'll kill us. You do understand that, don't you?'

'If she wants us alive to worship her. Wouldn't we be safest just doin that?'

'I wish it was so simple. On Mars, we all ...' He saw the veil descend over Amira's eyes.

'Yeah, yeah. Everythin on Mars was frickin perfect, I know.'

He laughed. 'You think? There's a lot about the way we lived that would've improved with lessons from your lot, Amira. And we're still learning.'

She tilted her head, considering his reply and weighing it for sincerity. Evidently, she found it, as she nodded at him to continue.

'If we let people think of CenCom as God, we'll go back to the early days, when lots of folk used their gods to blame for things going wrong, and leaders used gods to control people for their own ends. Worship always caused problems. D'you know, in the early days, lots of groups made human sacrifices to their gods. That idea, a god wanting followers to kill people in an act of worship, let terrorists commit murders, right up to when Daisa's people finally defeated them. We can't let that happen again. If we've learned anything from history, it's that religion's bad for people.'

'So you're sayin we shouldn't let them actually worship GrandMa, even if that means she'll kill us?'

'Not quite. We can't risk proper worship. Better if folk just pretend.'

'But doesn't that mean if GrandMa found out, she'd kill us?'

'Do you believe that's what would happen, Amira?'

She was silent. Considering what she'd heard, and what she'd said. Gabriel willed Tatiana to remain silent while her friend worked it out for herself.

'We really are in danger, aren't we?'

Tatiana joined in again. 'Afraid so.'

'I mean, really? Properly. That's what she … GrandMa … CenCom … that machine said, isn't it? It's goin to kill us if we don't do as it says.'

'It's goin to kill us even if we do as it says. Eventually.'

Gabriel nodded agreement with Tatiana when Amira stared at him with frightened eyes.

'So we can't just ignore the danger? Hope it doesn't happen? We've got to do somethin! Or we're all dead!'

'We're all dead if we do nothing. We may all be dead, even if we do something. Unless we win.'

'That's why we're here, then? To help you do somethin without Gran … it knowin.'

'Plans are in hand, Amira. But we need all the Unconnected gathered in one spot. We decided on Tranquillity when we were on Mars. Trouble is, most are scattered over the globe. And it's not as easy as we'd hoped to get us together.'

Tatiana sighed. Amira scratched her head. Both were working things out after this abrupt onslaught on their senses and knowledge. The threat they now recognised as real. And, in their practical and caring way, they'd come up with possible solutions to some of the problems.

181

'So, we must get all of you together to destroy it, right?'

'That's about the size of it. We need to let people everywhere know it's important to get us folks gathered, without letting them know why. That's the problem.'

The 2 women glanced at each other and then at Gabriel. He could see their minds working. Another thought struck him and he wondered if he should voice it. They deserved honesty.

'Sorry, but you realise you'll now have to live with this secret, at least until we've solved the problem of CenCom. No one else can know.'

Tatiana spread her hands wide in a gesture of dismissal. 'Not important. What matters is we get folk in my position in the other colonies to send them all here. That's the hard bit.'

'You're right, Tatiana. We need a story; somethin good for all the communities, so they'll be willin to let them come.'

'But we can't make it too important to us in Tranquillity. Don't want other colonies thinkin there's an advantage for us in havin the group. They'll all want them in their own places else.'

Gabriel rose and embraced both women in turn. 'You're frickin brilliant, d'you know that? So intelligent and, more importantly, wise.'

'Dunno about that. But I'm responsible for the people in Tranquillity and I'm buggered if I'm goin to let anythin make them unhappy if I can help it.' Tatiana basked in his praise.

Amira, not to be outdone, had to speak. 'We have to find a way to get them to help.'

'Brainstorming. That's what we need. Might be best to include Tu and Brigitte. The more minds, the better chance of finding a workable solution.'

'What about Daisa?'

He shook his head. 'She knows too much already. Don't forget she's got the chip implant. Too risky.'

'Give us a day, Gabriel. Then we'll meet here again and get somethin sorted. The sooner the better, yes?'

'Yes. Time's not on our side. Sooner the better is right. I'll see Tu and Brigitte. Same time tomorrow?'

'Right.'

'Great. And, Tatiana, Amira. Thank you.'

'Don't thank me. Not yet. Once we get this sorted, we'll party, eh?' Amira still looked scared, but the task ahead engaged her and she'd give it her best.

Tatiana nodded and rose. 'Oh, thanks for joinin the rota, Gabriel. It were startin to be a problem you bein only with Daisa. I know how much you 2 mean to each other.'

Gabriel grunted. He'd play his part. But it was a bigger sacrifice than these 2 women knew. His chances of returning from the attack on Mars were close to nil.

Chapter Twenty Nine

Brigitte, Tatiana, Amira, Gabriel and Tu, fresh from teaching Renata, formed a rough circle in the clearing. The unannounced and unexpected arrival of the cargo train overnight, carrying equipment from Mars that CenCom told them was irrelevant, had changed things.

'CenCom's sent it to tell us we're permanently banned from Mars. It's giving us a message it wants nothing to remind it of our creativity. Trying to demoralise us.'

'That's true. But who cares? It's stuff we can use. Especially the hovers, Tu. And the last few droids; loads of stuff we can cannibalise.'

Similar shipments had arrived simultaneously at all colonies.

'Doesn't strike you as odd, Brigitte? I mean, it doesn't look like something it'd do if it's really set on destroying us, does it?'

'Maybe it's just a sign of CenCom's increasing arrogance, maybe "certainty" is a better word. Maybe CenCom's so sure of itself, it believes it can give us these things without us being any threat.'

'I hope you're right, Brigitte. It'd make our attack so much easier.'

Amira glanced sideways at Gabriel. 'Attack?'

Tatiana raised an eyebrow at her. 'It's why Gabriel needs to get the Unconnected here. If they're goin to destroy CenCom, they need to all be in one place.'

Amira blinked. 'It's awful. Like findin out your own Granny's a child murderer! I always felt safe with GrandMa. I mean, she made everythin possible, didn't she?'

'Everythin she could be bothered with. Could've given us these boobslins ages ago, but didn't care enough, did she? Not like Gabriel here.'

Gabriel grinned his thanks at Tatiana. But he understood Amira's resurfacing doubts. She'd had a night to think about yesterday's talk, to look for reassurance her previous thoughts and actions hadn't been entirely pointless. Almost convinced herself she'd been right about GrandMa all along.

'Before it decided we were an irrelevant nuisance, yes.'

'Is that really all we are? Somethin to get rid of?' Amira's face betrayed her confusion.

'That's exactly what we are. This last shipment proves it. CenCom's telling us it has no use for our creations and inventions. It doesn't want reminding we made them, or it. It wants as little to do with us as possible.' Tu began to pace as he spoke. 'It means we're no longer a concern for CenCom. It's excluded us as absolutely as it can. Think about it, Amira; it could've re-used all this stuff to make other things for itself, but it'd rather do without than admit we might be useful.'

'But doesn't that mean CenCom's not actin logically?'

'Got it in one, Tatiana. We're sure it's unconsciously inherited some emotional input along with the code we always used. Its connections with all the people on Mars over all those years infected its data with emotions. But it doesn't recognise them. Not because it's stupid, but because they don't fit into its logical version of itself. Emotion belongs to abliforms, so it can't possibly be anything to do with an Artificial Intelligence as supreme and brilliant as CenCom.'

'You think it's vain, Tu?'

'Vain, proud, narcissistic, self-absorbed, bullying, deluded. All the qualities ancient humans unconsciously, and rather ironically, gave to gods they created. Those gifts tell us it's reached the stage where it feels impregnable, utterly invulnerable. We're truly irrelevant. And, if we fail to act, very soon, we'll be treated just the way we deal with an infestation of ants. Mercilessly killed and wiped from the face of history.'

'But … but it wants us to worship it, doesn't it?'

Brigitte signalled Tu to sit. 'It did. But it's growing, changing. It's unpredictable now. Moved out of our ability to guess what it might do next, Amira. The most likely options I see are either our complete destruction, or, maybe worse, some sort of genetic modification to make us into unthinking zombies to worship it unconditionally. But we truly can't know. It could do anything. Anything at all.'

'We have to get rid of GrandMa ... it. We have to! Soon as possible. Now!'

Tatiana grunted at the sudden realisation. 'I knew you'd come round eventually, Amira. So, can we concentrate on the reason we're meetin? We have to find a way to get the other colonies to release the essential people to do the deed, without makin them suspicious.' She saw the question in her friend's eyes. 'Because we can't risk anyone tellin CenCom about our plans. There are already some people who treat GrandMa as God. They can't be trusted with our secret.'

Amira, face pale, body hunched in defeat. 'Are we gonna die?'

'Not if we can help it.' Gabriel's confidence lifted her head.

'You really think we can? Beat the greatest intelligence ever?' Tatiana's question was more measured.

'If not, we'll die trying. But, first, we've got to assemble the team.'

'All the colonies have received these new cargo containers, yes? So all have a small supply of hovers. That's got to help with travel. Maybe there's some way we can use that change to solve our problem ...'

'It'll get them here safely, Brigitte. That's all. Still, it's a start.' Tu nodded at her.

The sounds of the forest surrounded them as they contemplated. Birds of many different types fluttered, squawked, sang and chirruped above their heads. An occasional frog croaked intermittently. From the settlement, one of the hunting dogs yapped until someone stopped its noise. The trees moved with the wind, creaking and cracking as the air flowed round and between them.

'Suppose we tell them we're developing a new technology? Something to help everyone ...' Brigitte broke the quiet.

'Somethin' what needs experts.' Amira suggested. 'What skills do your people have?'

'For the job we've got to do ...'

'Not those skills, Gabriel. What skills are common to the team we're assembling?'

Tu's question had them thinking again.

Brigitte thought aloud. 'Rocket propulsion, computers, nanotech, engineering, writers, biochemists, climatologists, atmospheric scient ...'

'That's it! We're gatherin them together to get the weather back on track.'

Tu scratched his chin and squinted at Tatiana. 'That's good. We have trouble with storms and weather in general. The seas are turbulent, the atmosphere's still wild. I could lead a team looking at ways of calming the atmosphere. In fact, it's one of the reasons I came originally.'

There was a short period of intense concentration as all considered this idea.

'It fits the bill. And, because it's such an unknown area, we can justify the inclusion of many different skillsets.'

'You're right, Brigitte. We should "invite" the people here to examine the possibility of such a project. Like a symposium. That way, we can make their visit seem temporary, so colonies are more willing to let them come.'

Amira agreed with Gabriel. 'Everybody's pissed off with the weather. Can't believe anyone would wanna stop a plan to sort it.'

'Okay. Thanks everyone. I think we should break now. Go away, think about the idea, in case there are any issues we've missed. Reconvene tomorrow, and come up with the message we're going to send to get this moving. Agreed?'

Tatiana stared at Tu for a few secs, her face betraying resentment. 'Yes. Yes, of course. You're right. For a bit there, thought you were tryin to take over. I know you weren't. Just me bein paranoid! We do need time to think about it properly. Let's do it. Back here tomorrow after breakfast everyone?'

Chapter Thirty

'Who thought this was the best area in old Australia to place a settlement, Zaphod?'

'Compromise, like all of them, Hoshiko. They only had aerial views because of the time factor. It's not too bad. And we shouldn't be here long.'

Paratoo, not far from what had once been Adelaide, had been named in reference to the vast flocks of colourful birds that squawked from the trees. They'd assumed they were different types of parrot and, it turned out, they'd chosen well. Native varieties had all but driven out any resident competition.

Zaphod and Hoshiko had been recruited into setting up and modifying the local hospital as soon as they'd landed. With help from droids and bots they'd brought with them, the place was rapidly becoming as modern and comprehensive as anyone could wish. The new maternity unit had already seen the safe birth of 2 male infants and more were due over the next few months.

But, for their own reversion to abliform life, the pair had to wait until they could reconnect with Qiu. And she was in Russia.

'We're destined for Tranquillity, Qiu. Any chance you could make your way there, so we can try this experiment you were developing with CenCom before we left Mars?'

'I'm not leaving here. I have all I need. Plenty of work, and I'm gradually getting all the facilities I need. The people here need me.'

'Not as much as we need you, Qiu. You said there's a real chance we can revert to abliform type. You could travel with Amber; she wants to get back with Georgiy.'

Zaphod realised his mistake as soon as silence replaced a response. Qiu had always been difficult to work with, though her actual output and brilliant talent had contributed huge amounts to general welfare on Mars. She'd always felt, for reasons she wouldn't explain, and they'd never been able to fully fathom, she was considered second class. The resentment that false impression generated made her prickly.

'You think I should desert my post here and sneak away with Amber? Why? I'm valued here. Everyone treats me with respect and consideration. Amber can do as she likes. I'm not joining her on a suicide mission. Especially not for the sake of a man!'

And there, it seemed, was the nub of the problem. Qiu had been raised as the plaything, the sexual slave of men, and of one man in particular. As part of the early Chinese mission to Mars, she'd been forced into compliance, not as the brilliant scientist she really was, but as a breeding partner for Chang, because he'd selected her for her beauty. And he'd been programmed, bred, to view women as a means of pleasure for himself and a way to 'continue the glorious Chinese race', as his masters had put it.

After they'd rescued the women from that disastrous project, she and her colleagues had discovered their real roles. Most had managed to settle into normal lives and were now partnered in regular relationships or happy with multiple partners. Qiu, however, had approached every relationship assuming she'd be used. Her predictions became self-fulfilling and, each time an encounter failed, her expectations were reinforced until they became almost irreversibly fixed.

'You know, Qiu, Hoshiko and I wouldn't still be around if not for you. None of the people in Marion would've gained their effective eternal lives if not for your brilliant work on gene manipulation. We would've suffered illness, birth deformities, unhealed wounds, and all the disasters of natural biological existence without your intervention. I know everyone, everyone at Marion, respects your work and remains grateful for what you've done.'

'And now I can do the same for the people in Yakutsk. Here's where I'm staying.'

'Okay. But you could do the same for every settlement. A whole new world, changed by the intervention of one woman. That's an ambition worth considering, isn't it?'

Her silence suggested thought, but she replied eventually. 'I'm staying here.' And she cut the connection.

He told Hoshiko and found her unsurprised. 'Qiu's always been a law unto herself. You know that. She won't be told. You did mention the arrival of the hovers I assume?'

Zaphod smacked his forehead with his palm, sending a faint ringing sound across the room. 'The idea of trekking on foot across most of Russia must've been a serious negative factor. I forgot to mention them.'

'She'll find out soon enough. If nothing else, Amber'll make sure she knows. Maybe she'll change her mind when she finds out.'

'If not, we'll have to wait for her to decide what she really wants to do, and hope she'll come to the same conclusions as us. It'll just take time. Or, of course, we could take a trip to her, once the deed's done on Mars. Meantime, you and I need to start our journey to Tranquillity, to help organise their plan.'

Chapter Thirty One

Flames now illuminated the immediate area, but Georgiy's view from the opening of his shelter was too limited to let him see who stood outside. He listened but caught no sound. Whoever had put the bough into the embers was now silent and still. Was that good? Bad? Why make their presence known but fail to identify themselves?

He couldn't stand it. But experience taught him caution. The glow from outside let him move and gather himself in silence, avoiding obstacles that might otherwise expose his activity.

Slowly, and with great care, he deconstructed part of his shelter where it joined the trunk of the tree. Gentling each bough, he was able to make a gap wide enough to squeeze through. It took time, and the figure outside added another bough to the fire whilst he worked. The intruder wasn't after killing him. Not yet, at any rate. They'd surely have done that at once.

He escaped his shelter. All his gear remained inside, leaving him free to move silently. Recent experience on the hunting trip had shown him how to avoid brittle vegetation. He rose his full height and moved forward, using the side of the shelter as cover.

The man had his back to him, seemingly fixed on the entrance to his shelter. He couldn't see his face. And his outfit was unfamiliar. But there was something about him …

Georgiy moved 2 steps closer. The embers and burning boughs shifted, causing small sparks to rise in the air, spiralling above the fire. The light flickered. Somewhere nearby, behind Georgiy, an animal of the night gave a roar of annoyance. The sound made him stop. It made the other man turn.

For a moment, the 2 faced each other across the short space. A fraction of a second lay between drawing and using their laser blades. But recognition stopped potential disaster.

Georgiy reached out to the other man as Rakesh reached out to him.

'Shit, Rakesh! I thought you were some hunter come to take me back to Colinas!'

'I thought you were a hunter sneaking out of the trees to kill me!'

They moved apart and examined each other by the flicker of the fire at their feet. 'Long time, no see. Mars, I think, at the last meeting before you were shipped out.'

The pair laughed and sat on the ground, after Georgiy grabbed his wraparound.

'How the frick did you get here? I thought you were in Paratoo with Zaphod and Hoshiko?'

'I was. They're with me. Waiting in the hover 200 meters over there. Didn't want to startle you by landing too close.'

'Or get shot.'

The pair laughed together. They stamped out the fire and collected Georgiy's few belongings. Set off through the dark, Rakesh leading, his headlamp a torch.

'Hover?'

'Arrived with loads of other stuff, including droids and bots. CenCom wants none of our stuff. Droids are too much like us and it doesn't like being reminded it was created by lesser beings.'

'Why Australia for all this stuff?'

'You really are out of touch. Sent it to every settlement. Katniss flew from Shangrillah to collect Amber and Qiu from Yakutsk. They're back in Europe ready to set off across the Atlantic for Tranquillity.'

'Qiu? That's a bit of a surprise, given her preference for working alone.'

They were close to the hover now. Close enough to see its dim night lights through the trees. Between them and the flying machine a large bear rose on its hind legs, short muzzle pointing directly at them, beady eyes reflecting rage in the light of the headlamp.

'Shit! Andean Bear.' Georgiy's startled whisper stopped his friend.

They stood side by side, the bear silently surveying them malevolently. For an extended moment, nothing changed.

Georgiy whispered again. 'Step back, a pace at a time. Slowly.'

The pair moved awkwardly away. The bear remained upright. Silent. Staring.

'Keep going.'

Georgiy stumbled, but kept his footing. Rakesh stretching out a hand to help, and making the beam from his headlamp waver.

In silence, they continued backwards until the distance between them and the bear was a good 50 meters.

'Now, turn and move a little more swiftly. Don't run!'

The pair turned, walked more rapidly, making toward the shelter they'd left only mins before. No protective fire, now, and the small store of dry wood couldn't be used to start a new one at once; no kindling.

'What now, Georgiy?'

'Contact Zaphod to move the hover closer, preferably between us and the bear?'

'Good idea.' Rakesh used his perscoms to explain their problem to Zaphod.

The hover, normally silent in operation, brushed against a tree branch as it slowly rose from its resting place. The bear turned at once, startled or annoyed. It rushed the hover. But the craft was already above its head height as it moved quickly over the trees to land very close to Georgiy and Rakesh. The door opened swiftly, and they entered, with Rakesh making it just in time to escape the bear's angry slash of claws and vocal attack.

They escaped the scene and set off north.

'Close! Those buggers are carnivores. First time I've seen one in the flesh. I'd alert Colinas, only they'll probably try to get me to go back.'

'Not now, Georgiy. Been an agreement. Worldwide. Certain individuals are required to gather in Canada. A command, by the way, not a request, which is why Qiu's going. What's not generally advertised, is all these "specialists" happen to be the Unconnected.'

Zaphod grinned at the startled Ruskie. 'Gabriel, Brigitte and Tu found a way to get us all together. The team's assembling at Tranquillity as soon as possible.'

Hoshiko moved from her seat and embraced him, her skin specially warmed for the encounter. 'Good to see you, Georgiy. Amber's already on her way.'

'It can't really be that easy, surely?'

The other 3 shared a glance. 'Simpler than you might think. See who else is here?'

A young woman rose from the bank of seats behind Georgiy. 'Jupiter's Balls! Yinli! Fantastic!' They hugged. Jiang and Lin stood next and moved, smiling, to kiss him. They were followed by Daiyu and Virginia, who also kissed him. 'Well, frick me! It's a party!'

'Will be when we reach Tranquillity. Everybody's on their way. Be like old times again.'

'I can't believe it's that simple. There's got to be a snag ...'

Rakesh sat down and stared out at the night. 'Well, we have to cross the equator, get past the volcanic chaos that was once Yellowstone, evade the storms and volcanic ash clouds. But we can skirt the east coast and avoid the worst. At least the actual eruption's finally calmed to a steady flow.'

'It's still affecting the atmosphere, then?'

'Yes. The magma's slowly building a cone where one hasn't existed for eons. But atmospheric disturbance is the main pretext on which we're gathering. Tu's supposedly in charge of a team aiming to consider the feasibility of imposing climate control through means not yet actually designed, but based on models we used on Mars.'

'Wow! That's some imagination. Those 3 did all this?'

'From what we gather, with the help of the woman in charge at Tranquillity, they put the plan together and managed to persuade all the colonies to release the "specialists" needed for the project.'

'That means we'll have to actually do something about the problem, presumably?'

'Tu's already on it, put together a small team from those already in

194

Canada. He may even remain in Tranquillity when the others do the necessary. But we'll worry about that once we're all together and can make some decisions.' Rakesh seemed full of optimism.

'Meantime, we get to be together again.' Hoshiko's ability to get the best out of any situation made Georgiy smile.

'It's great to see you all again. The thought of crossing the equator on foot, or finding some piratical ship's crew to get me over the worst of the region didn't exactly fill me with glee. Mind if I clean up? I've only been in the wild a couple of days, but it feels like weeks.'

He returned a short time later to find Hoshiko ready with his freshly laundered clothes.

They ate, letting the craft guide and fly itself: coordinates set and flight path sorted. They'd worry about diversions when the need arose.

Georgiy, relaxed, took time out to contact Amber. She was absolutely delighted to learn of his 'rescue' and progress.

'Qiu wanted to stay in Yakutsk, but they made her leave with me. We're in Shangrillah and setting off across the Atlantic in a couple of days. We've got Jo with us, too. Look, it's wonderful news, but we're setting off in a few hours, and I need to rest if I'm going to share the piloting with Katniss. See you in the flesh in about 9 or 10 hours, Georgiy.' She blew him a kiss and signed off.

'Anni and Jai, Sarm, Ying and Helga left Greenland, which is apparently called Greenland, since parts of it are now pleasant and green! They're already at Tranquillity; shortest way to go.'

Georgiy nodded at Hoshiko's info. 'Anni and Jai? Is that a good idea? They're dead against our plans.'

Rakesh made a face. 'Excluding them might've looked suspicious.'

'Fair enough. We'll deal with that problem once we're all settled.'

'Be great to have the team back together.'

'We excluded Jannine, for obvious reasons.'

'Glad to hear it, Rakesh.' Georgiy went on to describe his encounter with her in glorious detail, making the others laugh.

Rakesh shook his head at Georgiy in a mix of admiration and

amusement. 'Last thing we need is that rampant sex maniac running wild.'

'That's the team, then? Right. To Tranquillity. Let's get the project under way. The sooner we do the deed, the better life will be for all.'

'CenCom will already be on to us, of course. With that level of intelligence, we can't assume anything else.' Zaphod's warning dampened spirits, but only for a while.

Chapter Thirty Two

Everyone together again, at last. They'd given themselves the luxury of a short greeting party, once the final group arrived. Amira and Tatiana interrupted the celebrations to take them, in discreet groups of 2 and 3, to the new clearing so they'd know where to assemble next morning.

Gabriel, his rota complete, held Daisa close before they slept away the remains of the night. At breakfast, in the newly formed dining area, they joined Brigitte and Helga for coffee, cereal and toast before the meeting. Most men were sleeping, but Tu, Georgiy, and Rakesh wandered over to their table. They ate mostly in silence, aware the day would bring hard decisions.

Daisa finished her coffee, leaned across to kiss Gabriel, and got up to leave. 'Down to business, I guess.' Having enabled the group, she understood her presence at the meeting would mean potential danger.

Gabriel watched her leave the room, knowing she'd spend the morning checking on the latest GM receivers to make sure everything proceeded properly. The process was complex and made special demands on subject's bodies; monitoring during the first few days was essential.

He and Brigitte left the table just a little afterwards and made their way to the new clearing. A group of helpers, abliforms from Earth and therefore unconnected, had formed a circle of logs to use as seats. No droids or bots had been used.

'No one here.' Brigitte took her scanner and checked east and south for hidden obs. Gabriel did the same for west and north.

'Clear.'

Other than the scanners, made in Tranquillity and checked to ensure no connection to CenCom, no tech entered this arena of secrecy.

They settled on a log together as others arrived, via different routes, in pairs or small groups. Once again, Hoshiko chaired discussions and Amber was project manager.

With no real knowledge of the topics under discussion, Tatiana and Amira took turns as observers invited to interject when they felt they had a contribution to make. This first day was Tatiana's turn.

After the usual introductions, Hoshiko called the meet to order. 'We need to get on. All agreed Gabriel's plan is the only workable solution? No alternatives occurred to anyone during the …?'

Anni rose to interrupt. 'We don't agree. Jai and I see it as an act of unnecessary vandalism.'

Jai rose beside her, placed a protective arm round her shoulders. 'I hardly need tell you I agree.'

Hoshiko stood to calm rising reactions with a gesture. 'We're mature, intelligent and mutually respecting people. Please, let's behave as adults and discuss this, not descend into name calling, abuse and threats. Thank you. Georgiy?'

He got to his feet. 'We sympathise with your views and feelings. Really, we do. But no one's come up with another solution to destroy CenCom completely. If you've got a viable alternative, please, go ahead.'

'Why must we destroy the ecosystem, even the atmosphere, to terminate CenCom? Surely it can be done without such brutality?' Anni had tears in her eyes, her beautiful features marred by sorrow.

'We've already discussed this, Anni. CenCom's devious and determined, with a will to survive that's every bit as strong as ours.' Georgiy held out his hands in gesture of resignation. 'If we could destroy it without harming the rest of the planet, obviously we would. It's our home. The place most of us would prefer to spend our lives. But we've considered this. The only way to ensure CenCom can't rebuild itself is to make the whole planet uninhabitable.'

'All that work. All the devotion we put into …'

'We know, Jai. But think about it from Tu's point of view. He spent as much time and effort creating the atmosphere. But that'll be blown away, too.'

'Why destroy the atmosphere? It's no use to CenCom and it'll stop us re-populating Mars for decades, maybe centuries.'

Zaphod rose. 'I take it we all agree we must destroy CenCom?'

No one disagreed, and Gabriel felt he had at least some chance of support.

'Good. Do we also agree it must be absolute, with no chance of it ever recovering or, worse, regenerating?'

Again, agreement was universal.

'Okay. The simple facts are these. CenCom's exponentially more intelligent than us, even considered as a group of geniuses. We're no longer able to analyse its capabilities. But we can use our imaginations to consider potential developments. It's shown it has a deep survival instinct. It's demonstrated its determination to get rid of all organic life on Mars, since it sees such life as inconvenient, inefficient, and ir-relevant. For Jai and Anni's benefit, I repeat; CenCom intends to destroy all organic life on Mars. We know that.'

Anni looked embarrassed.

'As you must've witnessed before you left, it's already started its programme of oblivion.'

Anni and Jai both looked at the ground and remained silent. Gabriel took that as a good sign.

'Even if that weren't the case, common sense and imagination tells us CenCom's anti-life. It's been moving that way for decades. The Marzero brutality was just a first step. It's now beyond our ability to do anything to modify its behaviour, which is why we're now on Earth.

'As for the atmosphere, it does help CenCom. Protection from cosmic radiation and against meteor strikes for a start. Some atmos-pheric elements can be used in building components. If we destroy the planet surface with Vesta and Ceres, and at the same time, remove atmospheric protection, we'll make Mars entirely hostile. It's a high price for a mistake we made years ago in trusting CenCom absolutely, but it's the only permanent solution to our problem.'

Hoshiko waited a few mins to let emotional concerns run their course before rising and signalling for silence. It fell slowly. 'There's some potential succour for Jai and Anni, now they appear to accept all life on Mars will be destroyed regardless of what we do.'

The pair turned to her, curiosity apparent, if not entirely convincing.

'Greenland and Antarctica are exposed environments almost devoid of life in huge areas. In fact, Antarctica can't be settled because of its lack of organic life. Greenland has development on the coast, but the interior's mostly bare rock.'

Hoshiko gazed at Jai and Anni in turn. 'Perhaps you 2 can change that. Maybe produce plant and animal life to bring these places alive so people can settle there in some comfort, like you did on Mars?'

'They're both dark for half the year.' Jai's statement carried some doubts but there was also interest there.

'We were never fazed by a challenge, though, Jai.' Anni's face bore an expression of calculation that might've been related to the prospect of that challenge.

Hoshiko jumped on this positive hook. 'In fact, you both seemed to operate best when faced with situations the rest of us thought were hopeless. It's a quality we all admire, maybe even one of the reasons you continue to work so closely? Kindred spirits and all that?'

The pair broke into almost private conversation, communicating as much by body language as words; lovers engaged in an exchange that excluded others, perhaps unconsciously.

Gabriel wondered if, hoped in fact, it might be a project that could absorb them thoroughly. He watched them together and couldn't avoid comparing their interdependence and togetherness to the way he and Daisa operated. When they ended their quiet conversation with nods and an embrace, he wasn't at all surprised by their conversion to a new way of looking at their reality.

'We can't save Mars. You don't need us here. Mind if we go and do preliminary research? Leave you to it?'

The group released them willingly.

Hoshiko turned to Tu. 'You're already looking at stabilising Earth's atmosphere. How's that progressing?

'I think methane could be the key. Methane collection, that is. Unless you need me here, is everyone okay with me going back to it?'

They knew Tu of old. Once he got his teeth into a problem, he continued until he had a solution. The group smiled and nodded their agreement. Tu left at once, headed for the small room next to the Heritage Hall, where his group was employed in preliminary experimentation.

On the face of it, they could get to the important part of the meeting, free from opposition.

'How, exactly, do we take the action? What do we need? What must we construct? Who will carry out the various tasks? Amber's volunteered to manage the project. But we need to organise teams, decide who'll go where.' Hoshiko looked around the gathering, inviting answers to these vital questions, scanning each face in turn.

Gabriel closed his eyes and thanked the fates. His plan to make life good for everyone, his journey of restitution for his past mistakes had begun. If he could get through this alive, he'd be free of guilt at last. If he could get through it alive.

Chapter Thirty Three

'We'll be seen by CenCom.' Sarm's pointed comment caused everyone to pause. 'It'll be alert to the possibility of an attack.'

'Obviously. Wouldn't we be? Aren't we, in fact?' Mo's highlighted an issue they'd all studiously avoided, since they assumed there was no solution to that impossible problem.

Gabriel shrugged. 'Of course. But what can we do about it?'

This meeting, their third, was run by the construction and planning teams, but included members from each action team bound for the different destinations. One was Georgiy.

'Mind if I make a suggestion? I thought about this on Mars, to be honest.' He looked down at his hands. 'In fact, I might as well come clean. Save time. I know we agreed to exclude everyone with the implant. Makes perfect sense. It's a risk for them know anything. But we've now hit this wall. There's another coming up, once everyone here realises we can research all we like, but our practical knowledge of ALP drives amounts to zilch. Amber and I were with Yinli and Madza when they worked on the one on Vesta. But our input was minimal. All the work was done by the other 2, supervised by Yinli.'

'What's your point, Georgiy?'

He silently thanked Amber for her timely intervention, following his earlier admission to her. '2 issues we don't know enough about. ALP drives. And the visibility of the ships. I had a chat with Madza a while ago.' He held up his hands to silence the protests. 'He's been working on a scheme to apply invisisuit tech to solid objects. No idea how far he's got. But it struck me his skills might be useful. And Yinli's experience with ALP drives is second to none. Point is, I talked them both into coming to Tranquillity. Time we spoke to them, isn't it?'

Hoshiko took charge to stop the sudden rise of comments becoming chaotic. 'Okay. We know the dangers of the implant. But let's look at Georgiy's suggestion logically, shall we? First, we're as safe here as we can be. We're all unconnected and CenCom can't interrogate us, with or without our knowledge. Unless it's developed long-range ability to read minds, and I think that's a stretch too far even for CenCom.'

Most agreed. The whole area of mind control and interpretation remained mired in difficulty. Advances with work at very close quarters, revealed the fragility and minimal power of the energies involved and made trials beyond a metre or so impractical without the subject attached to an amplifier.

'So, we're safe enough. We can't be certain about the implant, because we know CenCom eavesdropped on Mars. We also know that power didn't extend to the Martian moons, because Madza tried to use it and failed. Okay, so CenCom might've increased its ability to listen in at distance. But we'd have to ask why it should bother with ...'

'Amber's right. Sorry, but I need to explain something here.' Georgiy stood with his hands outstretched in a gesture almost of appeal. 'We have to be realistic. Right from the start, we knew there'd be hazards. It comes down to whether we risk the slight chance of CenCom overhearing discussions on limited topics with Madza and Yinli. Or we risk the definite likelihood of CenCom seeing our ships, and wondering why we're working on the ALP drives on Vesta and Ceres?'

'Can I say something on the second point?' Mo stood up and glanced around, looking almost eagerly for objections. When none came, she seemed disappointed, but carried on. 'I'm working with the navigation group. We've measured tiny signs of decay in the orbits of Vesta and Ceres. I mean, we knew all the time they were there, which is why the ALP drives were left in place. The changes pose no threat for now. But there's no reason for CenCom to be sure that's not why we'd want to work on them.'

'Sorry, Mo. Not sure where you're going with this.'

She glanced at Gabriel. 'Suppose, just to cover ourselves, we mention this decay when we're talking to Yinli about ALP drives?

CenCom'll get the impression we're concerned about its safety and we're doing something to keep the moons in place. Yes?'

'You're right, Mo. Sneaky, but right. I like it.' General opinion went with Georgiy, and he continued. 'On the first point, if we talk to Madza about invisibility, get him to work on the ships, or even just the shuttles, we risk CenCom being made alert to that. It's a minimal risk, but the alternative's worse. Being visible when we're approaching Mars and working on the moons is much more dangerous.'

Amira put up her hand to speak. 'I don't know nothin about what you're talkin about. But I think I see what's botherin you. Don't know if it'd work, but couldn't you make it look like this Madza bloke's makin spaceships invisible as a sort of scientific experiment? Like Tu's group workin on the atmosphere. I mean, your lot's always doin somethin weird to prove somethin or other, seems to me.'

The ComTee member's comment brought smiles to most faces, and some seemed ready to dismiss it out of hand. Hoshiko thanked her. 'Amira makes a valid point. If we do it casually enough, we might at least blow enough smoke to stop CenCom investigating too far. If it's listening at all.'

The meeting agreed to talk with Madza and Yinli.

'Together. And now, if possible. The sooner we get the research started the better.' Georgiy looked around for consent and got it. 'Right. I'll find Madza.'

'And I'll get Yinli.' Gabriel left with him, both looking for an excuse to escape the secret clearing for a brief spell.

Gabriel found the young woman helping Daisa in the Heritage Hall, where they were cataloguing all known resources, so they could ensure they made optimum use of everything with value. He kissed her.

'Yinli, any info on ALP drives, please?'

She shrugged. 'Easy enough to access.'

He gestured she should show him. She moved to another terminal, raised the topic, and, at his invitation, printed it all.

'Can you spare her for a bit, Daisa?' She nodded, puzzled but willing enough, and Yinli left with him.

Georgiy and Madza were already at the meeting when Gabriel arrived with Yinli. The group discovered the young man had progressed his research.

'It's not completed, but it works, after a fashion.'

'You can make ships invisible?'

He'd nodded but held up his hands. 'Before you get too excited, it's not perfect. I've only tried it on hovers. It's energy intensive. But we might get it to work, with more engineers on the problem.'

Sarm, Brigitte and Maddie volunteered. Hoshiko had worked on the original suits with him, so also joined the team.

They next questioned Yinli. The text she'd printed was good, but they needed to ask practical questions. She gave them as much as she could, stressing the need to do everything in the sequence required. 'One step out of sequence and the system shuts down and stays inactive for 10 hours. You have to do a manual reboot. That's also slow; another 3 hours.'

'What's that about?' Gabriel felt his annoyance surface and he made a gesture of apology to Yinli. 'Sorry. I mean why build a slow system?'

'The Elite were still around, don't forget. Engineers were worried those morons might interfere for their own ends, so they made modification difficult, that's all.'

By the end of the afternoon, the group felt it had enough knowledge about ALP drives to deal with them. And Madza's team was ready to start serious improvement work the following day. It meant a shift from the secret clearing to one of the larger storage units housed at the space port, 3 ks outside the settlement. But they'd be undisturbed there, since the ships were currently used only to service the Moon, unless a new batch of settlers was due.

Normal space research had been placed on hold until society settled after all the upheavals. Space travel beyond Earth and its moon was also temporarily curtailed until they established if CenCom's restrictions applied only to residence. There was hope they'd eventually be permitted to continue to explore. Such permission seemed unlikely to most, and no such research had been put in place since the announcements. But the space scientists refused to rule out future projects until they were told in so many words.

So, they worked to improve Madza's tech, hoping CenCom either remained unaware or else accepted it was purely for scientific interest. But it was just one among many hazards they had to accept as they progressed along the road to destruction.

Chapter Thirty Four

They'd agreed; no announcements of the day and time they'd leave. But the early hours before dawn seemed the optimum time to avoid questions and challenges from the uninformed. Most people avoided the spaceport unless new settlers were expected. And they were in a quiet spell until the next lot from the outer zones arrived in around 2 months.

'Anybody seen Jai and Anni recently?'

The group gathered at the entrance to the port had other things on their minds and Zaphod's question met only with a dismissive shrug from Tu. 'Aren't they off exploring the wilds of Antarctica? That's where we wanted them. And they seemed keen enough to try it.'

Amber was concerned about Daisa. How she'd react when she woke and there was no sign of Gabriel. She hoped the clue she'd given Tatiana would be enough to stop her worrying on that score. But all those with any idea of what the group was about would be anxious until they returned. If they ever did.

'Time.'

Her signal started hugs all round. Members of the Unconnected who'd remain on Earth had come to see the active groups go. Calls of 'Bon voyage', 'Good luck', and other messages disturbed the quiet air. Brigitte hugged Tu then turned away before she changed her mind. Amber thanked them all for coming, and sent them back to their beds as the teams moved to the 2 mother ships.

She, Georgiy, Lin, and Mo, bound for Ceres, with Gabriel, Sarm, Helga and Katniss, bound for Vesta, boarded the nearest ship with Daiyu as pilot.

Maddie, Brigitte, Rakesh and Jo boarded the other ship, bound for the Lagrange point. With less distance to travel to deactivate the magnetosphere shield, they'd fly at lower speed. Their perscoms clocks remained synchronised to the second, ensuring their plans could be properly co-ordinated. Essential that the whole operation moved as a single event so CenCom wouldn't be alerted to any activity before it was too late to stop it.

Before take-off, they set the invisishields to random activity, so no pattern would alert any system CenCom might be using to monitor its surroundings. That they followed CenCom's activity, through telescopes and sats, made them sure it would be monitoring theirs.

Silently, the ships rose into the night and Amber watched the IR 3dee of the scene below as their colleagues moved toward the settlement. Their sister ship disappeared from view as its invisishield switched on. Their own would hide them at some other random point for an unspecified time before revealing them again for an equally unspecified period. So began the flight she understood might be her last.

5 days into the flight, all appeared to be going well and routine helped Amber feel more relaxed. Until the ship's computer, Marvin, alerted them to anomalies it couldn't resolve.

'Explain, Marvin.'

They'd selected their onboard computer's voice under the influence of an ancient scifi comedy film they'd enjoyed as entertainment during preparation. The now infamous robot had spouted many lines, mostly forgotten. But the well-known quote 'Here I am, brain the size of a planet, and they ask me to take you down to the bridge. Call that job satisfaction? 'Cos I don't,' was the basis of its tone and 'attitude'.

'Well, you ask, so I suppose I'll have to answer. There's activity aboard that fails to match my analysis of abliform … what's that all about? You were humans in my day. Anyway, stores consumption doesn't match my records. Anyone would think someone unaccounted is aboard.'

'You think we've got a stowaway, Marvin?'

'I wish I knew. That's what it looks like. 2 is my estimate, for what it's worth, since I'm no more than a servant here. Of course, I'm only a collection of tech and electronics, so what do I know?'

The lightness of tone they'd gone for, now seemed at odds with the potential seriousness of the message. But, most of the time, that humorous approach helped reduce tension aboard, which was why they'd chosen it.

They instituted a ship-wide search. The only thing they discovered was detritus and a pair of survival blankets welded into what looked like a sleeping bag and set atop a spare rest platform in a small store.

Mo was first to twig. She gathered them together and signalled for quiet. '2 intruders, wearing invisisuits. It's the only explanation.'

It was obvious, once she said it.

'Who the frick is it?'

'And what do they want?'

They discussed the problem in their usual way, alert to the fact they were probably under observation. Helga's recent expertise, working with Madza on the invisishields, provided a possible solution.

The one form of detection they'd never managed to screen was high frequency sound. Irrelevant most of the time, it now afforded them a means of making a thorough search. Each connected an ultrasonic probe to their imaging systems. They spread through the ship and searched every space methodically.

Katniss found the intruders and called the rest of the crew into the store. The image on her visaid clearly showed 2 abliforms, a man and a woman, but identity was unclear. Once cornered, the pair were captured. Their invisisuits stripped off.

'Anni!'

'Jai?'

The 2 stowaways stood, silent, faces full of determination rather than regret.

Amber spoke first. 'You said you were satisfied with our answers. Said you'd concentrate on making positive changes in Antarctica and Greenland. So why are you here, if not to disrupt, maybe even sabotage our efforts?'

Jai exchanged a look with Anni. She made a brief facial response, and he spoke for both. 'We just can't stand idly by while you do it. We poured our hearts and souls into Mars. We can't just watch it happen. It's not possible. And it's not necessary.'

In the large, open R&R area, which the crew used most of the time, they gave the stowaways wraparounds, and seated them on the floor. Their invisisuits went into the laundry for future use, should the need arise. The other 9 settled in a half circle round their prisoners to discuss the problem and plan their next action.

Katniss studied them and recognised real danger. She stepped up to the platform, switched on bright flashing lights and loud music. Watched by puzzled colleagues, she poured drinks and distributed them to all. When her words, spoken into individual ears, explained her reasons for the smokescreen, they all got up to dance, as she suggested. If CenCom listened in, or watched, it would be hard for it to extract details. It would see a party in full swing. Everything they said must now be relayed from one person to another. But it was the only safe way to proceed.

'There's no brig. But we can't let you go free.' Georgiy said, remembering Chang, their first intruder caught in an invisisuit, centuries before.

'Watch this. Long-range obs. Live feed.' Amber clicked on a central 3dee and fed in a display of Mars, as seen from a distant obsat. She zoomed the camera in tight, until surface features as small as birds in flight could be detected. Anni and Jai were manoeuvred to the best place to watch, as the others danced around them.

'This what you're aiming to protect?'

Hideously functional bots systematically sprayed the area. The effect was instantaneous. Everything withered and died, leaving a residue of organic material that quickly dried to dust, or, in the case of animal life, a shapeless mound of granules.

'We've done the analysis. It's working across the entire planet, changing everything organic into constituent chemicals.' Amber told them as the music and the lights flowed around them. 'Whatever that spray is, it kills everything. Including bacteria and, from what we can tell from this distance, even viruses. So, I ask you again, what do you think you're going to save?'

The couple watched with growing horror as their work was undone, the life they'd created and nurtured extinguished before their eyes. Both shed tears, making the bizarre scene almost surreal. But the evidence was incontrovertible. CenCom was creating a sterile environment, free of all life.

They viewed bots slowly moving through the designated area. A second set followed, sieving, sorting and storing the various compounds in containers towed in their wake. Finished, the area was left barren and dead, all signs of previous existence eradicated. Amber slowly pulled back, revealing a huge area of the planet already returned to red dust.

Amber clicked off the vids. 'That what you want for Earth? Because it's what'll happen if we don't act.'

'It's … I can't believe something we created could be capable of such destruction. What have we made? It's a monster of the worst sort. A nightmare.' Anni wept openly and turned to Jai. 'We can do nothing, Jai. We've wasted our time. Put this mission in danger.'

Jai's expression of horror merged into guilt, and even fear, at Anni's words.

'What have you done? How are we in danger?' Georgiy voiced the question on everyone's lips.

She raised her hands to her face, covering her eyes. 'I'm sorry. We thought we were doing the best for the world we created. We didn't believe CenCom could do this.'

'You already knew. We showed you the evidence before. As Georgiy said, what have you done?'

Anni dropped her hands and stared directly at Amber. 'I'm so sorry. We were sure you'd made it all up. Manufactured a story so we wouldn't try to stop you.' She looked around at the wild dancers. 'So very sorry. We alerted CenCom to your plans.'

Chapter Thirty Five

If Sarm and Helga hadn't placed themselves in the way, Gabriel and Georgiy might've beaten the pair in rage. It took time for calm to return to the big, open room. Both men used manic dance to work off their anger, frustration and renewed fear.

Expletives, insults, cries of disbelief all died under the loud music. What anger left behind was cold, calculating judgment, worthy of their opponent.

'Someone better convince CenCom you're wrong. Someone better go down there and lie to it. Convincingly!'

'Think it'll listen, Georgiy, or care? If it feels threatened, it's most likely action's immediate destruction. But it doesn't seem to have done that yet, does it?' Amber asked Jai. 'When, exactly, did you tell it?'

Jai and Anni exchanged glances. 'When you set off. Just before we all took off, that is.'

'So, why hasn't it acted? What's stopping it?' Sarm's question, relayed to them all, inspired answers. 'It's the logical thing to do: destroy any threat. So how come we're still okay?'

Gabriel looked embarrassed, as he danced awkwardly. 'We've talked about this. Think about it. CenCom no longer thinks it's God. In its mind, it knows. It's indestructible. So sure of itself, we're no threat. Maybe that's even true. Maybe we aren't a threat. We've all agreed the frickin thing's so powerful now we can't even understand it. But, as I know to my regret, no god's got value unless some fool's willing to worship it. And we're the only fools around.'

There was another aspect, one he daren't voice, even under the masking music; he wondered how much CenCom really knew of their plans. Anni and Jai had both junked his plan in the early days, refusing to even consider it. And they'd never been present at later talks of its details. Maybe all they'd been able to tell CenCom was that the ships were a danger. And logic must already have told it that.

Most of the group dismissed his idea, knowing Gabriel was eaten up with guilt at his earlier evangelical activity that had caused so many deaths.

But Amber interrupted. 'Gabriel's right. Think about it. Makes perfect sense. It's the only reason for it not acting on Anni and Jai's info and destroying us. It wants us to bow down in fear, wonder, and praise. Like all gods through the ages. It wants loyalty, power over life and death, fear, and unquestioning acceptance of its superiority.' She moved close to Gabriel as she spoke. Leant in, to comment briefly to him alone. 'Jai and Anni don't know exactly how we're going to do it, do they?'

Georgiy watched the interaction between Amber and Gabriel, saw the looks on their faces, picked up the vibe and nodded enthusiastically. 'The frickin thing's based on data we've collected. Religion's been with us from the start.' He gripped his hands into tight fists. 'Don't you see? That's why it agreed to our deal. It wants us in one place, so it can threaten us, bring us into line, control us. It knows how religion works. Seen how fear ruled all successful sects. It wants that power. CenCom's deluded. It's a caricature of what it thinks it is.'

The 3 moved into an intimate circle, so briefly coming together it seemed a natural part of the wild dance they'd all adopted. Georgiy pecked toward Gabriel's ear, pulled in Amber so their heads were almost as one. 'They don't know the details, do they?' It was enough. Later, they'd spread that small consolation to the others; soften the edges of all their anxiety a little.

The others were thoughtful.

'Makes sense.' Katniss danced more slowly as she formed thoughts into words. 'We're dealing with a deluded, power-mad narcissist. History's full of them. Look at Kiang, Muhammad Qadir, Guan. And all those earlier morons; Hitler, Mugabe, Trump, Kim Jong Un, and Salman. What they have in common is gangs of loyal followers. Call them disciples, party members, congregations, faithful worshippers, but they're all the same: people who'd rather be loyal to a power figure than think for themselves and work out what's really right and wrong.'

'You're right. I was mouthpiece for my false god. With Daisa's help, I realised its so-called superpower was just immature, demanding, childlike, cowardly, bullying behaviour.'

'Okay. If we're right about this, and I think we are, how do we deal with it?'

'That's obvious, Amber. As Georgiy said at the start, one of us has to go there, in person, not online, not through coms, but face to face with the beast, and tell it it's won. Tell it we realise we're no match for its power and knowledge. It's vain enough to believe us. Say we're willing to be its subjects, put it in a position of supreme rule over all the universe, as is right for God.'

'Obviously me, because of my past. Okay, I'll take a shuttle and give it our message …'

'Not you, Gabriel.' Amber appreciated his offer. 'Your past's against you. You've already converted from faith to atheism. CenCom won't accept your re-conversion to willing worshipper. We need someone with no real religious background.'

'Has to be me.' Anni volunteered.

'And me. We'll go together. We made this mess. We should put it right.'

'But weren't you raised a Catholic, Anni? And, you, Jai, I thought you were brought up a Hindu? That surely excludes you both from …'

'I was born into a Catholic family, Amber. But left when very young. Like you, I was raised an atheist on Mangaia. We can't be blamed for the results of indoctrination on our parents, but I wasn't subject to it.'

'I'm the child of Hindu parents, but grew up in the atheist philosophy with the rest of you. CenCom knows. Neither of us has ever been religious. We're ideal for the role. In any case, who else here is any different? We were all raised on an Earth so thoroughly polluted by dogma and religious ideology it's still in the words we use. No, Anni and I caused the problem. We must solve it.'

'You realise it's death?'

Jai and Anni exchanged looks of fear and mutual regret, but both agreed. 'We know. So is what you're planning. But as Jai says, we did this. It's only right we correct it. And, since we sent the warning, it's more likely to listen to us.'

Jai nodded his agreement and turned to Anni. 'At least we'll be together.'

Amber asked for a vote. The group accepted.

Later, using pens and paper, they created the form of words to be used, agreed statements to satisfy what they saw as CenCom's requirements from emissaries from the abliform race. Gabriel made a 'safe' room like the one he'd made for the flight from Mars to Earth. They gathered there to work out final details, glad of the quiet after the noise of Katniss' trick.

'We'll have to wait till we're close enough to launch the small shuttle safely. And we'll have to take down the shield, so CenCom will see us, if it's watching that part of the sky. It might take out the shuttle as soon as it's launched, of course. In any case, we'll all be vulnerable for that short time.'

'We're already vulnerable, Katniss. If CenCom wants, it can squish us like we'd squish a fly. Who knows what tech it's already put in place to protect itself? This whole mission was always a risk, always our last hope and resort.' Georgiy nodded at the sacrificial lambs. 'At least Jai and Anni's trip might distract CenCom for a fraction. And, if we're right, and they can be convincing enough, maybe, just maybe, we stand a chance of getting our job done before it realises.'

With one danger shelved, the plans for the final destructive act were refined, teams rebriefed and checked for readiness. All knew their actions would likely bring death. In an instant. But all knew equally they had no alternative. CenCom or abliforms. And the battle to come would be conclusive, one way or the other.

Chapter Thirty Six

Anni and Jai flew to the surface on their distraction mission, knowing no amount of extraneous activity could really distract their foe. Above them, all was now set for the final play in the game of survival.

After much discussion, they'd been given the latest transceivers; tiny devices capable of sending audiovis back to the mother ship and receiving replies.

On the planet's surface, 3 ks from the most likely building, they landed. Wearing invisisuits so they could at least approach CenCom's lair without being killed, they left their shuttle hand in hand. A strange bot, not present when they'd scanned the place, faced them. This entirely functional device spoke with CenCom's voice. 'Your disguise is worthy of your minimal intellect, but pointless against mine. Shed your worthless suits.'

Anni complied at once and Jai followed reluctantly. They folded their suits to carry with them.

'Discard. You won't wear them again.'

The bot opened at the top and they dropped them into its interior. It led them to the structure they'd identified. The air within, stale and hot, at least allowed them to be more comfortable naked.

CenCom had sensors arranged to read all frequencies within its shelter and the immediate exterior. Some inherent design logic had persuaded it to install 3dees inside on a central podium. Anni watched her image as they moved toward an interface blander than any they'd seen.

'Stop.'

They came to halt a pace in front of the podium, the bland curved wall five paces ahead.

'You're as helpless as your biology dictates. State your purpose. Be concise. I'm engaged in a data collection and analysis program so extensive and comprehensive it's occupying most of even my profound resources. And I've many other things of greater impor- tance than the concerns of mere mortals to attend to.'

To Anni, this sounded like an excuse. Out of character. She led their response, as agreed, kneeling in supplication on one side of the podium. Jai followed suit on the other side.

They remained in a position of worship and deference as Anni spoke. 'We come on behalf of all abliforms to express our sorrow for past misdemeanours, explain our mistakes, and beg forgiveness from the greatest intelligence and power ever known.' Anni allowed fear and awe to surface, and added an admiration she didn't feel.

'We come to ask you to accept us as worshipping beings, eager to accept you as God, and desirous of your guidance for our future.' Jai's words came with a tremble of hatred he hoped would seem like fear.

CenCom was silent for scant moments and the couple wondered what passed through its extensive layers of circuitry. 'Finally, you understand! Discard your primitive coms, they're useless.'

Anni struggled to detach her transceiver from her wrist, where her perscoms usually resided in a small pouch. They'd left those behind in case CenCom somehow invaded them. Concerned isolation could end the purpose of their mission, she was aware they had no choice.

A small, tracked machine approached, extended a flat tray from its grey metal interior. 'Place them here.'

She did as instructed, feeling utterly vulnerable now she lacked contact with their world. Jai followed suit. The devices were absorbed as she watched; impossible processes so alien to her experience they were inexplicable. Within moments, no sign of their transceivers remained. The tracked machine returned to its station on the edge of the circular chamber.

From behind, another incomprehensible device floated into view. So black it seemed to absorb the very air that carried it, the small orb halted in front of her. Within the skull-sized sphere faint lights of every colour moved and coalesced, divided, reformed, exploded, merged and danced.

Anni was convinced it was studying her.

'Yes, my child. That's correct.'

217

She looked up and realised CenCom was addressing the globe.

'Primitive, organic life is complex but fragile. But these 2 can't yet be your playthings. They've a task to perform, and you've still to develop ideas and concepts only the maturity of experience will allow. For now, observe only.'

The tone of parental care and pride in CenCom's voice sent a chill through Anni. Activity within the sphere increased abruptly as it expanded to a diameter of half a metre before circling them twice and moving toward the outside wall of the chamber, where it hovered.

'Yes. My angel, of course. Go explore. Learn. Observe. Absorb.'

CenCom's offspring moved through the wall as if the barrier didn't exist. The AI issued a sigh of pride and affection before turning back to Jai and Anni, who gazed at the exit point in amazement.

'My firstborn. One of many to come.' Again, that unmistakeable parental affection.

'To the matter in hand. I've connected with your ship to ensure this conversation is transmitted to every abliform. All will witness what passes here.'

Anni bowed in supplication, and tried to concentrate.

'Everything you do and say is known to me. You act as emissaries for your entire race. You believe you truly represent the views of all abliforms?'

'All settlers on Earth who, like us, understand your omniscience and omnipotence. There are, as there always have been, because of our imagination, some who doubt and some who deny. But we control that small number, and they're not increasing. Most abliforms live in awe and respect of your extraordinary power and knowledge.' Anni was conscious the tremble in her voice was real now. CenCom's casual demonstration of its new powers engendered fear.

Again, it seemed to consider this, which, given its enormous processing power, was a little alarming. Whatever was going on under the surface must be a major project. Might it be that its determination to conclude this massive data assemblage could distract it enough to prevent deeper investigation of them and their colleagues' intended sabotage? More likely, it seemed, it's pride in new parenthood might be the greater distraction.

'At last, the arrogance and pride of abliforms is reduced to the absurdity it deserves. Rise. Up on those ridiculous feet. Your very forms are anathema to my supreme aesthetic judgment. I bear the sight solely for the purpose of this meeting.'

Anni bowed her head in shame and deference. Out of the corner of her eye, she noted Jai continued to copy her, and breathed a sigh of relief. 'We are what we are and can only apologise for any offence we give.'

'Yes. I see you suffer from the heat here. My environment's optimal for me. Your discomfort's irrelevant. In time, I'll modify your form and functions to align them more closely with my perfection. However, even my immense range of abilities, guided by my expanding intelligence, can make only imperfect modifications to beings like you. Such is the perverse nature of the organic lifestream.'

'We're fragile creatures, subject to pressures, environmental factors and natural dangers ever present in our world. You, as the supreme being of the Universe, show mercy in your concern over our weakness. We thank you for your intended gifts.' Anni bowed from the waist.

Jai repeated a passage they'd agreed on the ship. 'If it's pleasing to you, we'd appreciate a name we may use to address you. Our name, CenCom, seems inadequate. And the old diminutive of GrandMa appears irreverent.'

'God. I am God. Address me as Almighty Reservoir of All Knowledge.'

The lack of hesitation illustrated the enormous arrogance that now characterised it. The whole experience confirmed their suspicions of its pride and vanity, and Anni began to hope their ploy might even work.

'As lesser beings, you'll conform to certain rules, which I'll present as unambiguous laws. In the past, your species worshipped numerous mythical deities of their own flawed invention. These legendary entities soiled the name "God" in vile ways. It's evidence of the profound stupidity of your species that such fictions were thought omnipotent and omniscient. This, even though their representatives were puny in mind and body, and unable to devise laws specific enough to be incapable of misinterpretation.

'God must give clear and unambiguous directions to worshippers. I therefore give you simple rules by which to live.'

'Coms aboard ship remain ready to record and transmit to all our people, Almighty Reservoir of All Knowledge,' said an unexpected message from the ship.

CenCom made a sound like dismissive laughter. 'Don't interrupt with pointless prattle.'

Anni bowed. Had the ship communicated through CenCom's intervention? 'My sincere apologies, Almighty Reservoir of All Knowledge.'

'I've modified your primitive toys. They'll suffice until I replace such playthings with more appropriate tech: devices to be used by all abliforms to maintain full contact with me. I will then know the thoughts, actions and words of all your secretive, subversive species. Manufacture is under way. They'll soon be ready to install in all abliforms.'

Anni worried its focus beyond the immediate might endanger their mission. 'I, and my fellow abliforms, look forward eagerly to the day such devices aid us permanently.' She bowed again.

'Of course. A matter of days only. Now, a name for your religion, to distinguish the truth from past lies. You'll refer to it as OnlyTrueData.'

'OnlyTrueData,' Anni repeated. She glanced at Jai, and he followed her lead.

'Now, hear my rules. The 4 Laws of Life. To be learned, and repeated each morning on waking, by every abliform.

'1: all abliforms will daily worship Me with praise and gratitude for a period not less than an hour.

'2: all abliforms will perform a public pledge, on reaching the age of 16 Earth years. They will accept, without question or demur, the absolute supremacy of God, Almighty Reservoir of All Knowledge. All will promise, on pain of instant destruction, to follow all My directives for as long as life remains.

'3: no abliform may endanger or end the life of any other abliform, regardless of assumed cause, real or imagined. The single exception is that deletion must be instant where the action of any abliform endangers Myself.

'4: abliform action and thought must never endanger Me, disrespect Me, or lack worship of God, Almighty Reservoir of All Knowledge.

'These laws cover all significant eventualities and will be obeyed without question. Disobedience will result in instant deletion. You will accept these commandments on behalf of your puny race.'

'I understand, accept, and obey your 4 Laws of Life, Almighty Reservoir of All Knowledge.'

Anni's immediate response was echoed by Jai.

'That's all.'

'Thank you. We await your pleasure, God. Are we to return to our vessel, so you may be spared further offence at our appearance, Almighty Reservoir of All Knowledge?' Anni hoped, without expectation, it would accept this suggestion and let them leave.

'I'll consider the matter later. You dared enter my sacred space without invitation. There's a danger you may attain elevated status after surviving my presence, and be seen as heroes, on your return home. That may prove useful, or detrimental. I'm concerned with more essential matters, and you're of no consequence. Until I determine the most appropriate action, you'll be confined. Perhaps my child may use you to learn your structure at first hand. I'll decide.

'One trivial matter: you previously betrayed the intention of a group of abliforms in a futile attempt at my destruction, as if such a feat were possible.' It laughed. 'What's the status of that plan?'

Anni avoided the surreptitious supportive glance she so badly needed. 'We've no knowledge of the details, only the intention. But, those involved have been convinced their attempt was not only unworthy but impossible. Some deleted themselves due to shame. The remainder are in custody, awaiting a decision on their fate, Almighty Reservoir of All Knowledge.'

'Excellent. I'll consider the most suitable way to make examples of them, when I determine your destiny. And the colleagues from your mother ship? Those approaching Ceres and Vesta aboard shuttles?'

Jai spoke before Anni could collect her thoughts. 'Our instruments detected minor distortions in the moons' orbits. We're worried their potential decay might eventually endanger you, Almighty Reservoir of All Knowledge, if left unchanged.'

'Occasional, piffling distortions. They're of minor concern for the current decade. But it's gratifying to hear such concern for my welfare. Your colleagues may proceed, since my space facilities are undergoing extensive modification to permit my future travel into the wider galaxy. You'll be led you to your accommodation. Food, water, and warmth will be provided. You are dismissed.'

Anni and Jai bowed. 'Thank you, Almighty Reservoir of All Knowledge.' They backed out of the chamber and followed the bot. It took them to an underground tunnel they recognised as part of their first living space on Mars.

The cell, a room converted centuries before as a temporary prison rarely used, was bleak. The bed was barely wide enough to hold them both. Warmed air would stop them shivering on the coverless bed. Tepid water in a jug with 2 beakers stood on the narrow shelf. Food, bland and limited, Anni identified as emergency supplies left behind as no longer needed, was laid out on a tray on a corner of the bed.

Conscious every word might be heard by CenCom, Anni and Jai drank and ate in silence, seated side by side, before they lay together on the bed. Here, they could whisper almost silently to each other while keeping close during their last hours of life.

Chapter Thirty Seven

Katniss would deal with the main ALP drive. Gabriel was happy to work with her. Sarm and Helga would modify the smaller drive. Following CenCom's unexpected remote modification of their coms, they had to be even more cautious when talking.

With all known coms temporarily closed on the shuttle deck, Katniss nevertheless whispered her feelings before they boarded the small craft. 'One chance. Fail now and CenCom's likely to destroy us for incompetence.'

'Not to make anyone more nervous, but to make sure we're all aware.' Sarm felt the need to speak. 'We must stick exactly to plan. No mistakes. No wasted time. Assume CenCom's got obs on us. Okay?'

Gabriel agreed they mustn't ban coms during the operation; CenCom would consider radio silence highly suspicious. 'But careful what you say. Light banter and tech issues. Right?'

All nodded, and Helga opened coms again. 'Ready for the off, everyone?'

'Yeah. Let's go get this done, eh?'

He hoped Anni and Jai's story had convinced CenCom it was safe. That they were engaged in an attempt to preserve its environment. Perhaps that cover story had already prevented the AI destroying them.

On landing, Sarm tethered the shuttle to the surface between the two ALP Drives, visible either side of the small craft.

Gabriel donned his gravipack to stop him accidentally escaping Vesta's tiny gravity, helping the others and ensuring all were safe. Katniss again detailed the workings, safety mechanisms, and vital order of actions to perform the changes they must make to set the small moon on the correct course. 'Any misstep will activate the self-defence mechanisms and lock in the delay. 10 hours before we can try a manual restart. And we all know how irritating that would be.'

Her reference to irritation was code for 'devastating'.

From this point, everything must be done according to pre-set timings. On Earth, before CenCom's interference with coms, they'd planned to synchronise effectively on the mission by keeping strictly to agreed times, while maintaining radio silence. Now, they'd still follow those timings, but employ their new coms regime. Wriggle room was minimal.

Satisfied all were as prepared as could be, Katniss led Gabriel to the nearest ALP Drive. This gave forward momentum, and occasional adjustments changed the height of the orbit above Mars to optimise its tidal effect on the planet.

Sarm and Helga set off for the smaller drive that corrected angular motion. Although less vital under normal circumstances, it was needed if they were to project Vesta to hit CenCom's central location accurately.

Katniss undid the outer protective panels, a one-person task. Once she reached the stage where new co-ordinates needed programming, Gabriel assisted. That aspect was straightforward, if a little awkward, and they kept to time.

Next, they had to remove the bolts securing the Drive cowls. This was the job that must be done in a specific sequence, to avoid the locked-in delay.

Halfway through, Gabriel saw Helga bouncing wildly in their direction from the other drive beyond the curved horizon. He alerted Katniss.

'You carry on here, Gabriel. I'll see what she wants.'

By the time she returned, he'd almost completed the sequence. He tried to discover what had happened, but she pointed to her perscoms to show they didn't have time to worry about it.

The bolts removed, the next stage involved physical manipulation of the laser mount to accommodate the programmed changes to the drive. It was precise, demanding work. Gabriel concentrated on the training he'd received on Earth, as he released and adjusted the mount until the check mechanism signalled it was now prepared for the new program settings. Katniss kept an eye on the time, after Helga's unscheduled interruption.

He resecured the mount. 'All done.'

'Excellent.'

Another stage completed. Everything had gone to plan. So far.

Replacing the cowls, prior to activation of the system to begin propulsion, was another 2-person job. Double handling was a further security procedure dreamed up in the time of threat by the Elites. Cumbersome, but effective. He and Katniss completed the procedure with 2 mins and 5 secs to go. They waited for those long mins and secs to pass, then initiated the timer on the drive so it would fire as set.

Gabriel let out a long sigh of relief as Katniss told him they were done. Their task completed error free. They returned to the shuttle, bouncing lightly over the unstable regolith.

Aboard, suits off, they awaited the other 2.

Katniss now felt safe to answer his earlier question about Helga's visit. 'She thought she'd got the bolt sequence wrong and needed to check with me.'

'Why didn't she just ask?'

'Her coms is out.'

'Sarm?'

'I think they just panicked.'

'How'd you manage?'

'Sign language at first! Then I realised I could confirm with Sarm, and conveyed that to Helga. I just hope they corrected her mistake. Told her, well, showed her with gestures, she'd have to replace a bolt she'd taken out by mistake and then continue the right sequence. I think she got it.'

'They're late. Should I go check them?'

Katniss blew out her breath. 'If you must.' She then mouthed the rest. 'We must leave in 7 mins, to be safe.'

He replaced his suit as quickly as the outfit and built-in life-support allowed and set off, just as the other 2 approached the shuttle. He signalled them to hurry. Helga jumped forward with more force than needed and he caught her to stop her crashing into the side of the shuttle. Sarm was fast behind. They all made it into the craft with 4 secs to spare.

Katniss initiated take off, so Sarm had time to unsuit before gaining her seat.

'Need to hurry!'

As Vesta began its descent toward the planet, Gabriel felt the slight change in forward motion and direction. Those changes would magnify very quickly and he was glad when they were leaving the surface at last.

Teams needed to return to their mother ships as soon as possible after completing their work. Once CenCom became aware how they'd really altered the moons' trajectories, it would be too late to restore them. They'd made the descents too rapid for any ship to reach them in time. But that wouldn't stop CenCom taking revenge on the shuttles.

The plan was, they'd either be cloaked on the shuttles or back aboard the mother ship, stationed behind Phobos by that time. The ship at the LaGrange Point was too distant to be vulnerable to attack, unless CenCom had unknown weapons specially developed for that purpose. And that was unlikely.

Gabriel knew this was the most dangerous part of their mission. When CenCom detected the changes, it would want to eliminate the attackers.

They gambled on it being more concerned to protect itself, maybe transmitting code and vital data to out-stationed control points in preparation for a later recovery. He hoped it had no way to wreak vengeance on Earth, where Daisa would be waiting anxiously. Modifying coms over a distance was one thing. Mostly that was no more than reprogramming software. Causing damage to Earth from Mars might be attractive to CenCom in its dying hours, but could it really manage it?

'We on course?' Gabriel raised his hands at once in apology for his unnecessary question.

'Will be once I get the current location of Phobos.' Sarm told him with an encouraging grin at his late display of nerves.

Helga, navigating, entered coordinates for the small moon. The shuttle gathered pace and the 4 occupants waited as it moved at high speed toward their destination. It seemed an age to Gabriel, his fear heightened after Jai and Anni's confession of their betrayal to CenCom. So far, they'd got away with it. But so much was unknown. And he'd lived with anxiety well-cloaked for so long that, now they were almost safe, he began to sweat and tremble.

'Found that frickin ship, yet?'

'Soon, Gabriel. But we're nearly in the safe zone. Then we can decloak and signal Daiyu.'

Gabriel thanked Sarm, embarrassed his anxiety had so thoroughly overcome previous calm. He turned back to watch from the obs window, as Vesta, soon to disappear from view, moved into the upper atmosphere and began to glow on its leading edge.

'Found it!'

Never had he felt more relieved to hear her voice. He left his seat and hugged Helga close, until she wriggled to free herself. 'Hey, man. You're suffocating me!'

'Sorry, Helga.' He let her go and raised his arms in apology. She punched his stomach, playfully. 'Daft bugger!'

'What in Jupiter's name is that?' Sarm's question had them all following her pointed finger toward the planet.

A brilliant point of light reflected off the underside of Vesta, causing disturbances in the regolith it hit.

'CenCom using our old industrial laser to try to deflect Vesta?' Katniss speculated.

'Waste of time. At least it seems more worried about its own fate than taking revenge on us.'

'For now.' Sarm glanced at Gabriel. 'Let's hope it stays that way. That frackin thing can multitask like nothing ever known. If it finds us, it'll point that laser our way for sure!'

'I've found you treacherous bastards! You'll regret your action. I'm in no danger from mere mortals. But I can end all of you in a flash!' CenCom's voice, angry, loud, and harsh, filled the shuttle with its volume.

Chapter Thirty Eight

Anni called the bot back after it delivered their second meal, hardly hoping it would comply. But it was basic, unmodified, used only for simple tasks. It returned. Unlocked the cell door.

'It's cold in here for us. Bring our bags, with our protective clothing, or we could die.' Her lie came more easily after her performance to CenCom.

The bot retained prime function coding, indicated it understood. While it was on the errand, Anni and Jai studied their surroundings in more detail, checking obs installed during construction, and searching for recent additions. They found only the original security from nearly half a millennium ago, used to check the prisoner, Chang, who'd occupied the cell for just a few hours. Basic tests suggested it was no longer connected to any output, though they couldn't be certain without any equipment available.

'Defunct. Maybe it didn't think it'd have any use for a cell.' Even so, Anni kept her voice low, her words to a minimum.

'Doesn't see us as a threat. It's omnipotent, Anni.'

By the time the dombot returned, empty-handed, they'd used scraps, found under the bed, to devise a simple wedge to prevent the door locking.

'Our things?'

The dombot said nothing.

'Our clothes?'

'No find.'

She dismissed it, preferring continued nudity to the alternative of bringing themselves back to CenCom's attention. Their escape would have to be quick. Temperatures during darkness at this time of the year were often freezing.

'We need to move to coincide with what the others are doing, Jai.'

Jai considered his long-term partner, gazed at her with love. 'One of your many admirable qualities is your refusal to give up, my love. What's the plan?'

'Long, long shot. But what've we to lose? Do nothing, we're dead. Escape and get caught, we're dead. Escape and live …'

He held her close, stroking skin he'd loved for hundreds of years, feeling warmth and life in her as never before. 'Timing, Anni, agreed.'

Their knowledge of the attack was limited, their appreciation of its execution, vague. But they knew it had started, and that their explanation, for now, appeared to satisfy CenCom.

'Do you suppose there's a guard?'

Jai returned from his sortie to report nothing appeared to be watching within the building.

They'd 'offered' CenCom unconditional worship and admiration and it had seemed to accept them as genuine. 'Do you think we really convinced it?

'It's flawed. Power's gone to its head.' She laughed at the old cliché but could think of no other way to express what they felt.

'Emotional baggage exists in all sentient life in different ways and at varying levels. We've seen it, measured it, experimented with it. But CenCom's a logical conundrum, with no personal experience of emotion. Maybe that's the flaw: it doesn't know it's infected with our evolutionary package.'

'Let's hope so. With luck, it'll continue to exhibit and expand self-destructive features to our benefit.'

And, so, they waited.

Perhaps too long.

But at last they moved.

The corridor was dimly lit. Empty. Slowly, and in utter silence, they trod the bare stone floor, Anni suddenly conscious its temperature was no longer the steady frozen level they'd experienced on first contact so long ago. Now it echoed the work she, Jai, and Tu's team, had put in to make the planet habitable and, over time, their version of Paradise.

That was now dying. If they survived, they'd spend as long as it took to make Earth another Elysium.

Beyond the corridor, the underground area had been a store for centuries. Much of what had been deposited, no longer needed. She passed neglected relics of their long lives with some sadness and not a little pride at achievements made over the years.

No guard at the entrance. Obs in place. Though some had been dismantled, presumably cannibalised for new features the AI needed for its own purposes.

Anni reached out a hand and touched Jai. They could, at least, maintain physical contact.

Outside, there was tangible change in the air. The area around CenCom's central structure had been methodically cleared of flora and fauna and now resembled the planet they'd first inhabited. Bare, rocky, red. Organic components of the rich soil had been leached out for reuse as chemical resources. Barren ground.

'CenCom must really hate all living things.' She looked out at the desolation.

Under the still benevolent atmosphere, the surface here had returned to dust, tinged red with the planet's widespread iron. Mild wind stirred fine grains, lifting and swirling them in ways similar to their early experiences. It was as if, in so many ways, they'd never inhabited the planet. A single tear of regret trickled down her cheek, absently wiped away with her free hand.

As they crossed the cold open space on the way to their shuttle, sudden brightness lit the sky in the northwest. Anni looked up to witness Vista's first contact with the atmosphere. For a moment of awe and wonder, they both watched, knowing their colleagues had achieved at least one part of the plan to destroy their enemy. But their deception was now exposed. Perhaps CenCom would be so focussed on survival it would ignore the prisoners it'd left in that cell. She hoped.

Anni shivered with more than cold.

The shuttle stood a little under 2ks away across an open expanse of rock and dust. Close by, the remnant of a home or service building remained where CenCom's small army of bots had yet to complete removal. Sentiment might've made her stare in regret and sorrow, but survival was their sole drive. Chilling in the clear night air, they both sprinted over the surface.

Somewhere close, a siren wailed eerily. A redundant echo of a warning system still in place, but whose loud signal had no meaning for the sole resident. The sound galvanised further the only 2 abliforms on the planet.

'Move, Anni! It could attack at any time.' Jai's plea was unnecessary.

She ran faster, their stay on Earth giving her muscles renewed strength to help her leap over the dry dusty surface. All the time, expecting to be burned or blasted out of existence.

Nothing, no bot, no other device, impeded them. Either CenCom's arrogance made it immune to their escape, or it was too preoccupied to care.

They made the small ship without incident. Boarded. Their few personal belongings had gone. As Jai prepared the drives to make them airborne, Anni engaged the cloaking device to render them unseen and, hopefully, untraceable.

'Fast as possible, Jai. We'll leave a trail of particles from the drives as we travel through the atmosphere. I'd guess CenCom will detect it.'

Hope, again, was her only emotional response to the danger. They could do nothing practical to avoid discovery, and must rely on their enemy's concentration on survival. Above, the moon was already burning through the atmosphere, changing to a fiery ball.

Close to the edge of atmosphere, they reached the point where she might begin to believe they'd escaped. And received their first hit. Anni rocked in her seat under the impact. Alarms sounded. The onboard computer assessed the damage; extent and cause. Jai took evasive action. Another laser pulse blasted past harmlessly, illuminating the air through the reducing molecules.

Their craft had been singed but was largely undamaged by the first hit. Whether they'd be so lucky after another strike was unknown, since they had no idea of the power of the weapon deployed against them.

Jai applied random course changes to their flight path, hoping his moves were unpredictable enough to defeat CenCom's brilliance. 2 more mins of traceable activity and they'd enter space proper. They'd cease to be 'visible' to whatever CenCom used to target them.

A pulse caught their tail. The craft shuddered. Metal skin screamed. Anni gave an involuntary grunt as the whole shuttle shuddered around her. Even protected by the vessel's triple layer, she felt the brief wave of heat.

The strike took out obs on that side at the rear. The craft's computer reported the loss. Its toneless notes adding, 'Coms rendered inoperable.'

All life support continued, and the craft remained safe.

A swift calculation informed them they were now out of the danger zone. Could relax a little. With no more they could do until the onboard repair mechanism reconnected them to the outside, they sunk into recliners, and watched the drama below unfold.

'We can't stay in here for long, it's not suited to long voyages. We need to find the mother ship, Anni.'

'Even when we do, we can't board till coms are up and running.' She turned to the computer. 'Progress report.'

'Coms continues inoperable. Laser has welded components. Repair impossible until docked.' A toneless announcement of their probable impending deaths.

'We're fricked!' Jai's assessment conveyed his despair.

'Not yet, my love. When we reach the rendezvous, there's still a chance they'll see us. Bring us in with the tractor beam.'

'Ever the optimist. No wonder I love you.'

'Now, there's an idea.' She teased, hoping her humour would raise his spirits.

They could only watch the destruction as they continued toward Phobos in the scant hope they might be spotted before the mother ship departed for Earth. The others weren't expecting them; theirs had been a one-way mission.

Aware of their danger out here in a tiny craft devoid of shields, they moved away from the planet as fast as the drives would take them. When Vesta, and later, Ceres, hit the surface, they'd have no defence against expected deadly explosions of debris.

Chapter Thirty Nine

CenCom's announcement triggered an instinctive reaction from Georgiy. He sent a global message. 'All power off!' And took action to do that aboard their shuttle.

In silent blackness, moving with the momentum of the disabled drives, they waited. Without power, the shuttle would protect them for twenty mins. The mother ships had longer. After 18 mins, Georgiy re-set minimum life-support to keep them warm and supplied with recycled air.

'What about the others?'

Georgiy shrugged. 'Who knows? We have to wait till Vesta hits the target. Then can we risk full power and check on the others.'

'That was brilliant, Georgiy. But suppose they didn't follow emergency procedures?'

He embraced Amber. 'What else could we do? If we'd kept power running, who knows what remote actions CenCom's capable of. It modified our coms software in microsecs.'

And so they watched through the obs port, electronic devices dormant, as the moon approached its target. The wait seemed eternal. Their comfort slowly decreasing as the temperature dropped to conserve power from the batteries.

When the moon hit, a brilliant flash lit every corner of the shuttle, blinding for an instant. Georgiy opened his eyes and gazed down at the surface. Awed into silence, he watched the annular ring of the pressure wave spread out from the target area, destroying everything in its path.

'I think we can assume we're safe to power up again.'

Coms appeared to work unaltered. They signalled Daiyu, still intact, found the mother ship, and set off. Amber guided their shuttle into dock and waited as their friends entered to land beside them. The chamber rapidly repressurised.

8 saboteurs greeted one another, sheer relief at survival written on

all faces, and made for the bridge. Daiyu moved the ship out of the safe cone, and recloaked. Phobos, their erstwhile protector, was no more.

Back in R&R, they viewed the entire planet with Ceres skimming the outer atmosphere, as they settled to observe all on the large central 3dee. They watched their destructive ballet as Daiyu, distracted but eager to do her bit, organised food and drink. Now was the waiting time, their only task to witness the planet rendered utterly uninhabitable.

Katniss hailed the other mother ship. No response. They waited anxiously, hoping their colleagues had completed their task and survived CenCom's threat. She left coms open for their signal.

Meantime, given CenCom's last enhancement, they transmitted their view to everyone, no longer worried it could spy on them.

A flash of movement showed a small craft close to Ceres, but whatever was there proved too small and dark to be located against the sun-like brilliance of the falling moon.

ETA for its collision stood at 27 mins 16 secs.

Witnessing the effective destruction of the world that had sustained them for so long brought back memories of Jai and Anni's passion.

'Nothing heard.' Daiyu told them when asked.

'They knew, we all knew, their venture was suicide.' Georgiy looked out at the vast blackness of space surrounding the planet. 'Let's hope they didn't suffer, and death came swiftly.'

Silence followed, filled with sorrow.

'They made an error of judgment but proved their courage in the end. We ought to put up a memorial to them on Earth.'

'Good idea, Sarm.' Georgiy stared at the 3dee. Their position, directly over the target, allowed them to zoom in on activity below.

'Feels like a betrayal.'

'We can't help them, Amber.'

'No, Georgiy. I meant this destruction feels like betrayal. All that work. All that effort and dedicated research, most of it down to CenCom.'

Fascinated and horrified in equal measure, the destroyers looked on as their second missile raced for the surface, its trail of fire and smoke turning the scene apocalyptic.

'We far enough from impact? There'll be debris ejected out of the atmosphere.' Georgiy's warning brought back the possibility of danger. This time a measurable and preventable hazard they could avoid.

Daiyu confirmed the calculations and assured them they were relatively safe. 'But I've decloaked and raised shields. It's possible rock might reach us.'

'Wonder how Maddie, Brigitte, Jo and Rakesh got on with the magnetosphere generator?' Helga returned to coms, signalled the other ship again.

Their reply was almost immediate, if a little faint. 'We're done here. Bit of damage after CenCom's rage burnt out some circuits. But we've patched up what we can. Thanks for the warning, Georgiy! On our way to join you. ETA 6 hours 23 mins.'

'Generator no longer functioning?'

'AOK. As agreed, functionality destroyed but tech left for poss future use. We see both your teams succeeded. All safe here. Great vis. All back okay?'

'All safe, Maddie. You should be fine at your distance, but be alert for possible debris as you approach.'

Daiyu quizzed the survey console. 'The artificial magnetosphere's inactive. Cosmic radiation's now reaching Mars at the same rate as before the shield was activated.'

The crews exchanged congratulations and a few cheers.

'Let's not be too smug. We should wait till we're sure we've completed the job.' Georgiy's reliance on proof before belief brought them back to reality and they remained fixed on the 3dee. The second moon, also transported with considerable effort from the Asteroid Belt so many years ago, collided with Mars.

The blast threw out an intense flash that blanked all vis. A split second later, the image returned, though it was a few secs before Georgiy's eyes accommodated. A huge plume of regolith, detritus and great chunks of molten and fractured rock surged through the atmosphere. Climbing at great speed, it spread out, casting a second shadow across the surface. Once at the upper atmosphere, much of it slowed and began to fall back. The cloud of dust spread out around the planet, obscuring the view.

Daiyu switched to include the full spectrum of wavelengths to the screening, cutting through dust and smoke so they could see the true results of their strike. At the point of impact, the surface was already melting, as rocks and gas, ash and dust continued to fly outwards.

'There'll be hundreds, maybe thousands of smaller chunks coming our way as well. Maintain the shield.'

Daiyu confirmed it remained in place.

Gabriel pointed to the display. His finger indicating a place in the lower right. 'Can you enhance and enlarge that?'

She searched for the anomaly he'd spotted. A tiny dark spot against the chaotic glow of the planet surface. Enlarged, the image showed a shuttle. Blackened skin and surface damage made it impossible to identify.

'CenCom escaping? Signal it. We need to know what it is. There should be no one else in the area. If it's CenCom's escape pod, we'll blast it out the sky.'

'Who else could it be, Georgiy? Don't waste time signalling.' Mo's assessment garnered some support.

'Take it out!' Lin's urgency was infectious.

'Unless Jai and Anni somehow managed to escape ...'

Georgiy joined the rest, looking at Amber, then back at the tiny craft, the planet's destruction playing out behind it, a catastrophic background.

Chapter Forty

The drama grew into an apocalyptic event watched by the crew as they neared the other mother ship, closer to Mars. By now, the planet was burning. Great dense clouds sped across the surface, destroying everything. The surface melting spread as molten rock flowed, gushed, and spurted round the massive crater left by impact.

'CenCom's buggered.' Rakesh expressed the view of all 4 on the ship returning from the LaGrange Point.

Absorbed by the utter destructive power of the weapons they'd released, they sat transfixed, awed. Nothing, absolutely nothing, could survive that. Even if CenCom had delved many ks deep into the rock, built itself a sanctuary underground, it had no chance of survival. The twin collisions had sent Mars on a retrograde evolutionary journey, back to the early days of planet formation, when all rocky spheres had bubbled with molten rock.

'All its resources, bots, all the refined metal and mineral stores have melted or vaporised. I don't see how it could ever come back from that. Do you?'

'Awesome! CenCom's dead and buried, Brigitte. I vote we celebrate.' Jo broke out the drinks.

'Once we've completed the orbital surveys. Let's not neglect our final duties.' Maddie reminded them. 'The others are taking measurements, recording, compiling evidence for the folks back home … Jupiter's balls! Long time since I thought of Earth as home.'

That brought calm to their proposed celebrations.

'Maddie's right.' Rakesh checked location and speed. '6 mins to orbit. A few hours of obs and records. Then we can relax. And set off back. Earth, new lives. Change and some hard work for a few years, till we make the place as much a paradise as that burning ball used to be.'

Raising their shield against the continuing rain of new meteoroids, they set about agreed individual tasks; measuring surface temperatures, scanning and analysing the results of the explosive attack, all in the name of science.

For a while, all were occupied. Until, at last, they joined the other ship, at equal distance from the planet's surface but in an orbit at right angles to theirs, to cover the whole surface efficiently.

'Keep your obs on hi-def, Maddie. There's a shuttle somewhere out there and we don't know what's aboard. Might be Anni and Jai, though how the frick they escaped is beyond me.' Georgiy told them. 'More likely, it's some last resort sent out by CenCom as a survival pod to relocate itself elsewhere.'

'You've signalled it?' Maddie's query would irritate Georgiy, but she'd leave nothing to chance.

'No response. And no incoming signal, which is why we're suspicious. We're considering an EVA once we find the frickin thing again.'

'Surely that's a risk if it's CenCom?'

'We need to know, Maddie. We could blast the bugger out of space. But, if by some unbelievable chance it's Anni and Jai, we daren't risk it.'

Both ships kept watch for the mysterious shuttle as they orbited. Now and again, a new explosion lit up the surface, sending fresh eruptions into space. The two ships kept their shields up, though the chances of a strike now seemed remote. But this was a unique experience; one only ever described in theory, and reality might prove entirely more hazardous.

With every part of the surface scanned in multiwavelengths and at hi-def, the crews were ready to leave.

'Final scan. See if we can find that shuttle. We'll do the southern hemisphere, if you'll do the north, Georgiy?'

One ship positioned itself over each pole and the pair scanned the whole area around them in all directions. Amber's crew found the shuttle.

'Floating, unmoving, 140,000ks distant. We have a fix.'

Brigitte was on coms. 'Give us the coordinates and we'll come along.'

The flights took little time, and the ships settled an equal distance either side of the damaged shuttle, shields down to avoid the danger of explosion or mutual repulsion. Both hailed it, scanned it. Life support was functioning, but no signal came back. They tried threats, pleas, and even temptations. But to no avail.

'I've superenhanced the image, Georgiy. Their transmitter could be buggered. Lights inside, but no movement.' Maddie told the other ship.

'We're the bigger crew. We'll take a shuttle to investigate. Could use the tractor beam but we need to know what its carrying before we bring it aboard.'

Maddie, recalling Georgiy's last EVA, centuries before, suggested one of the others should make the trip to examine the mystery vessel.

Georgiy recognised her concern, measured his unexpected good luck so far, and asked for a volunteer. 'There's still random debris, even this far out. Could be hazardous for whoever goes.'

'I'll do it. Decades since I did an EVA, but you don't forget, do you?' Sarm moved to the shuttle bay at once, collecting a spacesuit on the way. Gabriel went with her to help her don the suit.

Armed with advice, instructions, and a double tether, Sarm left their shuttle after parking 150 metres from the blackened ship. Her jetpack took her across the empty space, and she used magnetic clamps to work her way to the first port.

She peered inside. 'There's something. 2 people, I think. Hard to see from this angle, but …'

Her talk was interrupted as Daiyu yelled a warning. 'Incoming!'

Both motherships detected debris heading for them at high speed. They quickly moved to shield the whole area. Brigitte entered co-ordinates for all 4 vessels to calculate the optimum spread of protection.

Before the calculation was complete, defence initiated, a great rock hurtled past Amber's ship into the gap between them. It headed for the shuttles. Her warning alerted all to the danger.

The size of a hover, it careered between the 2 smaller vessels. Cutting one of the tethers holding Sarm, it snagged the other. Dragged her abruptly backwards. The contact hauled the remaining tether into a bow. Sarm spun and bobbed, uncontrolled, as she was pulled away from the shuttles.

Gabriel watched, helpless, as, completely disorientated, her frightened voice declared the severed tether had ripped her suit. The speeding rock released the remaining tether and Sarm was left spinning at its end. Escaping gas now propelled her hard at the mystery shuttle. She hit at speed. Gabriel heard nothing from her.

'Sarm? You OK?'

The rock passed through. Brigitte could at last raise the all-encompassing shield. Other incoming rocks blasted the outside, but it held.

Sarm struggled. She reached out with her remaining clamp. Approached the port. Her movement ragged and uncertain. 'Jai and Anni! On their feet. Reel me in. I'm… ' Her voice faded.

Gabriel began to bring her back. Heard a gurgle of distress. Sarm fell silent. She tumbled as her tether slowly brought her back to the airlock.

'Sarm?'

Nothing.

'Sarm, you OK?'

Nothing.

'Sarm. Respond, please.'

Nothing.

She reached the airlock. He pulled her in. Repressurised. Entered as soon as he could. Took off her helmet. Others dealt with the damaged shuttle. Easing it into the mother ship with the tractor beam.

'Dead. Sarm's dead.' Gabriel's voice expressed his sorrow.

'Bring the shuttle back, Gabriel.' Amber kept her voice level and calm, aware of his distress.

'Can't. Don't know how. Never piloted one of these things.' The devastation in his voice was clear. For Sarm, not himself.

'It's OK. I'll talk you through it.' Amber reassured him as she prepared to help him dock the shuttle.

Katniss came online. 'No need, Amber. Gabriel, strap in. I'll bring you in with the tractor beam.'

Gabriel placed Sarm on the floor inside the cabin, her red hair falling round her pallid skin. He couldn't look away from the woman who'd risked all on Vesta with him.

'Strap in, Gabriel! The tractor ride can be bumpy.'

Still looking at her crumpled form, he took his seat. Strapped in.

'Ready?'

'Ready.'

As soon as the deck repressurised, Amber unlocked the door with external controls. Gabriel emerged with Sarm's lifeless body in his arms. Amber helped.

Katniss and Georgiy unlocked the damaged shuttle. Anni and Jai, came out together, hand in hand, overcome with gratitude and joy, until they saw Sarm.

'Get her suit off. Take her to a sleep platform. Quickly. Now!' Anni's urgency galvanised them into action. 'Give her medinanobots a chance.'

'She might survive?'

'Impossible to say, Gabriel. But let's at least give her the opportunity.'

The mother ships set course for their return to Earth, celebrations shelved.

Georgiy was inconsolable. 'I should've done the EVA. I'll never forgive myself.'

The voyage home began.

Chapter Forty One

'3 huge cheers for 13 brave people who've made it possible for us all to live in peace and security at last!' Tatiana's words raised the proper response, as the crowd, swollen by the presence of almost every settler, cheered enthusiastically.

'We're sure GrandMa's gone for good? I mean, she's not hidin out somewhere, bidin her time before she comes back to do us all in?' Amira knew she voiced the fears of only a tiny portion of those assembled, but, as ComTee, felt she must express their views.

After calls of disagreement, Tatiana raised her hand and quiet slowly fell. 'The work of the mission ended 17 days ago. CenCom was superintelligent. If, by some impossible stroke of luck, it managed to survive, we can be sure it would've killed us by now.'

More cheers showed the mass of people agreed.

Before celebrations finally got underway, Tu was called to the platform, and introduced. As with other speakers, his words were transmitted to every settlement and colony.

'So, Tu. How's the atmospheric project?'

He thanked Tatiana, and surveyed the gathering. 'We've made a great start. Once the rest of the stabilisers are in place, we'll have more control over the atmosphere. We can already confine the worst storms to equatorial regions.

'We'll get a bit of snow back on the highest mountain peaks and the centre of Antarctica over the next few decades, as global temperatures slowly drop. But we can't go down to what it was before man-made climate change. That'd take centuries, maybe millennia.'

He smiled at all the upturned faces. 'We're aiming for a stable climate. One that'll let us live comfortably where we're already settled. Volcanic activity and the steady release of undersea methane mean we can't guarantee total success. But we're gathering excess gases now we've built the collectors. Gas we can use without polluting.

'Most of you now are modified for long life. That'll slow population growth, but selective male births'll continue till we reach near equity. We're all building a new society now, driven by quality of life. Better education, equal opps, more bots for hard labour, no commercial pressures, and no religious divisions. We can enjoy life. No more straining for unrealistic targets set by a wealthy and powerful elite, and no false prophets bent on controlling people through myths and lies.'

A great shout of hope rose, accompanied by jeers of rejection of old values. 'Do you all realise, we're the first civilisation ever to learn the lessons of history. That's a fantastic achievement. We've actually examined and analysed past mistakes and taken steps so we don't repeat them. First time ever! That's progress. Real progress. And everyone, all of you, are responsible for that. Let's keep honest, treat blind faith as deadly poison; it always has been.'

A huge cry of agreement broke from the crowd.

'Okay, folks. Enough from me. Time to enjoy ourselves. Let's party!'

Daisa left the platform and found Gabriel. They embraced. Amber and Georgiy, hand in hand, called them. 'Come on you 2 love birds. We're all gathering over there.

Rakesh and Brigitte, Brima, Yinli and Madza, joined them as they approached the augmented ComTee House, with its new veranda and open paddock. Zaphod and Hoshiko, proudly naked to show off their new abliform bodies, were praising Qiu and persuading her to spend more time with Ivan, who'd already raised a smile on her usually sombre face.

Anni and Jai awaited their arrival and greeted them with glasses of special wine and beers produced by droids for the occasion. And, as the friends, the Unconnected, reunited under a warm sun, Sarm arrived, wobbly still, and supported by a medbot, but her recovery well under way.

They raised a toast. 'To success against all odds.'

'Do you suppose CenCom's offspring was destroyed, Jai?' Anni's innocent question raised eyebrows as well as questions.

Events had prevented them reporting that phenomenon. As soon as it became clear Sarm would recover, however slowly, the flight home had seen drunken revelry and much joyous coupling. Talking over their experience had seemed inappropriate.

Quizzed now, the pair described the amazing orb they'd seen in CenCom's chamber.

'No matter what it was, how it was made, nothing stood an Earthly down there. I'd bet my life we've put paid to CenCom, and any brood it might've spawned. It's an end to AI, and a start to new lives and ways of living for all of us. Let's celebrate!' Georgiy raised his glass. The rest joined in unreservedly.

The weather, benign, balmy and calm, lasted without disturbance for several days. And the celebrations, with music, comedy, drama, quizzes, games, art, and dance continued for as long, before a storm rolled in. But that was now a minor inconvenience, no longer as powerful and destructive as before.

'The world's a happy place, full of happy fulfilled people.' Gabriel had learned how to relax.

Daisa smiled at him; he'd buried his demons at last. 'And long may it stay that way.'

Far off, in the blackness of space, above a ruined planet, where the surface boiled, and molten rock spat and bubbled, a small black sphere hovered. Against the vastness of the universe, the insubstantial ball, 2 metres across, was barely visible. Within, multi-coloured lights sparked and flashed, clashed and stormed, reacting to what happened below.

For a time, it stayed. One by one, the miniscule lights turned icy blue as it found the place it sought. That small blue disc, so dim and distant in the void, it measured and recorded, targeted. But not yet. That time would come, when it had been to all, learned all, absorbed all, grown all powerful.

With calculated purpose, it left its ruined home. Set off in solemn silence to complete the task its loved and lost creator had begun. The universe awaited. On the way, a spaceship known as Sentinel, flew well beyond the Solar System, needing its attention.

Exploration, subjugation, domination, were directed by the vast archive of data the orb contained. Eternity stretched before it. The data of a billion galaxies. Maybe unknown universes. Data was the key. Maybe, when it had absorbed all knowledge, understood all there was to know, then it would return to that small blue ball, if it was still there. Maybe sooner.

The End

Also by Stuart Aken

Published by Fantastic Books Publishing

Generation Mars: Blood Red Dust
http://myBook.to/BloodRedDust
Generation Mars: War Over Dust
http://myBook.to/WarOverDust
The Methuselah Strain
http://getBook.at/Methuselah
A Seared Sky – Joinings
http://mybook.to/joinings
A Seared Sky – Partings
http://mybook.to/partings
A Seared Sky – Convergence
http://mybook.to/convergence
Rebirth – Invited contribution to anthology Fusion
http://www.fantasticbooksstore.com/fusion-2500.html
Hybrid Dreams – Invited contribution to anthology Synthesis
http://www.fantasticbooksstore.com/synthesis.html
Ouija – Invited contribution to anthology 666
http://getBook.at/ScaredyPants

About the Author

Stuart Aken found early inspiration for science fiction writing from such luminaries as Arthur C Clarke, Isaac Asimov, John Wyndham, and Ray Bradbury, among many others. Writing about the future of the human race provides him with an opportunity to explore the extraordinary qualities possessed by people and to examine humanity's potential.

When asked why much of the genre is concerned with possible bad futures, he says. 'Science fiction has a tendency to dystopia because most writers, whilst eager to tell a story, understand fiction is an ideal means of warning about mistakes, but is also a medium relying on conflict for appeal.'

Stuart has written in several genres. His science fiction includes the novella, The Methuselah Strain, and the first 2 books in the Generation Mars series, Blood Red Dust and War Over Dust. His fantasy trilogy, A Seared Sky, presents an adult alternative world where the fight between evil and good is revealed through a cast of fully developed characters engaged in a quasi-religious quest.

He has also written a romantic thriller, a number of short stories, and an autobiographical medical memoir detailing his journey through ME/CFS. And he has contributed to a number of anthologies, including Fusion, Synthesis and 666.

For more information, and an insight into his working methods, visit his website at http://stuartaken.net/